S0-ADJ-946

DIRTY ENGLISH

ILSA MADDEN-MILLS

This is a work of fiction. Names, characters, places, brands, media, and incidents are either the product of the author's imagination or are used fictitiously. The author acknowledges the trademarked status and trademark owners of various products, bands, and/or restaurants referenced in this work of fiction, which have been used without permission. The publication/use of these trademarks is not authorized, associated with, or sponsored by the trademark owners.

Without limiting the rights under copyright reserved above, no part of this publication may be reproduced, stored in or introduced into a retrieval system, or transmitted, in any form, or by any means (electronic, mechanical, photocopying, recording, or otherwise) without the prior written permission of both the copyright owner and the below publisher of this book.

Copyright © 2015 by Ilsa Madden-Mills
www.ilsamaddenmills.com

Published by Little Dove Publishing

LITTLE DOVE

PUBLISHING

Cover Design by S.k. Hartley
Editing by Rachel Skinner of Romance Refined
Formatting by JT Formatting

First Edition: October 2015
Library of Congress Cataloging-in-Publication Data
Madden-Mills, Ilsa
Dirty English – 1st ed
ISBN-13: 978-1517687465 | ISBN-10: 1517687462

"You have bewitched me, body and soul."

–Mr. Darcy from Jane Austen's
Pride and Prejudice

PROLOGUE

A STABBING PAIN in my temple.

Fat and swollen lips.

A throbbing tenderness between my thighs.

Why did I feel like I was dying?

Muddled images flashed in my head, but nothing connected or made sense, just a big black hole of nothingness. Thanks, vodka.

The ache seemed to spread across my face. I groaned. *Had something hit me?*

Nausea curled as I got my bearings in the dark. Bit by bit, I figured out I was sprawled cross-wise on a bed that wasn't mine.

A small hotel room came into focus.

Careful to move my head slowly, I gazed around, taking in the battered nightstand and a rickety desk that had seen better days. In the corner of the room lay the beaded clutch purse I'd borrowed from my best friend Shelley for prom. Okay. *But where was she?*

My last memory was dancing in the gym. Maybe on top of a table?

My eyes went around the room.

Threadbare navy curtains.

A bed that reeked of stale cigarettes and body odor.

A bottle of Grey Goose.

My stomach lurched at the memory of that bitter taste sliding down my throat, and I swallowed to keep the bile down.

Was this a hangover?

I didn't know. I had nothing to compare it to.

Snippets of the night came in vivid clips.

Dinner with my boyfriend, Colby, and my friends Shelley and Blake at an Italian restaurant in downtown Petal, North Carolina. Lots of giggling. Colby sneaking in his flask so we could spike our drinks. Dancing under twinkling lights at the prom in the Oakmont Prep gymnasium. Getting in Colby's Porsche to head to the lake for an after-hours party.

No memories of the lake came to me.

Colby, though, I remembered him urging me to drink, pushing the bottle at my mouth on the way to prom and then later as we drove to the lake. *Don't be a pussy, Elizabeth. Drink it. Let's rule the world, babe.*

Rule the world was his thing. He was invincible, and I guess since his father was a Senator of North Carolina, he believed it. Being part of his inner circle, especially being his new girlfriend, made me feel like I was freaking royalty.

My tummy still fluttered from winning prom queen to his king. On stage when they'd set the sparkling crowns on our heads, he'd turned to me and told me he loved me. Crazy and giddy happiness had filled my heart. He loved *me*. The girl from the wrong side of town. The girl without a real family. The girl who was nobody.

I'd waited for someone to love me like that my whole life.

More flashes from the car came and I groaned.

I remembered the second sip. Third. Fourth.

Things got hazy.

God, I couldn't remember.

Colby giving me a little white pill.

Did I take it?

It was all so fuzzy.

Pink, sparkly sequins dotted my hands and I gazed down at them on the bed. My dress—the one I'd scrimped and saved to get by waiting tables at the local diner—lay in scattered pieces around me. My body was on display with my breasts hanging out.

I whimpered and tried to cover them, but my arms were too sluggish. Panic ate at me—and then an awful realization hit. The material had been ripped from bust to hem, the delicate spaghetti straps torn off. My underwear lay twisted around my ankles and spots of blood dotted the coverlet below me.

For a millisecond my brain refused to accept what was plain as day, but when reality finally settled in, horror pooled in my gut.

My hands attempted to move but only fluttered around my body.

Red marks. Bruises. Scratches. Teeth marks.

No. No. No. This was all wrong. This wasn't supposed to happen tonight.

Whispers came from a corner of the room. Colby.

My eyes found him standing shirtless in the bathroom, his back to me as he talked on the phone.

Pieces of his conversation came to me.

"She's out of it, man … like an animal in the sack … popped that cherry …"

His words hit me like a tsunami, and my breath snagged in my throat. I struggled to regain my equilibrium—to focus—lying to myself that this whole episode was a figment of my imagination.

Colby grunted. "I don't think she'll be able to walk for a week." A pause, and then he burst out laughing at something the other person must have said.

Something fragile inside me cracked and split wide open.

A sound tore from my throat, low and primitive, and his eyes swiveled to me.

I flinched, every muscle in my body jerking in revulsion.

"Gotta go." He hung up and stalked toward me, stopping at the edge of the bed to stare down at me with ice-blue eyes. A flash of annoyance crossed his face as his gaze skated across my body. "You made a mess."

Being from the trailer park, I'd had more than my share of scuffles with boys who wanted my attention and girls who wanted to boss me around, so I knew how to kick ass. Right then every nerve ending in my body wanted to jump up and claw his heart out piece by piece with my nails. He'd done this to me.

Rage burned inside, but I couldn't move.

My voice came out thin. Reedy. "You hurt me."

I struggled to sit up but collapsed backward.

He watched me dispassionately as I flailed around on the bed, letting the moments tick by, escalating my fear.

My tongue dipped out to lick dry lips.

He scooped up his white dress shirt from the floor, careful and steady hands buttoning it up, and that gesture, it said everything. He pulled on his pants and checked his sandy hair in the mirror. He wasn't drunk at all.

"What did you give me?" I pushed out. "Why?"

"Don't play games, sweetheart, you begged for it. *This* was consensual." He twirled his fingers around the bed, a look of derision on his face. "Whatever I gave you, you took it without asking."

"No, that's not true." *Had I?*

"Oh yeah, and you were the best lay I've had in months. Well worth the time I spent on you." He bent down until his eyes were level with mine. "Don't be telling lies about what happened here. No one would believe you anyway as drunk as you were.

Still are. I'm sure there're photos and videos from the prom to prove it." He laughed as if hit by a sudden memory. "Damn girl, you were crazy in the gym, dancing on the tables and yelling at people. Chaperones tossed us out, babe. If I didn't know better, I'd think you were a bad influence on me." He cocked his head. "That's what I'll tell everyone at least." He brushed at some lint on his trousers.

I shook my head. *No.* I was the good girl who'd scored the highest in her class on the SAT. I was the girl who volunteered at the local animal shelter—and not just for service hours. I didn't get thrown out of parties. I barely got invited to them.

He pushed hair out of my face, his fingers trailing down my cheek.

I flinched and jerked away as far as I could. "Don't touch me."

"Ah, and here I was hoping you'd be ready for another round." He chuckled, his hands fiddling with the ring I'd made for him a few weeks ago, a sterling silver band with our initials etched on the inside with a heart between them. I'd spent hours on it, engraving the letters and then fashioning the metal until it was perfect. I'd even used some of my college savings to buy the butane torch and tools necessary to make it good enough for him.

"You said you loved me." I hated the weakness in my voice.

His lips quirked up. "I tell all the girls I love them, Elizabeth. You just took a little longer to give me what I wanted."

A strangled noise came out of my mouth.

He sighed and zipped his pants. "Don't be upset. We both wanted this."

No, no, no.

He twisted his ring off and twirled it between his fingers. "I guess you'll be wanting this back now." He tossed it on the nightstand and it made a tinkling sound as it hit the wood, spun off, and fell onto the floor.

He checked his appearance in the mirror one last time to

straighten his jacket. "Well, I have to go, but I'll see you at graduation in a few days. Later, babe."

And then he walked out the door, shutting it softly behind him.

Thank God.

I sucked in a shuddering breath, my lungs grasping for more air.

To make sense of what had happened.

An hour went by. Another one.

Memories flashed like a horror movie you didn't want to watch but couldn't stop. Colby carrying me in the hotel and placing me on the bed. Ripping my dress. Groping at my legs. Hitting. Shoving. *Pain.*

I'd tried to say no, but the words hadn't come.

I'd tried to move, but I couldn't.

My body had been a frozen statue, and he'd moved me where he wanted. Twisted me. Ruined me.

I held myself together and watched the minutes tick by on the digital clock as my alcohol-soaked brain struggled to make my body move again. In tiny increments, I slid my legs down until they touched the floor, my toes clenching into the cheap, fuzzy carpet. Groaning, I forced myself to sit up and then immediately fell. I crawled until I got to my purse in the corner of the room and found my phone.

Panic drove me.

Any minute he could come back in here and do it again.

My hand shook as I pushed 911 but froze when the nasally voice of the operator came on.

"You've reached 911. Do you have an emergency?"

Shame. Guilt. Remorse. *Truth.*

Had I asked for it?

Was this my fault?

I panted, the throbbing between my legs reminding me of my sin.

"Hello? Do you have an emergency? Do you need assistance?" The voice was more insistent.

"No," I croaked and ended the call.

I gazed down at my ruined dress. Who'd believe a girl whose father was in prison—if he even was my father—versus the wealthy son of a senator? I was white trash, a small town girl lucky enough to get a scholarship at the prep school down the road.

Nausea rose again, more violently this time, until the contents of my stomach spewed out everywhere.

The smell of alcohol made me sicker.

Mocking me. Telling me the cold hard truth. I'd had a part to play in this scenario.

I clutched my chest, my heart hurting. Broken.

My muscles screamed.

My head banged.

I was done. Dead. Cold. Even my skin wanted to crawl away.

The sun crept up in the sky, the rays curling in through the dirty curtains. Dawn, a new day, but I'd never look at the sunrise the same.

Clarity happens to all of us when our heart jumps ship, and mine was no different.

Something dark slithered around inside me, crawling into the crevices of my soul and suffocating it. Everything I'd believed about myself ... about who I was ... about *love* ... unraveled, turning into something dark. Dirty.

Love is a knife that cuts out your heart piece by piece, feeding it to the boy you love.

Broken in more ways than one, I vowed to never fall again.

My body caved in on itself as I wept.

CHAPTER ONE

Elizabeth

Two years later

SWEAT DRIPPED DOWN my neck as I tucked blond hair behind my ears and groaned in the hot sun. It was Friday afternoon in Raleigh, North Carolina, and the only day I had to move into my new apartment before junior year started on Monday. "Welcome back to Whitman University," I muttered as I pulled yet another box out of the trunk of my beat up Camry.

For only being twenty years old, I'd accumulated a lot of stuff.

Most of it consisted of jewelry making supplies and books except for my furnishings, which I'd inherited from Granny Bennett when she'd passed this summer. A beige and green plaid couch, a kitchen table with ducks painted on the top, an old bedroom suite, and a collection of crocheted doilies in various colors was my inheritance from her. Not exactly Ethan Allen, but it had a certain style.

"Your apartment looks like an eighty-year-old cat lady lives here," Shelley called down to me as she popped her head out of my apartment to peer down over the railing at me. My bestie since prep school, she was a privileged rich girl, a sharp contrast to my own wrong-side-of-the-tracks upbringing, but she'd been there for me through everything. Even Colby. Her red hair had gotten fuzzy in the humidly, but it didn't detract from her prettiness. She pinched her nose and made a scrunchy face. "And it kinda stinks."

"Stop your complaining and get your butt down here to help. I'm melting in this heat," I said.

She snorted and made her way down the metal stairway. "You and your fair skin. If you'd get out of the house now and then, you might get some color. But no ... all you do is study and work at the bookstore. You probably have more colors of highlighters than you have dating prospects. Not to mention, you go to the library so much people think you work there."

I grinned. "I'm not that bad. I see people in class. I even talk to them sometimes."

She lowered her head at me. "Get real. If it wasn't for me forcing you to go out with me—like tonight—you'd hole up here and eat ramen noodles for the rest of your college career."

"Meh, sometimes I eat pizza."

She sent me a smirk and grabbed one of the boxes at my feet. We waddled back up the staircase and came to a stop at apartment 2B on the second floor. A two-bedroom with a balcony and a bathroom, it felt like a mansion compared to the dorm room I'd lived in all last year. I was on the corner and facing the setting sun, and I only had one neighbor on my left, 2A.

As if on cue, the thump of loud rap music blasted from next door.

I listened. Was that Eminem?

"That's loud and obnoxious," Shelley said. "Maybe it won't be as quiet here as you think."

I tried to be optimistic. "So? It's two in the afternoon, not two in the morning."

"They're just moving in, too," she noted, nudging her head at the pile of boxes sitting outside the neighbor's door, which I noticed was slightly cracked. She indicated the pile of books in one. "Looks like a nerd. Yuck. And here I was hoping you'd win the jackpot with a hot neighbor."

Making sure the new neighbor was nowhere in sight, I leaned over and hurriedly rifled through some of the titles: *The Great Gatsby, Wuthering Heights.* "Hmm, someone likes the classics. English major, maybe?"

She rolled her eyes. "Boring. What you need is a sexy neighbor who likes to have great monkey sex."

I shook my head at her. "See, you say 'monkey sex' and all I can think of are hairy animals in bed. Gross."

She huffed in a teasing kind of way. "Whatever. It's like every time you see a hot guy, you have FUCK OFF tattooed on your head."

Colby had been a hot guy and look what that had gotten me.

I shrugged, swallowing down those memories. "So? I don't want to fall for anyone. Ever. Love hurts. Remember?"

"Yeah." She nibbled on her lips, a hard look growing on her normally smiling face. She was remembering the hotel and the devastation that had followed. She'd been the one to pick me up that morning and take me home. The kind of girl who fell in love at least once a month, she was under the impression that if I could just meet the right one, then all would be well and I'd have my happily ever after. Crock of shit.

"Don't worry about me, Shelley. I'm good, okay? I don't need a guy in my life to make me happy. All I need is you and Blake—and the occasional hookup." Blake was my other best friend from Oakmont Prep who'd come to Whitman as well.

She smirked. "Your sex rules again?"

I nodded.

Here's the thing. I'd had sex since Colby. Plenty of times. The events of that night didn't ruin my sexuality, only my trust in men. So a year after Colby, I halfheartedly propositioned a guy from my science class and asked him to come back to my room. Connor had been his name, and I'd seen him checking me out more than once when we had a lab together. That day, he'd looked at me like I'd suddenly grown two heads—me having a reputation as a bit of a bitch when it came to guys flirting with me—but he'd been eager. We'd walked back to my dorm room, and while the sex had been horrible, a furtive and awkward encounter, it proved that Colby had not won.

He was *not* the last person to touch me.

My body was my own.

So was my heart, and I planned to keep it that way.

After that, sex got easy—as long as I was in control. Over the past year, I'd made it into a game with strict rules. Pick an average guy who wasn't popular or rich or too good-looking. Make sure he wasn't taken. Make sure he didn't drink or do drugs. Make sure he wasn't an escapee from the local insane asylum. Have sex. Never speak to him again. End of story.

It was about control. My choice. My rules.

I had to initiate the first move, and I had to be on top. Most importantly, I had to be in my own bed and around my own things. Sex with me was tame by most standards, I suppose, based on some of the crazy stories Shelley had told me about her adventures. But I didn't care. If they wanted me, then they'd follow my lead.

"Maybe I'll join a nunnery."

She grinned. "You don't look good in black."

"True."

"And you aren't even Catholic, goofball."

"Again, true." I smiled back widely. I didn't mind her teasing me. It was better than pity.

I moved past her and we went back into my apartment to unpack. I pulled out a picture of me with Granny on her front porch the day I left for Whitman freshman year. Most days, it

4

hurt to look at that photo, to see the skinny girl in the picture with the saggy jeans and wrapped wrists. But it was the last picture I had of Granny and me together, and that was worth something to me no matter how hard it was to be reminded of my foolish mistake with Colby. I set it on the coffee table.

We finished putting the dishes in the kitchen cabinets and then moved to the bedroom where she helped me arrange my closets. Later, we ventured into the extra bedroom, which was more like a tiny storage room. This was university housing and the apartments were notoriously small, but I managed to fit my jewelry supplies and a twin bed in there.

But I hadn't made any jewelry in two years. The metals I'd once loved to shape and mold had become a metaphor for my own stupidity in love.

Shelley fiddled with one of my drawing pads, a pensive look on her face. She darted her eyes at me and then back at the boxes against the wall.

I steeled myself for her questions.

"When are you going to get serious about your jewelry? What are you going to do when you graduate in two years?" She opened the book and flipped through the pages. "Besides, I really need a new necklace. Something with a butterfly. Or a heart." Her face softened as she looked up at me. "Remember the little friendship medallions you made us when we were fifteen—"

"Shelley, I'm not talking about this. I can't make jack right now."

She cocked her head. "Are you just going to give up on your dreams because you made a ring for Colby? It's been two years, yet he's still dictating your future. It's fucked up. At one time *this* was all you wanted to do—design and create. Do you honestly think you'd be happy in some job where you can't make something beautiful?" She sighed, a resigned look on her face. "I mean, you use sex with guys to say you're past him, but you're not. Not really. You're still punishing yourself for something that's not even your fault."

It was my fault. I'd been drunk. I'd taken his drugs. Willingly.

The familiar shame settled in my gut. I blinked rapidly. "You weren't in that hotel room. You know nothing."

She bit her lip. Nodded. "You're right, I wasn't, but I saw you afterward. I took you home and took care of you until your mom got back from Vegas. I know how wrecked you were. I—I just love you, that's all."

I exhaled and paced around the room, setting things out, arranging them. We'd gotten too serious. "Besides, butterflies and hearts are worse than tramp stamps. *If* I made you a piece, it would stand for something big."

She grinned. "Like what?"

"Maybe your phone number on something since you give it out so much to guys."

She pretended to be pissed but then giggled. "God, that is so true. I'm a slut."

We laughed. "Come on, let's go get the rest of my stuff." We made our way back outside my apartment and stood in the breezeway. I sighed as I looked out over the parking lot. I still had several more boxes to bring up before I could even think about relaxing.

She poked me in the arm. "Hey, I have an idea. Let's go meet your neighbor."

I shook my head. "No, it's move-in day, and I'm sure they're just as busy as we are."

She ignored me and tiptoed over to the door. Instead of knocking, she pushed the cracked door open and peeked inside the darkened apartment. "I don't see anyone. Maybe they're in the back on the balcony." A grin crossed her face. "Which gives us plenty of time to be nosy." She bent down and riffled through the boxes outside, pulling out a cap with a Union Jack flag on it, a pair of men's athletic underwear, a pair of men's black Chucks.

She went a bit crazy, pulling out fingerless boxing gloves—*that was interesting*—and a collection of postcards from London.

"Oh, your neighbor is definitely a guy. And hung." She held up a box of condoms. Super-sized and ribbed. Triumph gleamed in her eyes. "Magnums, baby. Score," she sang out.

My eyes scanned the door to make sure no one saw us. "Put that stuff back before they come out here. Are you insane?"

"Yes."

I groaned at her obvious disinterest in being caught, but I couldn't help venturing closer. I did want to know more about my neighbor who read the classics and listened to rap music.

She tapped her chin, eyes coasting over the contents. "Even with the musty books, he's not a terrible combo. I'd do him."

"You'd do Manson."

She laughed.

I snapped the postcards out of her hand and tossed them back where she'd gotten them. "Step away from the box, or I won't go to the Tau party with you tonight or wear that silly dress you spent an hour hemming last night." Shelley was a fashion major and took all sewing projects serious. I was her number one model.

She sent the box a forlorn look and pouted. "Fine, you win. Party pooper."

"Huh. You need me to keep you in line. You never would have survived freshman English if I hadn't been yelling in your ear every morning to get up."

She agreed—a little too easily—and we moved back inside and went to sit on the balcony.

"What's that you have?" I asked later, noticing a brown book she kept pressed against her side.

She glanced down with a feigned look of surprise. "Oh this old thing? I got so wrapped up in your new place, I must have forgotten to put it back in the box."

Right. I narrowed my eyes. "Really?"

7

She got a giddy expression on her face, ignoring my sarcasm. "Okay, you got me. It's Jane Austen's *Pride and Prejudice*. I snitched it from your neighbor. I mean, it's your favorite book because your name is in it." She let out a dramatic sigh and pressed the book to her heart. "Don't you see? It's fate. You and the boring neighbor dude are meant to be."

I shook my head. Sometimes she was too much. "That's it. No more silly romantic movies for you. I don't even know why we're friends. I'm revoking our friendship as of now." I snatched the book out of her hands. An old hardback with gold lettering, it was an older printing, perhaps even valuable.

What kind of guy hangs on to a book like this?

The kind that believes in love, my heart whispered.

I cracked the book open and turned the pages until I found the chapter where Mr. Darcy describes how he fell in love with Elizabeth Bennet: *I cannot fix on the hour, or the spot, or the look, or the words, which laid the foundation. It is too long ago. I was in the middle before I knew that I had begun.*

Sappy drivel. I snapped it shut. "I love lots of books. It's called reading, you know. You should try it."

"No need. I have my looks." She preened and flicked a strand of hair over her shoulder. "Where are you going?" she called as I marched through the living room and toward the front door.

I held the book up in my hands. "Hello! To return what you stole."

She threw her arms up. "It accidentally got stuck to my hand, I swear! There's a difference!"

"Uh-huh." I walked over to the neighbor's, but the door was shut, and the boxes were gone. I put my ear to the door, but all was silent.

The sudden blast of music from a car in the parking lot made me jump.

I leaned over the breezeway railing that overlooked the

8

parking lot and searched below until I found a rugged-looking black Jeep with the top off. The Beastie Boys song "Fight for Your Right" reached my ears. I blinked. Damn, it was loud.

The driver was a bulky guy with a black Union Jack hat pulled low over his brow, blocking his face from me, leaving only the ends of his brown hair showing as it curled around the sides. A pair of aviators rested on his nose. Even from here, I saw broad shoulders and taut, muscular forearms as he shifted gears on the manual transmission. I even caught the flash of tattoos on his arms but couldn't make them out.

Mystery neighbor? It *was* the same hat from the box.

I found myself leaning over further, arching my neck to see more of him.

Something about a big dude that read *Pride and Prejudice* made me breathless.

In my head earlier, as we'd gone through the boxes, I'd pictured my neighbor as more the Harry Potter type, a geek with black-rimmed glasses and a shy smile. *Wrong, wrong, wrong.*

Before he pulled out into the traffic, he turned and glanced back at the apartment building, his shielded eyes seeming to zero in on me. His car idled as he looked at me, and even though there were quite a few yards between us, I felt the physical weight of his stare.

I inhaled sharply, goosebumps making the hair on my arms rise up.

Had he seen Shelley going through his things? Shit.

The book! I looked down to see it was still clutched it in my other hand.

Dammit.

Feeling ridiculous, I tore my eyes off him and backed up slowly until he was out of my vision. I propped the book up against his door and bolted for my apartment.

"Who was that?" Shelley asked as I flew in the door.

I shook my head. "It wasn't Harry Potter, that's for sure."

CHAPTER TWO

Declan

NOTE TO SELF: arriving at the first frat party of the year at the Tau house with a black eye and without your usual girl-friend—now ex—raises a lot of questions and a shit-ton of stares.

The black eye was from a fight the night before. Right when it had looked like I was toast, I'd got in a heavy hook straight to the guy's jaw and a high kick to the gut. He'd gone down like a sack of bricks. It was my third win since uni had ended in May.

I rubbed my sore fists against my jeans.

The pain was worth every cent I'd taken home.

"Where's Nadia?" one of the honorary frat little sisters asked with a big smile when I came in the door.

I grunted. "Not with me. I'd check with the men's tennis team."

Her eyebrows went up as I marched on by. She obviously hadn't heard that Whitman's *It* couple had broken up over the summer. I'd ended it when I'd walk in on Nadia bouncing on top of some other guy's cock. I clenched my fists, remembering her deception. She'd known exactly when I'd be walking through that door, and she'd timed it perfectly, all part of her plan to force me to freak out and do what she wanted. Buy her a ring, go to law school, be like my wanker father. Never going to happen.

Her manipulations had failed, and I'd dumped her.

To borrow a saying from my dead mum, she was all fur coat and no knickers.

Most days I felt like my heart had recovered, but my faith in women was shit.

As far as I knew, Nadia was still with her new guy, some fancy tennis player from Brazil. Donatello or Michelangelo or something. Ninja Turtle? Yeah.

I pushed thoughts of her away and entered the large den which on a normal day would have a row of couches, end tables, and beer bottles, but now had a mass of bodies gyrating on a makeshift dance floor. Music blared, a strobe light ricocheted around the room, and red Solo cups littered the floor.

I wasn't a member of this frat—I didn't have time to get rat-arsed every night—but my twin brother, Dax, was the Tau President, so it was understood I was always invited.

Questions kept coming from partygoers as I crossed the room.

"Hey, Nadia isn't with you?" one of the girls asked. *That's right. She's a bloody slag and I'm done with her.*

"Dude, what happened to your eye?" a guy called as I passed. I sent him a dark look. *Seriously?* You don't know about the underground fighting? You must be new at Whitman.

I grabbed a bottle of water from the bar and twisted off the top to take a big drink.

"Dirty English is in the house! About fucking time," Dax called out as he jumped down the staircase and landed on the bottom floor, a distance of about seven feet.

"Bugger me, you're going to kill yourself doing that."

He tossed his head back and let out a deep laugh. "Me? Dangerous? Look in the mirror, arsehole."

I sighed, half annoyed, half glad to see him. Polar opposites, he was the happy-go-lucky one who partied while I was the serious one who dreamed of teaching mixed martial arts at my own gym and maybe getting a run at the UFC.

I peered into a face nearly identical to mine, except for the scruffy beard he had going on. His grin was lopsided.

"You're snockered, brother," I said.

He shrugged, ignoring me. "Where have you been? This party is off the chain, and I need my wingman."

I grinned. "Whoa. You're *my* wingman."

His lips twitched. "Let's try it out then. Pick a hottie and let's see who she wants more? I'm up on you by three already."

"You're keeping score?"

When you have a twin, everything's a competition.

Freshmen year, we'd pretended to be the other one for a week, even going so far as to wear long sleeves so no one saw my tattoos or Dax's lack of. We'd switched up girls for the weekend too. Damn crazy. They'd dumped us when they discovered the truth. I didn't blame them. But lately those days seemed like a distant memory. At twenty-one, I was close to graduation and about to be out on my own while he'd still be here trying to finish his degree.

Dax ruffled his hair back and checked his breath by holding his hand up and blowing. He rolled his neck. "Alright, the next pretty bird that walks through that door is up for grabs. The first one to get a kiss wins."

"Stakes?" I asked.

"The usual."

I smirked. "It's your dollar."

His eyes gleamed. "It's not about the money, brother."

I laughed. Dax had a way about him that always made you grin even when your ship was sinking fast.

Just then, I heard the front door open and saw Blake, one of the frat brothers, shooting out of his seat like he'd been shot in the arse by an arrow. Lorna, who'd been sitting in his lap, fell to the floor in a heap. I leaned down to help her up. Blake was a bit of a mystery to me, but Lorna was a popular girl and most guys knew her, me included.

"Ouch, love. You good?"

She dusted herself off, annoyance on her face as she took in the girls who'd entered the house. "Thanks. God, Blake is such a freak when it comes to her. I thought he was going to be with me tonight, but then he tells me *she's* coming. I just don't get it. She's not even that pretty. She's weird and slutty." She crossed her arms and glared. "He sees her across the quad and practically runs to her."

A bit more than I wanted to know, but I smiled to soften the blow of her being rejected.

I turned to see why the room had gone quiet.

Or maybe it just seemed that way to me.

She sauntered straight in the room like she belonged there, yet the bravado was fake—I could tell by the fluttering eyelashes and the way she clutched her purse like a lifeline.

I recognized her right away although I don't think she'd ever looked at me twice in our years at Whitman. Which was surprising. This was a fairly small, albeit prestigious, uni, and I'm used to girls flirting with me in the hallways and classrooms. After all, it's hard to miss the guy with the English accent who was voted Whitman's Sexiest Man on Campus by the sororities. But this girl, she lived in a bubble, and seeing her out at a frat party was like spotting a unicorn.

Her name was Elizabeth Bennett, and the only reason I knew that much was because we'd had a class together last year and the professor had called roll.

It *was* a memorable name.

I remembered turning to check out the girl with a heroine's name, but she'd bent her head over a textbook already. She'd sat in the back of the class all semester and never once spoken to me—or to anyone. Most people said she was stuck-up. Some guys even claimed she'd shagged them in her room and then had never spoken to them again.

I didn't get it. Or her. But I'd admit to a certain fascination.

She was beautiful in a chilly don't-touch-me kind of way with white-blond hair pulled up in a high ponytail. Dark eyebrows rose up dramatically and accentuated almond-shaped eyes, making the pale blue pop from clear across the room. Her lips were painted a deep red, and a sprinkling of freckles dotted her nose—decidedly, the only sweet thing about her.

From beside me, Dax whistled under his breath. "Bloody hell, who is that? I pick *her* for a good seeing to."

I edged in front of him. "I saw her first," I said.

CHAPTER THREE

I STOOD IN front of the Tau fraternity front door and gave myself a mental pep talk.

So what if this was my first college party? *I had this.*

It may have taken me two years, but walking into the biggest party on campus would prove that Colby had not won.

I could still be around alcohol and partying and not freak out.

Hadn't I watched *Animal House* and *Revenge of the Nerds* this week to prepare myself for the onslaught of college-age shenanigans?

Feeling fidgety, I adjusted the sterling silver bangles I wore each day. Two inches wide and embellished with my own infinity design, I'd made them in a metal working class before Colby happened. Now, I used them to hide the bundle of scars on my wrists where I'd tried to kill myself two days after the hotel.

I rubbed the cool metal, reminding myself I had two goals tonight.

The first was to walk into this frat party; the second was to find a guy, take him home, and christen my new place.

Any sober guy would do.

Like there would be any sober guys here.

Still ...

Something was off tonight, as if a heavy presence lingered in the air. Fate warning me that life was about to get rocky? Was I making a huge mistake by coming here?

"I can't believe you're actually going to walk in that door. On a normal Friday night, you'd be eating delivery pizza and avoiding my calls."

I took a breath and nodded.

Just be normal. Okay, don't be normal 'cause normal for you is being alone and grumpy and watching *Downton Abby* episodes curled on Granny's cat couch.

Just ... be cool, I told myself. Plus, if I didn't go in this party, Shelley and Blake were going to have me committed to some psyche ward for antisocial behavior.

We walked in and Blake rushed to meet us. He wore his fraternity jersey, looking boyishly handsome with his auburn hair and big grin. A big guy, he'd played football in high school and now played linebacker for the Whitman Wildcats. We'd dated in high school for about a second, but Colby had come along and all other guys had faded into the background.

His eyes gleamed with what I took as pride. "Hot damn, you made it! How are my two favorite girls?"

I smiled up at him. "The question is how's the party? Anyone OD yet? Human sacrifices going on in the back?" I pretended to be casual, but I stood on my tiptoes and peeked around his shoulders as I spoke, checking out the scene. I didn't let my gaze linger too long on anyone. My nerves were taut and ready to pop, and I hadn't even seen the entire place.

He shook his head, giving me a pointed look like he saw through my jokes. "Nah, we keep a tight watch on those things." He wrapped us both up in a big brawny hug, his rosy cheeks making him look almost cherubic. "I'm damned glad you're here. And I promise to take care of you." He tweaked me on the nose. "You especially. Now stop waffling and come on in."

The room blared with music and people stood everywhere. It was hot and noisy and my chest tightened. I skated my eyes through the crowd when all I wanted to do was run like hell. Thank goodness we swept on through to get out of the throng, and he led us out the patio doors to the backyard. Air. I inhaled and then choked on a cloud of perfume as one of the fraternity sisters stopped in front of us. Lorna something. I'd seen her around Blake before, and judging from the evil eye she sent me, I wasn't her favorite person. Whatever. I didn't care. Blake and I were just friends, but because we spent a lot of time together, some people might assume we were more.

She slid her hands over Blake's chest. "Hey baby, don't you want to come back inside where the real party is? No one fun is out here."

Shelley giggled and I kept my face a mask. Cool. Calm. I'd been around girls like her all through prep school. Pretty rich girls. The best way to deal with them was to never let them see you get flustered. Be a bitch right back. I smiled at her tightly as Blake leaned over to whisper something in her ear. She flounced off to go back inside, a little extra swing in her hips.

He crooked our arms together and showed me around, pride evident in his voice as he stopped periodically to introduce me to several of his brothers. Shelley knew most everyone already.

I took a look around the area, taking in the lit tiki torches, a makeshift dance floor with a DJ and strobe lights, and a huge pool. People roamed everywhere, most of them popular and Greek and not part of my crowd. A girl in a tiny red bikini did a cannonball into the deep end and came up holding her top. Almost immediately, guys whooped loudly and jumped in after her.

"This party is on steroids," I murmured.

"You good?" Shelley asked.

I nodded.

A tall guy—about six three—with dark hair and a jawline that could rival any movie star stopped in front of Blake. He did a bow thing and came up with a cocky grin and checked us out blatantly.

Shelley pushed her well-endowed boobs out. A notorious guy-chaser, she loved guys and was quite, er, free with her love. Didn't matter who they were. Tall, short, rich, poor, black, white, amphibian ...

"Who're your hot friends, mate?" the guy asked in an English accent, his words sleek in their delivery. Lofty.

My eyebrows went straight up, my interest piqued. Yes! I loved the way he talked.

Blake immediately stiffened. "They're with me, Dax, so hands off."

Dax? Nice name.

I shot Blake a quick look, but he avoided my eyes. He was a bit possessive when it came to protecting me, and a few times over the past few years I'd had to tell him to back down. I started to lean in and tell him it was fine, but the guy spoke first.

"What? Can't I even say hi?" He turned dark gray eyes at me. "You. Do you eat sugar all the time? 'Cause you are the sweetest thing I've seen all night."

A surprised snort came from me. "That's the worst pickup line ever."

He looked crestfallen. "Ah, angel, don't laugh—or snort—at me. You're killing my fragile ego."

"Truth hurts."

He grinned, not deterred. "Okay, this isn't a line, but have we met before? You seem really familiar."

I stuck my hand out. The more forthright I was, the easier it made things. "I'm Elizabeth Bennett, and we've never met because I'd definitely have remembered your accent. Unless it was in class and we never spoke ..." I arched my brow. "What's your major? I'm in the art department mostly."

He grimaced. "Psychology, but I don't go to class much. Maybe it was the Sigma party last year?"

"The one with the goats on the roof? Ah, no."

"The Delta toga party? The one where the cops came?" He chuckled. "Don't recall much of that one, although I do remember waking up in a pair of women's underwear."

Oh. "Sadly, no, but I did see the students who were arrested on the news."

He tossed back his head to laugh, calling attention to the strong lines of his throat. I let my eyes take more of him in, checking out the skinny jeans and the Vital Rejects band shirt that fit snugly to his muscled chest. He was gorgeous.

He knew I was checking him out, because he smirked, a knowing glint in his eye. He nudged his head at the crowded dance floor. "Wanna go dance?"

"Ever heard of taking it slow, Dax?" Blake snapped. "She just got here. Give her some space."

Shelley ignored Blake and looked at me expectantly, obviously wanting me to say yes, but I shook my head at Dax. "Sorry. I'm not your type." Best to rip the Band-Aid off fast.

"I'm every girl's type." His eyes skated over my white strapless sundress. "Especially beautiful angels who just fell from heaven."

"Don't angels have wings?" I asked. "Kinda hard to fall when technically you can fly."

He waggled his eyebrows and held up the Solo cup he carried in his hand. "No one's splitting hairs here, besides my lines get better the more I drink."

Ah.

I stiffened but nodded. Trying to be polite. "Hmm, well, I usually spend my Friday nights doing homework while I wear granny panties. I also binge watch Masterpiece Theatre, crochet knit hats, and do calculus when I get bored. I don't usually come to parties. I don't even talk to guys who drink, so I'm *really* not your type."

He rolled his eyes. "Just one dance, love. We don't have to get married."

"Good thing I'm stone-cold sober. Looks like I'm the winner here, brother. You can pay me later," said another accented voice behind me, and I whipped around to see a replica of Dax. Only with bigger muscles.

Another Brit?

Only this one's voice was huskier. Sexier.

"Twins?" I squeaked.

They smirked and nodded simultaneously. In the same exact manner.

I blinked. Oh. They were double trouble, sex on *two* sticks.

The sober one pushed dark brown hair off his forehead and stared at me. His face was classically handsome, the jawline angular and defined, but that's where the carbon copy stopped. Every inch of this guy's arms not covered by his black shirt were covered in colorful tattoos, and I got lost trying to trace the designs, from ivy branches to skulls. My eyes paused on the blue dragonfly tattoo on his neck. Odd seeing something so light-hearted on such a bulky dude.

He wore tight designer jeans, black motorcycle boots, and a shirt that clung to a chest that had obviously seen its fair share of the inside of a gym. *Intense* was the word that came to mind when his silver-gray eyes met mine, sweeping over my face, lingering on my bare shoulders. Warmth spread and I got hot as if I'd just stuck my finger in a socket.

What *was* that?

One thing for sure, he was pure hot male and if you could put it in a bottle, you'd make millions.

Get away from the hotness and tell your ovaries to settle down, my brain yelled, but I stupidly ignored it.

Something about him had me riveted. Maybe it was the black eye.

I immediately pictured him in a bar, turning over chairs and tables and kicking other big dudes' asses.

I took a tiny step back. *Remember the rules.* No hot guys. No popular guys. No rich guys. I was fairly certain he'd check all those boxes.

The sober twin flashed even, white teeth. "In case you're wondering, I'm the oldest by two minutes. I also get better grades, as you might have guessed." He tossed an arm around his brother and rubbed his head good-naturedly.

"Yeah, but I'm the babe magnet," Dax said. "You're just coasting on my bloody coattails, trying to pluck the birds I found first."

The bigger one laughed. "Keep dreaming, baby bro. I don't need to coast. I *am* the sexiest guy on campus."

"Whatever. I'm Dax, in case you missed it," he said to me with a grin.

I looked at the other twin. "And you are?"

"Declan," he murmured in his low voice, his accented words like silk, the vowels soft and rounded.

I shivered.

Declan.

One simple word that I felt all the way to the roots of my scalp.

Butterflies danced in my tummy. I yelled at them to settle down, but they didn't listen.

His full, sensuous lips kicked up in a grin as I repeated it. "That's a beautiful name," I said, "the way it rolls off my tongue."

"It's Gaelic and means *full of goodness.* Ironic since most call me trouble." He smiled. "Elizabeth, right?"

I nodded and he put his hand out for me to take. I rested mine in his much larger warm one, not surprised by the tingles that zipped down my spine. Reluctantly he released my hand, his fingertips sliding against my palm in a sensuous sweep. I let out an uneven breath I must have been holding since the moment he stepped into my vision.

Was his reaction the same as mine?

His facial expression hadn't changed at our first touch, yet he'd moved closer to me, the expensive scent of his woodsy cologne permeating my senses.

The conversation picked back up with the others, but Declan and I just stood there silently. I glanced at him. He glanced at me. He smiled. I smiled. And right there it felt like we were having an intimate moment, just the two of us as we stared at each other while the world carried on. His gaze kept coming back to me, almost inquisitive as if he wanted to ask me something but didn't know how. There was a connection between us, and I'm not stupid, I know it wasn't love at first sight—maybe lust—but he was definitely the hottest guy I'd been this close to in two years.

He was exactly what I needed tonight, the complete opposite of Colby's blond and preppy Ralph Lauren looks. Perhaps it was time to take my rules a step further, to prove to myself I could be with whomever I wanted and keep control of the situation.

As long as the fortress of my heart remained under lock and key, I was good.

He turned away from me when a pretty girl walked up to him, and just like that I changed my mind. *Player?*

He looked back to me a minute or two later, a sheepish smile on his face. "Sorry about that. I taught her some self-defense moves last year, and she was telling me how she'd used them on her older brother this summer."

Oh. I took in his broad chest and biceps. "You're a trainer?"

He nodded, an earnest expression on his face. "Yeah. I've taught in some of the local gyms, but I'm opening my own soon."

"Is that how you got your black eye?"

He considered me carefully. "No."

I studied him harder, my gaze boring into the masculine planes of his face. Instinctively, I reached up and delicately touched a red place near his hairline. A cut? He winced and I immediately dropped my hand. "So sorry, I—I don't know why I did that."

Stop touching the hot guy! I yelled in my head.

He shrugged. "It's fine."

"You use your fists a lot?"

"Yes," he said softly.

I sucked in a sharp breath. Dangerous. Sexy. Trouble. *Why was I still talking to him?*

Blake sidestepped between Declan and me in such a way that it felt forced. "You want a drink, Elizabeth? There's beer and some punch, although it's probably spiked. I can scrounge around and find you something though."

"A water would be great."

"Yes," Shelley said emphatically. "She may not drink, but I do. Bring it to mama. Anything will do."

Declan surprised me by saying he'd get them for us, and I watched him move away, his lithe frame moving with the easy grace of someone used to holding back power like a sexy jungle cat who prowled around and took what he wanted ...

I'd like to pet that jungle cat, rub his silky fur and make him purr ...

I slapped myself mentally.

Jungle cat? Make him purr? What was wrong with me tonight?

"Don't mess with him," Blake whispered in my ear as if he'd read my train of thought.

I shot a look over at Dax and Shelley to make sure they hadn't heard his comment, but they were involved in a discussion about music.

"Why? What's wrong with him?"

He narrowed his eyes, a flash of annoyance on his face. "*Are* you interested?"

"Get real. I study. I work. I sleep." Occasionally I have sex.

He nodded, his expression growing serious. "Maybe it's time to move on and trust someone."

I arched a brow. "But *not* Declan?"

He opened his mouth. Shut it. He held his hands up as if to placate me. "Don't get me wrong. He's cool. But you're exactly his type, physically any way, and I saw the way he looked at you. He's on the rebound, and I just don't want you to get hurt. He's a senior and popular—and well, no one knows *you*."

"Wow. That hurt. Thanks for the vote of confidence." I crossed my arms.

He groaned. "It's just … I've seen him go through girls like frat boys and their beer. He's a user and once he's done with you, he'll toss you out. You need a nice guy."

My mouth tightened. "I thought Colby was a nice guy and look how that turned out." I sighed. "Are you actually jealous?"

He flushed. "I just know how guys think. Declan's a jerk and you need to avoid him and not do anything stupid."

"And if by stupid you mean let a guy get me drunk so he can do whatever he wants—I think I learned my lesson." Blake and I had been arguing a lot lately, and it was always about stupid stuff. Something was off between us. "Whatever. I'm going to find a restroom."

Shelley's eyes were big as I turned to walk away, but Blake grabbed my hand and pulled me back. He grimaced, hazel eyes apologetic. "I'm an asshole. I'm sorry. It's just—I remember what you looked like, all messed up and crying, and then you tried—"

"Just stop," I snipped. "Please. I don't need reminders of my mistakes."

He reddened, his shoulders dipping down. "I can't do anything right by you tonight. Forgive me, Elizabeth?"

God, what was wrong with me? He'd always been there for me.

"Of course. I'm sorry for snapping," I said as his big body leaned in to give me a hug. We embraced tightly, his strong arms encircling my waist as I tilted my head up and met his eyes. They were glistening with some kind of emotion I took as remorse.

"It's okay," I murmured and kissed his cheek.

We pulled apart but not before I saw Declan look over his shoulder at us from his place in line at the bar. A strange expression crossed his face, but then it was just as quickly gone.

I couldn't help but notice that my gaze wasn't the only one following him around the patio. Almost all the girls. And a few of the guys. He laughed at something someone said on the way back to us, his long legs eating up the ground in big strides. People everywhere clapped him on the back as if congratulating him. He'd nod and smile. Those who didn't know him seemed to scurry to move, nodding their heads at him, giving him passage.

He had *presence*, as Mom would say.

My mom had dated a string of men with presence—drug problems, felonies, heavy fists.

I groaned. I was spending way too much time analyzing this guy.

But my mouth had other ideas. "So what exactly is Declan's type," I asked Blake, turning my eyes to him.

"Blond hair, long legs, smart. Mostly sorority girls with attitudes and rich daddies. In fact, his ex, Nadia, is here somewhere." He gazed around at the crowd as if to find her.

I snorted. "Rich girls? I'm here on an academic scholarship. I think I'm safe."

"Safe from what?" Declan asked me as he approached us. I startled. He'd moved a lot faster than I'd thought. He handed me a chilled bottle of water, his warm hands again connecting with mine, his fingers lingering.

Sparks went off on my skin.

Did he carry some kind of electrical current machine around in his pocket?

He handed a Solo cup of beer to Shelley.

I tried to focus my eyes away from him, but the darn things kept returning to him, searching his face and taking in the details. He had a three-inch white scar above his right eyebrow and I found myself wanting to touch it, to trace it with my fingers and ask him what had happened. He was preoccupied with me too, giving me long glances but then looking away and rolling his neck as if what he saw in me made his shoulders tight.

Ha. I bet he had a line of girls waiting to work those kinks out.

But still that didn't stop me from following him to the back of the yard when he suggested it, saying we could talk without everyone in our face.

Blake went off to dance with one of the fraternity little sisters. Shelley checked with me to make sure I was okay and when I told her I was fine, she and Dax headed out to dance.

We stood with our backs against the fence and watched the party, laughing every now and then at something crazy someone would do in the pool or on the dance floor.

"Do you think we're the only sober people here?" I asked. I'd noticed he'd been drinking water too.

He shrugged. "My father drinks a lot, and I don't want to be anything like him."

I heard the tension in his voice, and because I wanted to ease him, I opened up. "Hmm, no family is perfect. My dad's in prison—or at least the man my mom tells me is my dad. I've never met him, but he's there for murder."

His mouth parted, a look of surprise on his face. That I was the spawn of a killer? "Bugger, that must have been tough."

"He beat a guy to death in an alley outside a bar while he was on probation for selling drugs. He got life." My gut tightened as I took in his black eye. "My mom says he was a hothead. Maybe it's a good thing I never knew him. People who use their fists scare me."

His body tensed at that, but it didn't stop me from babbling on and on. Maybe it was because he was a stranger, and I figured I'd never see him again. "My mom, on the other hand, wanted to be a Vegas showgirl but then she got pregnant with me. I guess you could say I ruined her life." I shrugged, pushing those memories away. "So, how did you end up here? Are you an athlete?" My eyes lingered on his broad chest. Again.

He grinned. "No."

Oh.

"I'm originally from London. My mum was English and my dad's American—he was the ambassador to England years ago." He seemed to gather himself, adjusting his stance, his eyes suddenly everywhere except on me. "They divorced when I was a toddler, and when I was ten, Mum died from cancer. Dax and I moved here to Raleigh to live with my dad. I guess you can say we've been Americanized in the past few years. At least I got a dual citizenship out of the union." Hardness grew in his eyes. "He ripped everything away from us and then forgot we existed when he got remarried. I don't see him often. He doesn't care."

I held my water bottle up. "A toast to shitty parents."

A large blue dragonfly landed on my arm, its stick-like body vibrating. I'm not the kind of girl who screams bloody murder when an insect shows up. The artist in me preferred to study everything in great detail.

"Oh. Look how pretty it is," I said, but he'd already seen it and had leaned in closer, the smell of him male and potent.

"It tickles," I giggled after a while, and he shooed the creature away, his gentleness surprising me.

He watched it fly away and then sent me a considering glance. "It's funny—every time I see a dragonfly, I think it's my mum's spirit. She loved them. Crazy-like. She even had this charm bracelet someone had given her, and you'd think she'd have different things on it, but all she bought were dragonfly charms. She had magnets, knickknacks, even paintings." He rubbed his jawline. "On the day of her funeral, we were at the burial and one landed on Dax and then flew over to me. It hovered around us the entire time and wouldn't leave. It was strange yet comforting—" He swallowed and then continued. "The day my father showed up at our house to move us here, one followed our car for miles. Weird, right? I—I just always think it's her looking out for me."

"That's beautiful. Is that why you have the tattoo on your neck?"

"Yeah. To always have her with me."

Him, him, him, my body said. *Pick him tonight.*

I fidgeted, switching my water from one hand to the other.

"Hey, you okay? Did my story bother you?" His eyes watched me, landing on my lips.

I licked them. "Uh, no, it's just we seem to have this *thing,* like a connection, and I was wondering if maybe, you know, if you weren't busy later, and you know, if you aren't with anyone else, and if you think it's cool, and if you're attracted to me and like sex, then perhaps you could come back to my place?"

I closed my eyes in horror. Kill me now. Shit, shit, shit. That came out so wrong.

I popped my eyes open to see Blake jogging over to us. Thank God. Someone to rescue me from my stupidity.

I chanced a look at Declan for a reaction to my offer, but his face was a cool mask as he watched Blake approach us.

Had he even heard me? What was up with him?

Blake stopped in front of me, not looking at Declan. "Come on, you love this song. Let's go dance," he insisted, grabbing my hand and tugging.

I cleared my throat and got my nerve back up. "Why don't we all go out and dance? Declan?"

Declan sent me a conflicted look, his eyes going to my hand enclosed in Blake's and then back to my face. A muscle ticked in his jaw. "No, thanks," he said coolly.

What was that?

"Go on. I'll be out there in a minute," I told Blake, who immediately sent me a sulky look but stalked back to the dance floor.

I turned to Declan. "Why don't you want to dance? No rhythm?" I grinned to lighten the suddenly dark mood he seemed to be in.

"Are you Blake's girl?" His words were clipped.

"No. I don't date anyone. I have fun, that's it. And in case you missed it, I just propositioned you. Horribly."

His face softened as he touched my hair briefly and then dropped his hand. "You shocked the hell out of me, you know. It was surprisingly … earnest and cute."

Cute? The worse adjective ever for a girl. A death knell sounded.

"I shouldn't have done that. I got caught up in the night and you …" Obviously, he wasn't interested.

"Don't think I'm not into you," he said rather huskily.

"But?"

"It's not a good idea."

"Whatever. I should be running like hell from a guy like you anyway."

His eyes zeroed back in on mine. "Why?"

"Long story."

He shifted closer to me, his hand brushing mine. "Maybe you can tell me that story someday."

And then out of the blue, tears pricked at my eyes at his tenderness, and I hurriedly blinked them away before he noticed.

He exhaled, seeming to be uncertain about how to proceed. "Look, I've seen you around on campus. You keep to yourself and underneath you seem, well, fragile—and honestly, I like my girls and sex hard. I'd be all over you, and somehow I'm sensing you aren't down with that." His intense eyes searched mine. "Putting everything out there, I just broke up with someone a few months back, and I wouldn't want to use you."

I got hung up on *I like it hard*, and repeating it in my head made sweat pop out.

"Maybe I want to use you, and I'm not fragile. No one hurts me anymore," I said, but before he could reply to that, Shelley yelled from the dance floor.

"Elizabeth, get your ass out here and dance with me." Her arms waved at me to come on, her lithe body gyrating around several partners.

When I turned back to Declan, a pretty girl with blond hair cut in a sharp bob had come up and crooked her arm through his. Thin with big boobs, she wore stilettos and a soft periwinkle dress that probably cost more than my rent.

She took a look at me, dismissed me with a sniff, and turned to Declan.

"Hey, babe, I need to talk to you." She ran her fingers down his arm.

His entire body stiffened, a cold look on his face as he peered down at her. "What do you want?"

"You," she whined. "Just give me a chance to explain ..."

Oh. The ex?

He flicked his eyes to me and nodded. "It was great to meet you, Elizabeth. I'll see you tomorrow."

Tomorrow? Since when?

He sent me one final look, turned, and walked away with the other girl.

Just like that, my night with Declan was over.

Was I disappointed? *Yes.*

Was I going to let it ruin my first college party? *No.*

CHAPTER FOUR

Declan

ELIZABETH BENNETT WAS the most awkward person to ever come to a frat party.

Not only had she came through the door like she was going to an execution, but she'd asked me to shag her in the most unsophisticated manner I'd ever seen in my days at Whitman. I could live for the next hundred years and my ears would never hear a come-on *that* bad.

Weird or not, no one could deny she was hot as hell. The entire time we'd talked, I hadn't been able to stop staring at her blue eyes or the way her dress plunged down to the deep V between her breasts—which was frustrating.

I wasn't here to meet some girl and start something. I didn't need the distraction.

And the Blake dude?

What in the bloody hell?

He was crazy in love with her, and she had no clue. Or did she?

I followed Nadia as she led me back into the house. I should have shoved her off me as soon as she'd sidled up next to me with that forlorn expression on her face, but truthfully, I'd needed to distance myself from Elizabeth and Nadia had been a good excuse. Surprisingly, seeing her hadn't crushed me like I thought it might. Now that we'd been apart for a while I'd had time to think and I could see how incredibly wrong she'd been for me. Most of our relationship had been based on sex. A shallow girl who only looked out for herself, she'd been the wrong choice all along, but I'd been swayed by her body and the way she'd fawned over me.

We headed into the library toward the back of the house. A secluded room, it was where the frat held most of their meetings and formal gatherings. I figured there'd be less of a chance of anyone walking in on us if things got heated. Not that I'd lose my temper with her. That wasn't my style. I'd never gone off on a female—thanks to the good influence of my mum.

I took my frustrations out on the punching bag at the gym, not on girls.

I knew Nadia's game. She'd come to the party and seen me with Elizabeth. She wanted what she couldn't have. Typical.

We made our way into the center of the room and before I could even ask her what she wanted that was so important, she had her tongue down my throat.

It felt good for half a second, and then I reached behind me to untangle her hands and remove her lips from mine.

"Don't do that," I snapped.

"Declan, I know you hate me," she whispered, staring up at me, "but I've missed you so much. Please don't push me away. It's been an absolutely horrible summer without you."

"Mine was pretty good," I bit out. "I got rid of a cheating girlfriend and worked my arse off getting the gym ready. Ditching you was the best thing I did."

She closed her eyes, a flash of pain on her face, and when she opened them, tears swam, making them shimmer. "I know we ended terribly, and it's all my fault, and you shouldn't even give me the time of day, but it's been so long since I've seen you—"

"Where's Donatello?" I said curtly and crossed my arms. "Go find him."

She bit her lip and let out a choke. "Oh, God, Declan, my mom has cancer. She was diagnosed last month, and I've been a basket case ever since, and all I could think of was talking to you, and I *can't* because you won't return my calls." She swallowed, her hands twisting in the fabric of her dress. "With what you went through with your mom, you're the only one who gets how scared I am. I—I just needed to see you tonight and tell you."

Her mum?

I scrubbed my jaw, remembering Mrs. Brown as a sweet lady who resembled Nadia, only softer and always asking if I needed anything when we'd been at her parents' house a few times for dinner. I exhaled and pinched the bridge of my nose. "I'm sorry for your mum. Cancer sucks more than anything I know."

She sniffed and snuggled into my chest, so I ended up wrapping my arms around her.

"God, you smell so good," she murmured against my chest.

I stared down at her. "Nadia—"

She cupped my face. "Don't talk. Just kiss me, Declan."

CHAPTER FIVE

Elizabeth

THE SONG ENDED and I took off to go back inside. I told myself it was just to find a restroom, but I also really wanted to see where Declan went. Stalker? Maybe.

I wandered around until I passed one of the smaller rooms and out of my peripheral gaze caught a couple embracing.

I stopped and backed up to get a better view.

I really shouldn't spy, but it was Declan and Nadia who stood in front of a chair, giving me a view of their torsos as they held each other. She pulled his head down and kissed him hungrily as her hands ran through his hair. He let it go on for a while but then disentangled her hands as he said something I couldn't hear.

Holding my breath, I leaned forward to try and catch their conversation.

I don't know why I cared so much. He'd turned me down and let me know I wasn't his type, which was damn ironic considering I'd rejected his brother—not that it had fazed Dax in the least.

Yells and whoops reached my ears as a sudden influx of

partiers came into the house. Declan and Nadia turned toward the door, and afraid of getting caught snooping, I ducked down to my knees.

Had they seen me? I closed my eyes.

How had I gotten myself in this mess?

Because you had to pee, I responded to myself. And because you came to this stupid party.

Praying the chair hid me, I moved in a slow duck crawl toward the hallway and hopefully a toilet.

Black Converse shoes stopped in front of me, and I looked up into the amused eyes of Dax. He peered down at me with a quizzical look. "Enjoying yourself?"

Think fast, Elizabeth.

"Just looking for my contact," I said, patting the hardwood floor. "It popped out while I was looking for the restroom."

"Ah. You need some help then? It's rather dark in here."

"No, I'm fine." Pat, pat.

A few ticks went by.

I kept crawling around. Playing cool. Hoping he'd walk away. *Praying.*

I chanced a look up to see him watching me in amusement.

"Are you sure you don't need help? That floor is terribly dirty."

"I don't mind a little dirt. Improves your immune system. I ate it daily as a toddler."

He laughed. "Why don't you just confess you were staring at my brother and Nadia? Besides, I can see straight down your dress when you're on your hands and knees. I don't mind the view of your tits but figured you'd want to know."

Dammit!

"Fine." I stood up, brushing my dress down. "For your information, I don't wear contacts. I just happened to be walking by and saw them, and you have to admit, they're intense. It's like a soap opera. Obviously I lack social skills and I'm nosey."

"Indeed."

His lofty English accent only made my mortification worse.

I buried my face in my hands. "I should never have come to this party in the first place. I'm way out of my comfort zone, and your brother ... well, I tried to flirt—pick him up, to be honest—and it blew up in my face."

"You fancy my brother?" His tone was surprised.

I peeked through my fingers. "And by fancy you mean like?"

He smirked. "As you Americans like to say, *duh*."

I bit my lip. "I barely know him."

Dax looked over my shoulder, eyes narrowed. "He's coming out now. Let's pretend to be madly in love."

"What?" *He was crazier than I was.*

He sent me a long look. "Let's give him something to think about ... make him jealous. Kiss me."

I held my hands up to ward him off. "I don't kiss guys with liquor on their breath—and probably a venereal disease."

He clutched his chest like I'd broken his heart. "Oh, you're funny, but trust me on this. Declan likes *you*. I saw how he was talking to you. Kiss me, love, just do it." His voice was insistent.

Alarm bells went off. I clenched my fists.

"*No*."

But he wasn't listening.

He gathered me in his arms, his strong arms cupping my shoulders and pulling me closer. He pressed his lips to mine, his hips maneuvering me against the wall behind me.

The smell of alcohol on his breath slammed into me.

My stomach lurched. Memories hit.

The sharp sting of vodka.

My dress torn around my body.

The slice of razor on my wrists.

I shuddered, bile crawling in my gut.

Dax lifted his lips from mine and stared down at me. Confusion dawned on his face. "Elizabeth? You've gone white as a sheet."

His voice came from a distance, and I shook my head, shoving him to get away from me. Inhale through the nose, exhale through the mouth. *Just breathe.* I dug down deep, reaching for that part of myself I knew was strong. A survivor.

I'd had years of counseling. I knew how to handle a freak-out.

He touched my arm, and I flinched, my palm flashing out to strike him hard across the cheek, the sound reverberating in the quietness of the hallway.

He cupped his cheek and stared at me with a stunned expression. "That is not how I saw this ending. Bugger, I had no clue you weren't into me." He put his hands on my shoulders with a light touch. "You okay?"

"Get away from me," I hissed and shoved at his broad shoulders. He released me, and I leaned against the wall, my hands digging into the paneling to stay standing up.

Suddenly strong hands were pushing Dax even further away.

Declan stood between us, his face dark and angry. His silvery eyes swept over me then focused back on Dax, a muscle twitching in his jaw. "What's going on here? What's wrong with Elizabeth?"

"It's fine," I whispered. It wasn't.

Declan swiveled his eyes back to Dax, who held his hands up. "I went in for a kiss, and she wasn't excited. That's it."

His eyes flared as he shoved Dax away from him. "Don't be such a prick, Dax."

Dax flushed a deep red as he glared back at Declan. He exhaled and fixed his gaze to me, a contrite look on his handsome face. "Look, I'm truly, truly sorry. I didn't know kissing me would make you want to barf. I just wanted to be able to tell Declan I'd kissed you first. We have this thing where we take bets on who can get a girl ... Sorry, you probably don't want to hear that right now."

I wasn't even listening to him, focusing instead on breathing.

Declan touched my hand. "You okay?"

Okay?

Hundreds of miles and years away from Colby and that hotel room, yet it haunted me. Shame beat me with her whips. I hadn't had a reaction like this in months, mostly because I kept my environment in strict control.

But, I'd wanted to be a normal college kid for a night. I'd just wanted to be like everyone else.

I straightened up from the wall, my gaze encompassing them and then bouncing away. I felt embarrassed. "I'll be fine."

Declan didn't agree, his stormy eyes still flashing at his brother.

Nadia came out to the hallway, adjusting her dress, making me wonder what I'd missed.

"What's going on?"

No one answered.

Dax just shrugged and fidgeted while Declan kept his gaze on my face, his eyes seeming to devour every inch.

Even in the midst of having a near panic attack, something about *him* had dug into my skin.

Leave. Go. This party is not for you.

"I need to go," I said, crossing my arms and rubbing them. "It's late."

"Don't go," Dax said. "I swear to keep my hands to myself if you'll just stay."

"Don't pressure her," Declan said. "Can't you tell you scared her?"

Nadia's eyes bounced from me to Dax to Declan as she tried to figure it out, but I didn't want her to.

My mortification grew.

I needed away from this party, away from the guy who'd kissed me, and away from the guy I couldn't have and certainly didn't need.

"Let me give you a lift home," Declan stated more than asked, his voice soft.

No! I couldn't take being close to either of them anymore. "I can take care of myself."

Nadia chimed in. "I can take her home. I'm leaving anyway."

"No thanks," I snapped at her. I would not be maneuvered by a jealous ex simply because she was afraid I'd take her man.

She held her hands up. "No need to be bitchy."

"That's enough, Nadia," Declan said.

She huffed. "I'm just trying to help."

No she wasn't. I didn't know her personally, but I knew girls like her. They were the ones who'd talked about me after prom, the ones who'd gossiped and posted on twitter and Facebook about all the horrible things Colby had told everyone about me in the hours following the hotel. Suddenly girls who'd I'd thought were my friends had labeled me as a slut and a troublemaker.

Before Declan could protest any more, I turned on my heel and walked away. I found Shelley back outside on the dance floor where apparently she'd never left. I pulled her aside and said I was ready to go.

"Is everything okay?" she asked me, her face flushed from dancing.

I didn't want to see the disappointed look in her eyes, so I lied and told her I was just tired. She offered to drive me back to the apartment, but she'd been drinking and was having a great time, and I didn't want to always be the friend who required extra attention because she had mental breakdowns over stupid stuff.

After some cajoling and assurances that I could find a way

home, she went back to her dancing, and I got my phone out to call a cab. Next time I'd know to drive myself.

No, wait, there wouldn't be a next time.

This was my last party.

Blake appeared at my side as I hung up my phone. "Where in the hell have you been? I've been looking everywhere for you." He took in the way I clutched my purse. "Leaving already?"

"Sorry, I have a lot to do at the apartment. Can you take care of Shelley if she's too trashed to drive? Make sure she gets back to the dorm?"

"Of course." He sent me an anxious look. "Just don't disappear on me like that. I searched all the bedrooms for you. Who knows what could have happened when you were with Declan Blay."

Declan? He'd been the nicest of the entire lot of them.

I didn't have time to argue with him. I just wanted to go. "I'm fine. I'll see you soon."

He grabbed my arm to stop me as I turned, uncertainty written on his face. "Elizabeth, wait. There's something I need to tell you that I should have said a long time ago ..."

No.

I put my hands to his lips. I suspected what he wanted to say, and I wasn't ready to hear it—or respond to it. "Don't. Not now. I can't handle any more tonight."

CHAPTER SIX

Declan

FROM THE SIDE of the Tau house, I watched her long legs walk across the yard and ease into a cab that had pulled up to the curb. Her shoulders were hunched as if weighted down with burden. Her huddled posture sent alarm bells all through me. Her reaction had been extreme. I got angry at Dax all over again. He was impulsive and rushed headlong into everything without thinking, so it wasn't a surprise to see him making a pass at a pretty girl, but it was *her*, and for some reason it bugged me.

Acting on impulse, I jumped in my Jeep and pulled out to follow her home. Some unnamed emotion made me anxious to make sure she got home okay.

It wasn't like I didn't know where she lived.

I followed the cab until it reached the apartments, and I pulled in at Minnie's Diner across the road to let my Jeep idle as I watched her get out, pay the driver, and then make the trek across the carpark. She made a solitary figure as she trudged across the pavement, her white-blond hair blowing in the wind that had kicked up from an incoming storm. One of the streetlights was out, and I noticed she seemed keenly aware of the fact, her pale face peering over her shoulder as she made her way up the stairs. She walked briskly down the hall, the mere swing of her arms telling me she was on alert for anything. She was aware of the dangers of walking alone at night.

Had Dax been the one to cause all that reaction?

I suspected not. She fit the mold for the kind of girls I'd seen in my self-defense classes. Scared. Vulnerable. Hiding behind her pain.

Elizabeth Bennett had been hurt in the past by someone, and whoever he was, I wanted to bury my fist in his face.

She stopped at her door and dropped her keys. I got jacked up at the way she bent over in her dress, her heart-shaped arse straining against the material. My eyes lingered on her shoulders and how they contrasted with the white of her dress. She was hot, and it had been hard as hell to tell her no tonight. She slipped inside the door, giving me a brief glimpse of the soft curve of her face, and I immediately regretted my sexual urges.

Right then all I wanted was to take that bruised look off her face.

She went inside, so I pulled out and parked in our own lot, planning on heading inside myself. There was no need in going back to the party, even though Nadia had insisted we talk tonight. And with thoughts of her, I reminded myself why it was a shitty idea to even be attracted to any girl right now, especially one as gorgeous as Elizabeth.

I got inside just as my phone pinged. Father.

I read his text: **Dinner at my house tomorrow. Dax has already confirmed. We need to discuss your after graduation plans and inheritance.**

I barked out a laugh and tossed my phone on the couch.

And that proved how well he kept up with me.

He had no idea I'd used my half of Mum's money I'd got last year to buy a gym.

I needed to punch something. I stripped off my shirt, yanked on some gym shorts, and picked up my gloves. I couldn't hit the bag without music, so I cranked up Nelly on my speakers and went for it.

CHAPTER SEVEN

Elizabeth

A THUNDERSTORM LIT the night sky.

I sat on my bed and watched the lightning, its lines jagged and sharp in the distance. Before long, the wind picked up, the gusts bending over the small trees in the landscaping below my balcony.

I picked at Granny's quilt on my bed.

I was alone, but like the storm outside, winds of change were blowing in my life. I just didn't know where they'd take me.

Shelley sent me a text, responding to one I'd sent her earlier to check on her.

Blake got me home. Why did you leave so soon? What happened with you and Whitman University's Sexiest Man on Campus? Did you guys have monkey sex?

No monkeys. Please! What's wrong with human sex? And Whitman's Sexiest Man? Wow. Cheesy, I tapped out.

He's hot and rich and sexy as hell, she texted. **Rumor is he only had eyes for you tonight. According to Blake.**

I ignored that and tapped out, **Nite. Let's do lunch soon. I**

owe you for helping me move today.

I set my phone down and snuggled back down in the bed.

While the storm raged, my neighbor moved around his apartment, making a racket as he cranked up some music, the beat of the bass loud through the thin walls.

Okay, I could handle some late night music next door. Easy. I quickly reminded myself this was the weekend and these *were* university-owned apartments.

But isn't he being inconsiderate? Whatever. I flip-flopped over just as a rhythmic thumping sound reached my ears. *Thump, thump, whack, whack.*

Great. Was he having a freaking party over there?

I groaned and buried my head under my pillow. That didn't help. I tossed in my bed, antsy. Angry even. I replayed the night, remembering my rejection from Declan. I rose up to beat on my pillow to make it softer.

Bloody Brit. He knew *nothing* about me.

I'd seen the darkness on the other side that night in the hotel, and I'd faced it down, dealing with it the only way I knew how. I was *not* fragile.

But you've changed, a small voice inside me said. *You're bitter. A shell.*

I blew out a puff of air and flipped over on the mattress to find a more comfy spot, but it was pointless. Ugh. After fifteen more minutes of music and thumping noises, I jerked up and slipped a white cotton robe over my nightgown. I burrowed through a pile of shoes still in a box in my closet, bumping my head in the process, which only made me more pissed. Finally I found my pink rain boots and shoved my feet in.

I was putting my foot down with my new neighbor. If I didn't, then he'd likely party every single night, and I couldn't have that. I stepped outside my door, and since there was no overhang along the doorway, I got drenched in about five seconds. Cursing, I ran the short distance to my neighbor's apartment and banged on the door with a heavy fist.

The thumping stopped, then the music.

I put my hands on my hips and schooled my features into an irritated glare. Kinda hard to look tough when you're being pelted with rain, but I did my best.

The door opened wide and I squinted at the brightness.

"Excuse me, but your music is way too loud and you seem to be knocking out the walls—" I came to an abrupt stop. Blinked, resisting the urge to rub my eyes. *"Declan?"*

Dressed in black gym shorts and nothing else, he leaned against the doorjamb, his body glittering from the sweat that dripped down his well-muscled chest and straight down to the V of his hips. Oh. My. I inhaled.

He should come with a freaking warning label.

Just perfect. I must look like a drowned rat.

He pulled me inside the door and slammed it shut after a bolt of lightning lit up the sky. "What the bloody hell are you doing out in this?" His molten eyes swept over me, and I swallowed at the lump that formed in my throat.

Once again I felt a tug between us, that mysterious carnal push that had me imagining us in an erotic kiss while he pressed me against the wall and pounded …

Whoa. I stopped that train of thought.

"What are *you* doing here?" A ridiculous question, but my brain was fried.

He set down the red boxing gloves that had been dangling from his hands when he opened the door. "This is my new flat. I moved in today, same as you."

He was the guy in the Jeep with the Union Jack hat.

"You saw me on the balcony today and recognized me at the party and didn't say anything?" My voice had gone up an octave. "Don't you think that's weird?"

He raked a hand through his dark hair. Sighed. "I felt it best to not mention it after seeing how Blake reacted to me. He won't be happy to know we're neighbors." He cocked his head. "He's a territorial dude. You sure you aren't with him?"

"I'm not with anyone. Ever."

He took that in, his eyes raking over me. "So, did you come over here with the intention to seduce me? Because if you are, you're doing a rather kick-ass job."

What? I looked down.

My robe had come apart, revealing my now practically see-through white gown thanks to the downpour outside. Short, filmy, and made of silk, it had been a gift from Shelley.

I stiffened. "I'm here because someone keeps beating on the wall and playing their music so loud that I can't sleep. Oh, it's you." I smirked.

He grimaced apologetically. "I was working out pretty hard with the punching bag. Sorry. It's been a crap day. My new gym is stressing me out, plus my father sent me a text …" His eyes ghosted over my skin. "You're soaked." He turned and left the room, giving me a glimpse of scars on his back before he disappeared. My mouth parted. *What had happened to him?*

He came back with a towel, which he draped over my shoulders and pulled the ends closed. He smiled softly. "I'm sorry for bothering you. I like my music rather loud."

And his women and sex hard. Oh yeah. I shivered.

"Okay." My voice was husky, my heart hammering at his nearness.

But it wasn't fear; it was pure lust. Declan was a man who hit all my buttons.

He seemed to realize how close we were standing, and he shifted, taking a few steps back from me. "Was there anything else?"

I laughed. Someone was ready for me to go, and for once, I wasn't the one being overly cautious around the opposite sex; it was the guy. "No, that's all. Sorry to bother you. I'll go. Just try to keep it down."

"Wait," he said, as I put my hand on the doorknob.

I turned back. "Yeah?"

"About earlier with Dax. I'm sorry for it. I'll hold him if you want to punch him in the nuts."

I smiled at that visual. "It wasn't your fault."

"It's just—he's a good guy." He shrugged. "I've been taking care of him my whole life even though we're the same age. He can be careless but doesn't mean to hurt anyone intentionally."

I nodded. "No, of course. I'm glad you were there. Thank you."

He smiled. "My mum always said I was the stronger one. She told me to watch over him."

"Oh."

He smiled and sucked his bottom lip in with his top teeth. The entire thing—his sweet words, his sexy face, his luscious lips—I wanted to kiss him.

My chest rose.

My palms got sweaty.

An entire colony of butterflies fluttered around in my tummy.

"If you really want to make me feel better, maybe you'd like to erase Dax's kiss from my memory with one of your own?"

He froze, his alert gaze lingering on my lips as he licked his own. "Yeah?"

I nodded. "Most definitely."

"Now?" His husky voice assaulted my senses.

"Why not?"

The apartment swelled with silence as his eyes ate me up, as if he were trying to figure me out. God. What was wrong with me? Was I this desperate? I prepared myself for another rejection.

"Come here, Elizabeth," he said in a soft yet commanding

voice.

The towel around my shoulders dropped to the floor, and my feet crossed the space between us, eager for him. For this.

He cupped my cheek, his fingers trailing down my jawline to my neckline where he toyed with the buttons on my gown. "I can't tell you no again, Elizabeth. Are you sure?"

A whisper of something sang through the air. Electric.

I nodded and put my hands on his shoulders and stood on my tiptoes, my mouth settling on his, my tongue dipping out to taste his secrets. He smelled masculine, like sweat, and the warmth of his chest pressed against my wet one. He didn't move, until suddenly he did, his arms sliding around my shoulders, brushing the base of my spine as he gathered me close.

I sank into him, sighing at the way one of his hands moved to tangle in my hair.

Deeper. Decadent.

He became the instigator. His mouth roved over mine, his breathing heavier as he sucked at my lips playfully and then attacked again, his tongue tangling with mine. Owning me. Tendrils of desire curled inside me.

His hands moved down and tightened around my waist, digging into my hips. Sharp with need. He said my name against my mouth.

He felt so good, hard against my soft, and I wanted to revel in my success, in the way he wanted me, in the way I wanted him.

I moaned. This was good. Hot. Erotic. This was progress.

Until it wasn't.

He tore his lips away and rested his forehead against mine. "You make it hard to stay away when you come in here with pink boots and wet knickers—which clearly aren't granny panties." His voice was like liquid amber, gold and warm, wrapped in sex.

"Why would you want to?" I breathed. "Come to my apartment and spend the night with me." I touched his face, my fingers stroking the softness of his sensuous lips. "Just one night and we can make this shitty world disappear."

He exhaled. "A one-night stand?"

"Yeah."

He cupped my chin. "Someone hurt you, didn't they?"

My lips tightened. No one at Whitman knew about Colby except for Shelley and Blake, and I sure as hell wasn't telling him. He'd judge me like everyone else had in Petal, North Carolina. "That's none of your business."

"I see." His eyes searched mine until I felt like a bug under a microscope. "What if I wanted more than just one night?"

"Then your hands can let go of my hips now."

He removed his hands slowly, the tips of his fingers grazing mine. "This may surprise you, but I don't sleep with every girl I kiss."

I'd been rejected. *Again.* "Blake said you got around, that you used—"

"And you believed him?" His voice was incredulous. "Dude is in love with you and he saw exactly how we looked at each other tonight—"

"*Looked at each other?* What are you talking about? You refused to dance with me and then you ran off with your girlfriend. Not to mention I just kissed you and you didn't even care." I threw my hands up.

"I wanted to fuck you the minute you walked in that party," he snapped.

"Then why don't you," I bit back, tossing back my shoulders.

"You think you want me?" he said tightly. "You can't handle me, Elizabeth. I can see it in your eyes. You're scared of something, maybe not me, but something."

My eyes went to his black eye.

He let out a harsh laugh. "Ah, that's what you're afraid of.

You want the real truth? You told me tonight you didn't like violence, but I'm an arsehole who uses his fists. That's who I am."

I didn't believe that. I sensed a good guy in him. "What do you mean?"

His gaze was intense, dark and low, his face struggling as he fought to find the right words. "I'm in a fight club for money. I show up at warehouses and fight other blokes. Sometimes I beat them so bad they need medical attention. A few times, *I've* been beat to unconsciousness. I'm everything you need to stay away from."

I inhaled, anger and lust and excitement all riding me. Anger that he was pushing me away, lust for the alpha male in him, and God help me, the fighting thing repelled me and excited me at the same time. "I don't want to stay away from you. I want you to fuck me and stop making excuses for why you can't."

My words seemed to snap his taut restraint.

He pulled me back in his arms, his lips fusing with mine unerringly. His tongue plundered me in a sensual way my body had craved for years. I wrapped my arms around his neck, my anger morphing into all-out desire as he turned us and pressed me against the wall.

Yes, yes, this is what I craved.

A passion to remind me that I was *real*, not just some sad excuse of a girl who chose to exist on scraps of love.

Before I knew it, he'd shoved my robe off, his hands sculpting my shoulders, massaging them as he ravaged my mouth. I reveled in the warmth of his hand on my neck as his mouth skated down, kissing the hollows of my throat, sucking on my collarbone.

"Like this?" he asked, his voice dark and gravelly. "You want me to take you up against this wall?"

"Yes," I moaned. Gone. Past caring as long as he kept his hands on me.

Out of control, my brain whispered, but I beat back the dark warnings as his warm hand found my breast and squeezed, his fingers rolling my nipple between his thumb and forefinger.

I gasped in pleasure and arched my back to get closer to his body, ignoring the fear that pricked at the surface.

The rules girl in my head stamped her foot and yelled at me. I ignored her.

But even if I wanted to stop right now, I couldn't. My tongue tangled wildly with his, my hands pulled at his hair, spurring him on, his hand palming my breast and then tugging. Sharp sensations of need went straight to my core.

"Is this what you want? Something quick where we just take what we want and forget each other the next day?"

No. Not that. Not like the way he said it, like it was something dirty.

"Yes, like that," I whispered against his shoulder, my mouth on his skin, tasting him as my teeth bit down. I pressed against him and rocked. Friction. *More.*

He grunted and hoisted me up until my legs looped around his hips, his shorts and the hard length inside pulsating against my skin. He moved sinuously, his long legs supporting my weight as I squirmed to get his body closer to the place I wanted.

I clung to him, a fire building under my skin, in my blood. I rocked wildly and reached around to grab his ass and shove him against me.

Take me.

Make me forget. Make me feel good.

"Elizabeth, you're so hot," he said hoarsely. "I can't stop, love."

We'd passed the point of no return. He was hungry for me, just as much as I wanted him.

His mouth skated down with his hands as he took my nipple between his lips and sucked.

I groaned, the sound primitive and loud in the quiet apartment.

Hot fingers slipped under the waist of my panties, finding my wet core and massaging the wetness.

"Yes," I whispered, gripping his arm and moving him faster, showing him what I wanted. More, more.

"Slow down, love," he whispered and played me effortlessly with his fingers, dipping in and then out, finding the sensitive nub and flicking it and then teasing me by darting away.

But I didn't want to go slow. I wanted fast and hard and rough before I changed my mind.

"Declan." I bit his neck, making him grunt. "Make me come."

He kissed me harder, his tongue fucking my mouth like I wanted his cock to. "I want you so bad I can't think straight," he whispered between kisses.

"Me too."

I'd gone over the edge when it came to him.

I'd lost all sense of where I was ... who he was ... *my past.*

Yet ...

Darkness inched in bit by bit. This wasn't some guy from my calculus class I could control. This wasn't some nerdy guy who'd thought he'd won the lottery when I propositioned him.

This was Whitman University's Sexiest Man on Campus.

He was part of the beautiful people—just like Colby.

He was everything I shouldn't want but did.

Suddenly there was space between us, and I realized I'd been the one to shove him off me. He obliged readily, I acknowledged thankfully as he panted from a few feet away, his face red, fists clenched tight at his sides.

My own chest heaved and I looked down at my nightgown, its straps pushed down, exposing my bare breasts still rosy from his ministrations.

God. *Things had gone too far.*

I gazed back at him, but he was already in the kitchen pouring a glass of water and chugging it with his back to me. I studied the taut lines of his shoulders and the tightness in his stance, recognizing he'd let go when I asked.

No matter *who* he was, he wasn't Colby.

Yet how could I have been so stupid? He was a dangerous fighter with enough sex appeal to blow up a building. *He was entirely wrong for me.*

Tension escalated as he still didn't turn around, but his voice came out rough, like it had been dragged over gravel. "Get out of here, Elizabeth."

I sucked in a shaky breath. "I'm sorry—"

"Go!" His body heaved.

I turned, bolted out the door, and slammed it behind me.

CHAPTER EIGHT

Declan

"WHERE'S NADIA? SHE'S usually here with you," my father said as I stepped into the study where he and Dax already sat in leather club chairs. My stepmum Clara and my stepsister Blythe played on the floor with a puzzle.

I shrugged noncommittally at my father, knowing it drove him bonkers.

We'd just finished a five-course dinner with rather stilted conversation in the dining room, where my father had talked about his business projects and the various vacations he and my stepmother, Clara, planned to take in the coming year. My four-year-old stepsister, Blythe, had been fed by the nanny in the kitchen while the adults chatted.

My family lived a prestigious life, which I guess wasn't surprising considering he came from a long line of privileged military men and she was the daughter of a real estate mogul.

My mum, on the other hand, had been a secretary and merely a casual fling that had resulted in a pregnancy. He'd married her when she'd refused to have an abortion and then he'd promptly given her a small house, a lump of money, and divorced her. Most of that had been to save his career and reputation.

Mum should have been the one living in this huge colonial mansion with a pool, tennis courts, and a stable full of Arabian horses, not the younger version Father had replaced her with.

The sharp ache of a distant memory touched me, one of Mum lying on her bed. Weak. I'd been upset—even angry—with her, too naïve to see her illness. All I'd focused on was that the giggly woman who'd made the best shepherd's pie, the woman who'd come to my martial arts classes and cheered me on, was missing.

God, that cut deep, and I closed my eyes, wishing I could jump back to that one point in time and tell her I was *sorry*, that I didn't mean any of the stupid shit I said.

She hadn't told us until the very end.

I'm dying and your father is coming to take you away.

She died a week later.

A man I hadn't seen in nine years had shown up at our house the next day, his face a mask of iron, his eyes dismissive as he took in our small house filled with the belongings of two messy boys. He'd heaved a great sigh and told the packers to forget bringing anything with us. We'd left behind our cozy home in London for a mansion in Raleigh, North Carolina.

It had been the beginning of my hell.

"Declan, I asked you about Nadia."

Still I didn't answer, my eyes touching on the huge plate glass window behind my father's desk, and I recalled how angry he'd got with Dax one summer in high school over his failing grades. He'd shouted loud enough at Dax that I'd heard them and came in to see my father waving his fists at him. A big barrel-chested man, he'd got in our faces plenty of times, but had never used his fists. I don't know if he would have that day, but I didn't give him a chance.

Rage had driven me to use my own fists. We'd wrestled on the floor of the study, his hands connecting with my face more times than I care to remember. Sweat and blood had flown, and when he tossed me off him and I'd stumbled, the force of it sent me straight into that window and right out onto the concrete drive.

I'd ended up in the hospital with a concussion and over a hundred stitches across my back.

To say things had been rocky between us since was an understatement.

I turned to face his hard stare. "We broke up this summer."

Wearing a frown, he set down his tumbler on a coaster. "Why? She's the perfect girl, plus I like the thought of you going to law school settled in a steady relationship."

Perfect?

I'd rather have *imperfect*.

It dawned on me that perhaps I'd been drawn to Nadia because dating her had been a small attempt on my part to do *one* thing to please my old man.

My father sighed. "What stupid thing did you do to lose her?"

"Caught her screwing a Ninja Turtle."

Clara gasped, her eyes flashing angrily as she looked pointedly at Blythe. "Really, Declan. Have you lost all sense of decorum?"

I grimaced down at Blythe, who looked up at me with big green eyes, her curly brown hair in angelic ringlets around her face. My dad might be a wanker, but she was innocent and completely unaware that her parents were arseholes. "Sorry, poppet. I forgot you were there. Forgive me?" I grinned and pulled out a pack of gum I'd picked up on the way over. "Look, I brought you a treat. It's orange sherbet, your favorite."

She took the gum in her small hand. "Which Ninja Turtle was it?"

I laughed. "Donatello."

She pursed her lips. "How do you screw a Ninja Turtle? Do you twist his neck?"

Dax barked out a laugh from across the room.

I smiled. She was as cute as a button. "Yep, that's exactly how you do it. Want to sit with me?"

Truth was I needed a buffer between my father and me.

She nodded and climbed into my lap as I sat down in one of the chairs.

He got right to business. "Dax has informed me he isn't going to graduate on time—I'm not surprised considering his dismal grades—but I hope you will be walking the line this spring, yes?"

I nodded.

He sent me a pleased look. "At least someone is studying around here."

"Dax's got other skills," I reminded him. "He's the president of Tau and head over so many bloody clubs I can't keep track of him."

"Yes, we're all aware of Dax's penchant for social activities."

"Right here," Dax muttered. "I can hear you loud and clear."

Our father stiffened and swiveled his cold eyes toward him. I saw the moment Dax drew up, radiating nervousness.

I patted Blythe's hair, trying to keep my fists from clenching.

Dax had always been the weaker one, and Father picked on him the most.

"I bought a gym," I announced.

Dax's eyes flared wide and he shook his head rapidly back and forth. His eyes said, *No dude, no dude, don't fucking do it! He's going to flip.*

Too late now, mine said.

I ignored the flush that started taking up most of my father's burly neck, easing up to his face.

I sighed. "I got my half of the inheritance from the barrister that handled Mum's estate. Law school isn't going to happen. I know it's what you had planned, but fighting—training people—it's what *I* want to do. Someday I might want my own shot at a UFC championship."

Tension ramped up the room.

Clara fluttered around him. "Now, Winston, don't get upset. Here, let me get you another Scotch."

His gray eyes bored into me. "You wasted your inheritance on a sweaty gym for white trash karate wannabes?"

I stiffened. "We have all kinds who come in to take classes. Blacks, Hispanics, a few Muslims—"

He slapped his palm down on his armchair. "Don't get smart with me, Declan. You will apply for law school at Harvard like you should."

I set my cup down. "It's done. You can't get money back that I've already spent."

"No son of mine is going to toss away a first class education and a high IQ to be a common laborer."

I let out a resigned sigh and poked Blythe in the side, making her giggle. "You better go see your mum. It's time for me to go."

As usual, I'd made him angry. I just couldn't be what he wanted.

I was never good enough just the way I was.

AN HOUR LATER I was at my gym.

Built in the late seventies, it had been constructed in the historic part of town that was being revitalized. Several of the neighboring homes had been re-modeled and upgraded with young and hip families moving in.

No matter what my father said, the gym *was* a good investment.

Anybody can pop up a gym and say its MMA qualified, and it didn't mean shit, but Front Street Gym would have real credentials. Max was one of my trainers, and although he'd got his start in traditional martial arts, he'd transitioned over to Brazilian Jiu-Jitsu, Muay Thai, and Krav Maga in his later years.

As for me, my mum had put me in classes starting at four. I held a black belt in Brazilian Jiu-Jitsu, a black belt in Tae Kwon Do, and a blue belt in Judo.

Max had taught me everything else I knew.

I unlocked the double metal doors and stepped inside, my eyes taking in the updates the contractor had been working on for the past week, installing new plumbing in the restrooms and lockers, revamping the front office. The final step would be putting in a flat for me to live in. I was bleeding money to get this place opened—literally. I imagined Front Street with every punch and strike I took, knowing that in a few months this place would be open and running and I'd finally be free of my father.

I bent down and rubbed my hands across the new red sparring mats that had been delivered last week. Some of the new workout machinery had been installed as well, and I checked out everything carefully. I made the rounds of the building, checking the windows, outside doors, and smoke detectors. Paranoia ran high when I was this close to tasting happiness. And I couldn't put my finger on it, but it was as if something was waiting out there in the darkness, panting its nasty breath, waiting for the right opportunity to yank away my slice of good.

CHAPTER NINE

Elizabeth

TWO DAYS AFTER the party, I drove a few miles down the road to meet my mom at a truck stop off the interstate.

I hadn't seen her in nearly four months, and we only lived three hours apart.

The diner smelled like old grease and deep-fried onion rings, reminding me of my childhood when my mom would bring home takeout from the restaurant where she waited tables.

She waved at me from a red booth at the back.

I walked her way, feeling anxious.

Some people think God puts difficult people in our lives for a reason, to make us better people as we sharpen ourselves on the knife of their shortcomings. That was my mom. She'd destroyed my trust a million times as a child, and eventually I'd learned to stop counting on her. My kindergarten graduation, my first middle school dance, the day I got my acceptance letter to Oakmont Prep, the night with Colby ... she'd been gone, off on an adventure with whomever she was seeing. Like a stray dog that whines for scraps, I'd been begging my mom to love me my whole life.

Yet out of my shitty childhood, a strong drive had been forged in my heart.

To be *more*.

More than the trailer I'd grown up in; more than my alcoholic mother and absent father.

Today she'd put extra effort in, hot-rolling her natural blond hair in big waves and pulling it back with a bejeweled butterfly clip. She wore a pink gingham sundress and her lips were painted a glossy pink. At thirty-nine, she still managed to look farm fresh.

She jumped up to greet me, a bright smile on her face.

"You're too skinny," I commented as she gathered me up in a hug, my hands feeling the bones of her spine poking through.

We pulled back, and I studied her face more closely, taking in the hollowed neckline. A tingle of foreboding went over me. It had been a year since her last rehab for alcohol and drugs, and I'd held out hope she'd last longer this time. "You clean?"

"Don't be ridiculous, Elizabeth, I'm fine. Right as rain." She laughed at my frown. "Don't worry. I can take care of myself."

We sat down together.

Her eyes gleamed with a happiness I hadn't seen in a long time. "I can't wait for you to meet my new boyfriend, Elizabeth. He's in the restroom right now, but he's got real class and is the sexiest man I've ever dated." She rolled her eyes. "Yeah, I know I've said that before, but I mean it this time." She squirmed in the booth, excitement written on her face. "He's even going to take me on a one of those cruises to Mexico soon."

"Fun." I smiled through my disappointment. I'd thought it would just be us today. "Is he employed?"

She nodded. "And he has dental. What else could I ask for?"

"A washing machine maybe, or I don't know, a home to live in?"

She'd sold her trailer a year ago and had been bouncing back and forth between boyfriends' and friends' houses.

An older man sauntered out of the restroom area in a flowery print Tommy Bahama–type shirt unbuttoned a quarter of the way down, wiry chest hairs poking out like crazy. He was so abundantly hairy I wouldn't have been surprised if a small monkey lived inside his shirt and was reaching up to say hi.

Balding but hiding it with a greasy combover, he walked toward us, his eyes raking over me, lingering. Long muttonchops came down each side of his face.

My whole body went on high creep alert.

He stopped at our table and his eyes bounced back to my mother. "Yo, baby, you didn't say she was a looker like her mama. Guess I hit the jackpot today. Now, who do I sit next to?" He let out a belly laugh.

I stiffened.

But this is your mother, I told myself. Be respectful. Give her a chance.

She laughed and blushed. "Stop flirting and sit down and meet my daughter."

He slid in next to her, and my eyes went back and forth between them.

I'd seen a myriad of men come in and out of our trailer growing up. A few had been decent to me, but she'd never wanted those. Nope. Most had been grade-A assholes, and she'd loved them the most. In my teens—and after a particularly bad episode where I'd found a hidden video camera in my bedroom—I'd managed to avoid a lot of them by staying at Shelley's most nights.

"Didn't know you were bringing your boyfriend," I said, not able to hold back.

"Now don't be that way, Elizabeth. This is *Karl*." She preened at me expectantly. "He owns a used car dealership in Rockport and even gave me a new Impala for my birthday." She pointed out to the parking lot. "Look, there it is. It's even got leather interior."

"Hmm." I was still reserving judgment.

"Hell yeah, I did, 'cause this hot piece sure does know how to treat a man right." *Sure* was *shore* and *right* was *riiaght*, the county twang heavily pronounced, his words elongated.

He leaned in and they kissed each other with visible tongue.

"Nice," I muttered.

The waitress showed up to take my order, and they separated, Mom straightening her blouse and Karl wiping his mouth and leering at me.

He placed hairy arms on the table. "So you one of those smart girls? I heard you got yourself a scholarship to Whitman with a free ride?"

I nodded. Warily. "Yes, but I get financial aid to pay for living expenses. I work too," I added.

"Good for you, but these are bad economic times we're living in. Gotta make a buck where you can." He took a sip of coffee, eyes skating over me. "Maybe you need to get yourself a sugar daddy like your mama here."

"I'm fine just the way I am, thank you." My fists clenched under the table.

It was decided. Karl fell in the asshole category.

They had ordered before I came, and I watched him chew his eggs nosily, wiping his mouth on a napkin as he finished. "Well, if you ever need anything—like a new car or a loan, I can take care of ya. Any girl as pretty as you who's related to the love of my life, well, I wanna do good by. Maybe adopt you after I marry your mama." He nodded emphatically as if I had no other option but to agree.

My eyes flared. "You're getting married?"

She shrugged, her thin shoulders making me wince.

I looked only at her. "You think that's a good idea?"

Karl stiffened. "Of course it is. That's what you do when

you fall in love."

The waitress finally set down a coffee for me, and I busied myself drinking it.

How long did I have to stay here?

I powered on. "So how did you guys meet?"

Mom leaned in over the table, eyes glowing. "It was fate, Elizabeth. I was at Club Raven, you know the one out on Highway 89 where all the locals go?"

I nodded. It was her favorite honky-tonk.

"So in walks this big hunk of a man here and from out of nowhere, someone played Journey's 'Faithfully' on the jukebox and *bam!* His eyes met mine and when he came over to ask me to dance, I nearly fell off the barstool. He bought me a slew of drinks and we laughed and played pool all night." She sighed, hooking her arm through his as she gazed into his eyes. "It was love at first sight."

"What an epic romance. Sounds like a movie ... maybe even a country song."

I didn't say a good movie, but I really did try to keep the sarcasm out of my tone.

Karl took a sip of coffee. "So, your mama and I have been talking about how to get some real cash, you know, to start our marriage off right, maybe buy us a big house and later expand my car dealership."

"Yeah?" I didn't see how this related to me.

He cleared his throat. "So we thought you might help us."

"Me?" I was dirt poor.

"Yeah, she told me about you and Senator Scott's son back in high school. How he took advantage of your good nature and all. And well, one thing led to another and we came up with a plan."

The entire room spun and I wanted to vomit. I heaved in deep breaths and clutched the table, fighting the panic. *Why had she told him?*

She shushed him by flapping her hands at his shoulders. "I told you to let me bring that up. She's sensitive."

I wanted to crawl under the table. "What gives you the right to discuss my personal life?" My voice was sharp, my wrists itching.

She pouted. "Baby, it's water under the bridge now, right? In the past. You're over him. Why look at you. You're a big time college girl now. You've left all that behind."

Left it behind?

He'd ripped my heart out and sent it through a wood chipper.

I'd never be over that night.

"You can't let him get away with it," Mom insisted. "Something should be done about what happened to you."

What?

I shook my head. Emphatically. My nails dug into the seat, trying to hold it together in a public place when what I really wanted to do was run away screaming. I didn't want to think, talk, look at, or dwell on Colby Scott ever again.

"What does this all have to do with me?"

Mom lowered her voice. "In case you didn't know, it's an election year for Senator Scott."

Karl leaned in. "So, if we play this right, we can *all* come out ahead." A glint grew in his eyes. "We just tell your story to dear old dad and claim we have evidence against his son. He'll give us money to shut up about it, and we'll all be richer."

They wanted to blackmail the Scotts.

They wanted to dredge up the past and air it all out for everyone to see.

They wanted everyone to be reminded of what a slut I was.

Never.

"You deserve retribution. Don't you want to make him pay?" Mom said.

Make him pay? A strangled laugh came out.

Revenge is hard when the person I blamed the most was myself.

Revenge is even harder when the person you despise is at the top of the food chain and you're a bottom feeder.

"No, I don't," I snapped louder than I'd intended, causing a nearby table to glance our way.

I didn't care.

I slapped my hand on the table. "The Scott family has run Petal and this state for generations. They control the police, judges, everyone. You can't do this. It's the most stupid thing I've ever heard, and I refuse to help you."

A few beats of silence went by.

Karl held his hands up. "It was just an idea. That's all. If you say no, then I guess we don't have a leg to stand on. We can't exactly say we know what happened when you aren't willing to tell your side of the story."

"Never in a million years. Don't ever bring it up to me again. Got it?" I felt the muscles in my jaw clenching.

Mom let out a brittle laugh. "Let's have some pie. Okay? That will make it better."

Karl just stared at me. I stared back.

I jerked up from the table and looked at Mom. "I'm done. I came here hoping, I don't know, that we could be a real mother and daughter for once—but I guess not." I opened my purse, pulled out a ten, and dropped it on the table. "This is for mine. I trust you can get your own?"

Her lips compressed. "Elizabeth Nicole Bennett, you will not walk away from me. I gave birth to you and I deserve some respect. So does Karl. He drove me here to see you."

I shook my head, feeling the last vestiges of my control slipping away as my voice grew louder. "You don't get it, Mom. You weren't even there the day I came home from the hotel. You were in Vegas. You didn't see how *broken* I was."

She paled. "I got there as soon as I could, baby girl. I was trying to get a dancer's job, to get ahead and make a better life for us both. You know I could have been great if I hadn't gotten pregnant and then your dad …" Her voice broke.

I turned to go, but she grabbed my wrist. "Wait, don't be mad at me, Elizabeth, for trying to make us a better life. Just think about what we said … okay?"

No!

I pulled away from her and pivoted, my nose crashing into a warm chest.

Strong hands clasped my shoulders, and I tilted my head up, up … straight into a pair of stormy gray eyes.

CHAPTER TEN

Declan

OOKIE'S KITCHEN WAS a dump but homey. It was mostly a stopping place for truckers off the interstate, but it was where Max liked to meet and talk shop, mostly about the underground fighting.

We strolled in the double glass doors.

Arlene sashayed over to us in a pink waitress outfit with a white apron. "My Brits are back," she said with a smile. "Been missin' you boys." She nudged her head toward the back. "Max's next to the window. He's waitin' for ya."

"Thanks, love," Dax said as he swooped down and picked her up in a bear hug and kissed her on the cheek. She blushed and popped him with a dishrag.

He watched the sashay of her hips back into the kitchen. "There's not a woman alive who doesn't want me. I think I'm going to change my name to Sex Lord."

I snorted. "Yeah, that's a real turn on."

"Jealous?" he asked.

"Extremely."

He grinned. "Don't be. Not everyone can be as wonderful as

me. You got your fists, I got my sexing abilities—which in my opinion is a hell of a lot better. Make love not war, bro."

"That so?" I chuckled.

Max caught my eye and waved us over. He was in his late forties with thinning hair and a trim physique, and I'd met him at one of the local gyms where we'd both taught classes. Over the past three years, we'd grown close, and hiring him to work at my own place had been the next natural step.

We ordered and talked about the gym and the updates. If all went well with the renovations, then Front Street would be ready for business by January. We'd have a soft opening at first and then a grand opening party in February. The flat at the back would be finished a bit later, perhaps in June, since my first priority was to get the doors open for business.

"What's new with Nick? You got anything?" I asked a bit later. Nick was the guy who ran the underground fights in North Carolina.

"Yeah. I've got some small fights lined up in the next few weeks for you, but Nick wants to schedule a big one for Halloween. He's got a warehouse lined up as the venue with heavy spenders coming, not just college kids." He slapped down a portfolio and then slid it over to me with two fingers. "Don't be afraid to say no."

Dax shifted in closer, peering down to take in the photos of a blond behemoth posing next to a makeshift octagon. "Bugger."

Max rubbed his whiskers. "They call him Yeti. He played linebacker for UNC Charlotte but got kicked off for hazing freshmen players. Third strike."

"Nice lad," Dax murmured.

I studied him analytically. "It takes more than bulk to beat me. He needs skill. What's his record?"

"Three knockouts and one tapped out." Max sent me a rueful look. "Don't be fooled by the football. He's been working with a mixed martial arts trainer, hoping to hitch a ride to the

UFC. He's not like these pansy boys you've been grappling with on the weekend. He's serious."

"Style?" I asked.

Max grimaced. "Signature move is a guillotine choke until you black out. If you don't, he pounds your face till you do."

Nice.

"What's the purse?"

"Two thousand if you lose," he said.

"I won't lose." I couldn't.

He grinned at my confident manner. "If you win, you get twenty-five percent of the purse, not to exceed fifteen grand. And bragging rights, of course."

Fuck. That was the most I'd ever fought for.

"Take a look at this." He pulled out his phone and handed over a YouTube video of Yeti and another man. "The guy he's fighting is Lorenzo, a Cuban from Miami. Tried to go pro in boxing but opted out to make some fast cash first. Yeti nearly killed him a month ago."

We watched the blond monster tear the Cuban apart in less than five minutes using his Thor-sized fists to pound him into the pavement.

Dax shook his head. "No way. He's bigger than you and you're a giant. Let me give you any extra money you need. I have my half of Mum's inheritance."

I shook my head. We'd already had this conversation. "That's yours, and if Father found out, he'd disown you. You don't want to piss him off anymore."

It's funny, but Dax had cleaved to the new family while I hadn't. He adored Clara and Blythe, and losing family after Mum would kill Dax.

I rubbed my hands across a coffee stain on the table and stared down at the video.

Raised voices came from a booth in the back of the restaurant and we turned to stare.

A blond girl stood up from the booth, her shoulders stiff, hands clenched at her side.

Elizabeth.

What the hell? I squinted, taking in her companions.

Dax's eyes followed mine and then came back to me as I rose up from the table.

"You're going over there?" he asked. "Why?"

"Because she looks like she needs help—and I happen to like her."

He cocked an eyebrow. "You just met her."

I ignored that.

He shrugged. "Fine, I'm not missing this." He made as if to stand, but I pushed him back down.

"You stay here. If we both show up, it looks pushy. Give her some space. Plus, she's probably still angry with you."

He held his hands up. "Alright, I can take a hint when I'm not wanted. I'll chill and watch from across the room."

"Who is she?" Max asked.

"A girl we met at one of the frat parties," Dax answered, his eyes scrutinizing me oddly, as if he were trying to suss me out. "Declan seems to have a crush on her."

"Fuck you."

He chuckled. "I don't blame you. I do too."

Max grunted. "Huh. Well, anyone's better than Nadia. I never liked that girl. All she wanted was to ride your coattails."

Dax's eyes shifted over to Elizabeth. "You better hurry if you want to talk to her. She's about to bolt."

I ate up the distance between our tables. She turned, her face planting itself in my chest, her body flush against mine.

Heat ran through me, my groin tightening at the contact. Since the night in my flat, she'd weighed on my mind. Mostly with visions of me pounding into her. Against my wall. On the kitchen table. On the floor.

"Whoa," I said, taking her shoulders to steady her. "You

okay?"

She peered up at me, and my fingers itched to smooth out the worry lines I saw on her face. "Declan? What are you doing here?"

"Just having breakfast. Small world, huh?" I smiled down, resisting the urge to question her about the shadows in her blue eyes. She nodded, still visibly upset, as I stared over her shoulder at the table she'd left behind. A woman who resembled Elizabeth gaped at us while the man's eyes narrowed in on me.

I glanced back down at her and spoke softly. "Do I need to kick anyone's arse?"

"No," she said, a look of desperation flickering across her face. "Just get me out of here before I say something I'll regret."

I didn't even pause. Whatever she needed right at that moment, I wanted to give it to her. I took her hand and led her through the maze of the restaurant, sending a wave to Dax and Max as we passed their table.

Elizabeth didn't even see them there.

We went out the doors, and she came to a halt in the carpark as she looked around in a daze. Her shoulders hunched in on themselves and she let out a frustrated sound, her hands digging through her purse. "God, I'm so frazzled I don't even remember where I parked."

I wanted to march back into that diner and find out exactly what had happened.

"What's going on? Who were those people?" The lady had to be her mum, but I wasn't so sure about the man.

She inhaled at my question and turned away from me, as if she didn't want to face me. "I appreciate you coming over to help, but I—I don't want to talk about it."

"You're hurting, Elizabeth. Sometimes, it helps to talk." Shit, I didn't know what else to say. I felt like a blundering wanker. But I wanted to make her feel better.

"You want me to talk? I'll talk. I'll tell you that my whole life is ruined and some days it's all I can do to remember the girl I used to be. I've never had much, but two years ago I lost everything. My innocence, my creativity, then my Granny, everything." Her voice trembled, rippling with pain. "And you'd think she'd understand, but no, I'm always the one reaching out and begging her—my mother—to just see *me*. She wanted to abort me. She doesn't think I know that, but I overheard her telling Granny once." She covered her face. "God, I shouldn't be telling you this stuff. It doesn't even make sense to you."

I picked up her hand and took the keys she'd clasped in her fist. "Come on. I'll drive you home. You shouldn't be alone."

She sniffed, and I braced myself for tears that never came, and frankly, I wasn't surprised. She might be vulnerable, but I sensed the steel underneath.

She sighed and gave me a curious look. "What about your car?"

"I came with Dax. He can drive by himself." I would send him a text before we left.

I waited anxiously while she decided.

She sighed and sent me a wry half-smile. "Thank you. I'm glad you were here today. You always seem to be right where I need you."

I nodded and scanned the carpark until I found her white Camry. We walked over to it, and I opened the passenger door for her. Her blue eyes roved over my face as I buckled her in, our arms brushing. Sparks.

This girl. *Her*. What was it about her that had me twisted up in knots?

Since the moment she'd walked in that party, I hadn't been able to get her off my mind.

Shit. But she was all wrong for me. I mean, she was skittish as a colt. How in the hell would she ever fit in my world?

She won't, the cynic in me said.

"Why are you so nice to me?" she said suddenly as I set her

purse at her feet. Her eyes searched mine. She continued. "I mean, I made a fool of myself at your party, then I came in your apartment and hit on you and then pushed you away right when things got heavy ..." She swallowed and gazed out the window. "I'm sorry. I'm a real bitch."

I exhaled and bent down on my knees next to her seat. We stared at each other.

Breathlessness mixed with exhilaration hit me, as if I were about to take a dive off a cliff straight into an ocean below. I pushed a strand of hair out of her eyes. "I'm nice to you because you're worth it, Elizabeth."

CHAPTER ELEVEN

Elizabeth

THAT AFTERNOON I took a nap feeling as worn and thin as old paper, as if I'd been folded and refolded a million times.

Visits with Mom tended to do that, but today had been the worst ever.

I made a mental note to call her tomorrow after the dust had settled to make sure she and Karl had given up on their plan.

I groaned and rolled out of bed from my nap and got dressed, pulling on a pair of black eyelet shorts and a halter top. I brushed my hair in a ponytail and applied makeup with a heavier hand than usual. My body was jumpy and twitchy. I needed out of the apartment, but I couldn't think of a single place to go. Blake and Shelley had gone to lunch together earlier, and I hadn't heard back from either of them.

After pacing around the apartment, I peeked out the balcony window to check out Declan's place. He'd mentioned going to work out on the way home and then seeing Dax, so I assumed he hadn't returned.

The minutes ticked by. I paced past my extra bedroom a few

times but nothing eased me. Something insistent clawed at my brain, itching to get out. Finally, I stepped inside the extra bedroom and turned the light on. My artist pad sat out on a small desk with a myriad of colored pencils next to it—just waiting for me to draw.

Not thinking about it too much, I walked over to the pad and opened it, thumbing through some of the old designs I'd created. After a few minutes of mulling, I grabbed one of the pencils and twirled it between my fingers.

I licked my suddenly dry lips, feeling the tendrils of inspiration for the first time in ages.

And the thing is, my hand seemed to know exactly what I needed to create. Something vibrant. Beautiful.

I closed my eyes and pictured the tattoo on Declan's neck.

I recalled the reverence in his voice when he'd talked about his mother.

What must it be like to be on the receiving end of that kind of emotion—from Declan?

With furious fingers, I drew half a dozen different dragonflies and then used colored pencils to decorate them. Some were big, some were small, but all had that ethereal quality I imagined a dragonfly had.

I pictured engraving a dragonfly on a bracelet. Or a plaque on a necklace.

No, no.

But the more I thought of it, the more I realized I was thinking way too much about Declan and not just the dragonfly. Frustrated, I set the pad aside.

I didn't need to think about him.

He was exactly what I didn't need.

I stood and paced, shaking my hands out.

God, I needed a release.

I needed someone inside me.

And that person could never be Declan. I wanted him too

much.

Because today in the car when he'd said I was worth it, all I'd wanted to do was wrap my arms around his strong shoulders and sink into him. I'd wanted to unbuckle my seat belt and crawl in the back with him. I'd wanted to trace my tongue over every inch of him, my hands following, learning the map of his body, committing it to memory.

But I can't!

Which is why an hour later I found myself sitting in the bookstore café, sipping on a soda as people came and went.

It wasn't my night to work, but then that wasn't why I was here.

I found an easy mark, a cute-in-a-geeky-way kind of guy. I studied him, recognizing him from an astronomy class last fall.

Medium height and lean, he strolled among the stacks with an intense expression. In one hand he had a notebook and periodically he'd pause at one of the chairs at the end of each row and sit down to jot notes.

Studious. Not over-the-top hot. Perfect.

I left money on the table for my drink, gathered my purse, and made my way over to him.

A dark corner of my mind whispered *yes, he was the one tonight,* but my heart was silently judging me. I ignored my stupid heart and stopped in front of my mark.

I leaned against the shelving. "If I had to guess, I'd say you are a TA prepping for our first week of classes. Your professor must love you." I smiled broadly.

He glanced up from his seat, swept his eyes over me appreciatively, and stood. He grinned in a self-deprecating kind of way I found endearing. "Uh, yeah, but the professor I work for barely knows I'm alive. I do all this work with no recognition."

"That sucks." I stuck my hand out. "Elizabeth Bennett, by the way. Sorry to interrupt, but I had to come over and say hi. We had a class together last year? You sat in the middle and I sat in the front." I laughed. "Truthfully, I always wanted to talk to you, but when you left class you always had a girl waiting for you in the hallway." This part was true. He was always on my list of possibilities, but I never fooled around with guys with girlfriends.

He leaned in and took my hand briefly, giving me a clear view of his soft brown eyes. "Harry Carter, astronomy major. I remember you, of course. You wore lots of jewelry to class. Yeah, that was my ex. We broke up this summer." He made a little shrug, his shoulders dipping. "Her loss, I guess."

And check. No attachments.

"My gain." I grinned.

He laughed, a gleam in his eyes as his gaze lingered on my legs and then moved up to the red halter top. I was tall and slim, but my breasts were a good C cup.

"What are you doing here?" He leaned against the stacks, calling attention to the nice set of arms he had. Hmm, closer up, he was definitely hotter.

"Hanging out. Looking for a guy like you." I peeked at him from underneath black lashes and laughed. This part was always so easy, mostly because I wasn't being myself. I pretended to be someone else.

Someone who didn't carry pain around.

I bit my lip. "Sorry, I tend to talk before my brain can tell me to shut up. That was way too forward and you probably think I'm a flirt—but I'm not. It's just—I go with the truth. I'm upfront and some people kinda freak out about that."

"No, I like it." He cleared his throat and waved his hand outside to the street. "I was actually about to go have dinner across the street. You want to join me?"

"Sure." Success.

WE LEFT THE bookstore and along the way I explained to Harry how I didn't drink and never spent time with guys who did. He seemed on board with it, and we found a quiet booth in the back of the restaurant and ordered hamburgers and fries. Before long, a local band set up and started playing, and the lights went low. Harry scooted his chair close to me, his leg pressed firmly against mine. I reciprocated, brushing my arm against his when I could, letting my fingers touch him as often as possible. Before dinner was over, his hand was tucked into my upper thigh, his thumb caressing my skin softly.

The way he made me feel and the way he gazed at me was nice, but something was off. There was no fire, no burning need. I forced myself to carry on though.

He asked me to dance when a slow song came on, but I said no. I immediately regretted it. He was the one for tonight. Right? Why was I being so wishy-washy?

"Kiss me," I whispered in Harry's ear a few minutes later as we still sat at the table.

Feeling like I had something to prove.

He leaned down and captured my lips, his tongue slipping into my mouth with just the right amount of pressure. Light, nothing hard or hot.

Flashes of Declan kept popping up in my head, and I remembered how just the tiniest brush of my hand in his had been electric.

Where was he tonight?

Why did I care?

He'd made it plain he wasn't into one-night stands.

And that's what *this* was all about. It didn't have to be spectacular like I imagined sex would be with Declan.

Mmm, Declan … his big body covering mine, his sensuous lips caressing my mouth, his hands framing my face as we kissed …

"… next Friday night at the bonfire. Want to come?"

I startled as he toyed with my fingers, his head bent low as he gazed into my eyes.

I tried to piece together what conversation I'd missed. "Oh, sorry. I can't."

Disappointment flashed on his face. "You're distracted. Am I that horrible of a kisser?"

Suddenly everything felt wrong. Him. Dinner. The touching. The kiss.

He kissed me again when I didn't answer, his lips more insistent this time, his tongue massaging mine. He groaned and I put some effort into the act, parting my lips and rubbing his leg with my hands, skating close to the growing length in his crotch. Our hands were hidden, and I pushed on him, making him moan. He put his hand on top of mine, grinding it on top of him.

"I want you, Elizabeth," he whispered. "Right now. Let's get out of here. Mmm?" He nipped at my lips playfully while his eyes begged me to say yes.

But …

Something was niggling in the corners of my brain.

Don't do it.

"Actually, I need to go." I pulled away from him and put some distance between us in the booth. He wasn't the guy on my mind, and it wouldn't be fair. I needed some time to think. Maybe I'd rushed into this a little too fast. "Look, it's great touching base with you, but I—I didn't realize it's already kinda late. Classes start tomorrow."

His face fell. "Seriously? After all that?"

I picked up my purse. "College calls, and I'm serious about my studies. Maybe we can run into each other again." I looked at my watch. "Plus you have a professor to impress tomorrow."

He let out a heavy sigh and rose up from the booth, looking at me intently. "That's too bad. I kinda felt like we were just getting good here." He blushed. "You're a gorgeous girl, Elizabeth—and nice, of course. I'd really love to see you again."

"Sorry, I can't." My voice had sharpened. "I need to get to my car and get home."

He shrugged it off and we each paid our checks and walked outside together. It was dark, and I dreaded the walk back to my car at the bookstore. We walked in a strained silence. His car was a few rows over from mine and after telling him goodnight, I turned back to mine.

He grabbed my hand and tugged me back.

"What are you doing?"

"Come on, babe, don't you want to hang out some more? I don't want this night to end."

Babe? Didn't want this night to end? Hmm, Harry was more of a player than I realized.

"I have to go." I eased my hand free. Clingy guys made me itchy.

"Wait. Can I get your phone number at least? I mean, it kinda feels like fate, us meeting at the bookstore ..."

Fate? Ha.

Fine.

"You can give me yours."

I'd never call it.

He wrote out his digits on a piece of paper, and I tucked it absently in my shorts' pocket.

I said goodbye *again*, got in my car, and left. Tonight had been a mistake.

Ten minutes later, I pulled into my complex and parked. My eyes went straight to Declan's Jeep. He was home, and part of me wanted to knock on his door and just ... I don't know ... talk.

I made my way up the staircase to the breezeway that led to my door. I fished around in my purse and found my keys just as a loud male voice came from behind me on the breezeway a few feet away.

"Elizabeth, wait a minute!"

I turned, half expecting to see Harry. I was ready to tell him off for following me home like a creeper, but the truth dawned on me as I watched the handsome guy jog over to me.

I froze for a second and then snapped myself out of it. I tried to shove my key in the lock but fumbled and dropped them to the ground.

There he stood, Colby Scott, tall and handsome, wearing black pants and a black shirt, his hair swept low over his forehead, ice-blue eyes glittering at me. He looked the same but thinner and harder, a tightness around his face as his chin jutted out.

Of course, I'd seen him in passing in Petal after the hotel. Once at a gas station when I was filling up my car to head back to Raleigh and another time at the local Wal-Mart. He'd leered at me but had never spoken, and hearing his voice now was a shock.

"Don't come any closer to me or I will scream this place down and someone will call the cops." I bit the words out, but inside I quaked.

He held his hands up. "Hang on. I'm not going to hurt you. I just wanted to pop by and say hi. In case you haven't heard the good news, I'll be a Whitman student come Monday. Got kicked out of NYU, I'm afraid—too much partying apparently. As you can imagine, Dad wasn't too thrilled about that." He sent me a wry grin, as if expecting me to smile along with him. "Anyway, I just got settled into an apartment nearby. I couldn't be this close and not look *you* up, Elizabeth. We dated once. We had some good times. Aren't you glad to see me?" His low southern drawl washed over me in waves. Making me ill.

Was he crazy? Didn't he know what he'd done to me?

My gut churned as the entire world tilted on its axis, and the only way I was able to stay upright was by leaning against my door.

Panic beat at me.

God. Don't pass out.

"Get away from me. Now." I panted, the air growing thin. My heart thundered.

Had he been waiting for me in the parking lot?

Even if I wanted to scream, I couldn't seem to muster up the air to do it. Somehow I managed to bend down and snatch my keys.

He smiled, raking his eyes over my body. He came closer. "You're still as pretty as ever, Elizabeth. I hope we can catch up real soon."

My hand clutched my keys as the fear escalated higher. I made a fist with my keys and showed him. "Don't come one inch closer."

He laughed and placed his hand up on the wall behind my head. "You're not going to do a damn thing. You're too scared. Besides I'm not here to bother you, only to get a welcome to Whitman from you. Does everyone here know what a sexy little thing you are? How you like it? Hmm?"

I snapped away from him, using my hands to push off his chest.

If I could just get to Declan's door.

CHAPTER TWELVE

A FEMALE'S RAISED voice penetrated my brain and in my half-asleep state, I pictured Elizabeth in my bed, lying back against my sheets …

Her voice came again.

Shit.

This was no dream.

I sat up from the couch where I'd fallen asleep after the gym and glanced at the clock on the telly. I groaned as I clicked on the lamp. Barely eleven. I scrubbed my face, my muscles screaming. I'd been at the gym most of the afternoon working on sets and sparring with Max. Dax had come by to watch, and later on we'd ended up catching dinner together.

A male's voice came next, and I perked up

Who was that?

The greasy guy from the truck stop came to mind.

I jerked up, not bothering to put a shirt on.

As soon as I stepped out the front door and into the breeze-way, I caught a clue. A guy I didn't recognize had Elizabeth cornered with his body, a hard look on his face.

"Get away from me," Elizabeth yelled at him, her face ashen.

I saw red. Bloody hell, I saw every fucking color imaginable.

Without pausing, I rushed and ripped into him with a palm strike straight to his face. Hard. His neck snapped back and blood splattered in the air.

His body got airborne as he lost his balance and landed on the concrete of the breezeway, nearly toppling over into the carpark below.

Elizabeth gasped, but I didn't look at her.

With tightly clenched fists, I loomed over him, doing a mental checklist: five eleven, blond hair, newly broken nose, a Rolex on his wrist. I fished around in his pockets, but his wallet wasn't there.

"Don't hurt me, man," he said, opening his eyes with a wild look on his face as he took me in. He swallowed, wiping at the blood that dripped from his nose to his mouth. "I was just saying hi to an old friend. Nothing's going on."

I didn't like the look of him, from the expensive cut of his clothes to the petulant droop of his mouth. And then his eyes slid over to Elizabeth as if drawn there. Incensed, I kicked him in the ribs with my bare foot. "Don't look at her. Get out of here before I rip your throat out."

He scrambled up to his knees and crawled away a few feet until he jumped up and took off running. I watched him dart across the carpark and then cross the street to Minnie's Diner where he'd parked in a darkened area.

He squealed out onto the street and drove away in a black Porsche with tinted windows.

I turned back to Elizabeth.

"Are you okay? Did he hurt you?" I rushed over to her and tilted her chin up.

She took a deep breath, her lashes fluttering as she tried to gather herself. She gasped in air then slowly let it out.

"Panic attack?" I asked softly, careful to keep my distance from her as she inhaled and exhaled.

She nodded and spoke around her breaths. "Yeah. Only happens when I feel out of control."

I gave her a few minutes to gather herself and watched as she took deep breaths, her color slowly coming back to her face.

"Who was that guy? Did you know him?"

Her eyes flared wide and then she looked hurriedly away. "Just—just someone I met tonight at the bookstore. He—he followed me home, I guess."

She was lying. But why? Was she protecting him?

"He said he knew you." I clenched my fists. Was he one of her one-night stands gone wrong?

She blushed a bright red and clamped her lips shut.

Why wouldn't she confide in me? God, I didn't want to upset her when she was already freaked out.

I sighed and looked around the breezeway. Okay. Changing gears. "Can you tell me what happened?"

Her tongue darted out to lick her lips. She nodded. "One minute I was thinking about getting into my apartment, and the next he was just there. He didn't touch me, but if you hadn't come out ..." She shuddered. "Thank you. Again."

"You get a name?"

She stiffened. "Why?"

I shrugged. "I have a friend with campus police. Wouldn't hurt checking in to see if any complaints have been filed about him."

She let out a deep breath as if steeling herself. "Colby Scott."

"Okay." I smiled gently, filing that name away as I took the keys from her hand and pushed her door open for her. I'd be doing my own investigating as well.

She blinked at the door, not moving.

I cupped her shoulders, consciously keeping my hands soft. "Hey, it's over, okay? I showed up in time, and I'll make sure it doesn't happen again." She rested her head on my shoulder, and shit, I got angry all over again. I should have hit him harder. "I think we should call the police and file a report. He followed you here, and that's not cool."

She tilted her head up and looked at me. Her lips trembled. "He didn't actually do anything."

"But you felt threatened, right? That's enough to report him. Maybe I should just go pay him a visit myself."

Her eyes widened. "No," she bit out. "It's over, and after what just happened, he won't be back." She swallowed. "And don't you do anything on your own either, Declan. I don't want you getting into trouble because of my stupid mistakes. Besides, he could stab you or shoot you or hit you with a two by four ... just don't."

I grinned at her. "A two by four? Is that what people fight with in Petal, North Carolina?"

She smiled—just a little—and damn it made my heart glad.

She wavered for a moment at her door, her glance falling on my hand. "You were so fast, and I didn't even know you were there—until you were. I wish I could do that."

I gazed down at her, assessing. "If you want, I can show you how to hit, but I'd need to touch you. Are you good?"

Emotions flitted across her face and her mouth opened but then shut.

"Elizabeth?"

She covered my hand with hers and looked up at me with those soul-wrenching blue eyes I could drown in. "When it comes to you, Declan, I'm never afraid. Why don't you come inside and show me?"

Heat poured into me.

"Okay." I followed her into her flat. A lot like mine, it had a big living room with a small kitchen to the right and the bedrooms in the back. "Your place is cleaner than mine."

A few minutes later, after she'd got us some water to drink, we stood in the living room and squared off across from each other. I showed her a few basic self-defense stances, and then got to work on her hands. I took her right one and curled it around until she had a nice tight fist.

"First rule is to make sure your thumb is on the outside. Never tuck it inside your hand when you hit because you'll break it. Keep it tight, but not so tight you cut off the circulation."

She nodded and came in closer. I held her hand, adjusting it, my fingers pressing into her skin as I shaped her fist. The fresh citrus scent she wore made my cock twitch.

Down, boy.

She watched me intently, the electric current between us seeming to ramp higher.

Did I notice that her eyes had darkened? That her breathing was heavier? Yes.

I sucked in a ragged breath. *Keep control, man.* She might be gorgeous and sweet, but she wasn't the one for me. I needed someone who wanted the same things I did.

"When you hit, use a linear motion, not a wide swing. Your opponent is less likely to see a straight punch. Tilt your fist down slightly and protect the fingers. Your goal is to hit with the first two knuckles."

"Okay." She made a fist and held it out.

I bit back a groan, picturing her holding my cock, sliding those soft hands over my hard length.

I cleared my throat. "Good. Now, use a quick jab when you hit, keeping one fist up to protect your body." I took a step back and demonstrated a jab while she watched, her eyes big as saucers.

"You're beautiful," she said, her voice full of awe. "And, I love how you move. I could watch you forever. Of course, you are half naked." She blushed and bit her lip. "Sorry. It's just ...

you have to know how great looking you are, and then you're so fit and muscled up, and well, the sex appeal factor is just off the charts. But all that aside, you're a nice guy too, and ..." She trailed off, her tongue dipping out to caress her lower lip. "Sorry. I'm talking awkwardly. Again. I seem to do that a lot when you're around. I'll shut up now."

My heartbeat had kicked up, and part of me wanted to kiss her, but what kind of guy would I be if I made a move on her after what had just happened?

I rubbed my mouth. Her chest rose more rapidly and her eyes glittered with a heat that had been banked for far too long.

She wanted me.

A few beats of silence passed.

A car horn blared in the distance but neither of us moved.

All I wanted in that instance was *her*.

I gazed down at her mouth. Licked my own. "You need to stop looking at me like that if you don't want me to kiss you, Elizabeth."

"God, please, kiss me." Her eyelashes fluttered down and that was all I needed to close the small distance between us and press my lips to hers, my tongue diving in to take control of her mouth.

She tasted like mint. Like perfection.

My hands snaked around her waist and I tugged her against my chest, my mouth plundering the softness of hers. We kissed for a long time, our mouths learning each other, neither of us in a hurry to rush, yet the intensity was well off the charts.

Sweet yet hot.

I wanted to prolong the kiss, drag it out.

But you can't kiss forever.

We pulled apart after a while and stared at each other. I rested my forehead against hers.

I wanted her.

But what did she want?

The soft echo of rain falling and splashing on her balcony hit our ears.

She closed her eyes, a soft smile on her face. "It's funny that we're kissing and now it's raining. Two of my favorite things."

"Yeah?" She was slowing us down. I went with it. I didn't want to rush her. Not yet anyway.

She nodded. "I love the sound rain makes, how it taps against the roof, rhythmic and steady like a heartbeat. The best place to hear it is on a metal roof, lulling you to sleep. My trailer had a roof like that. Rain made me happy as a kid, just to get caught in a downpour so hard it's like a white noise all around you. The best is when it catches you without an umbrella or rain boots and you go splash in a puddle." A small smile flashed across her face. "I miss that feeling of being free and young, like I'm a superhero and nothing can touch me. We're all so innocent as kids, and then life happens and we grow up and make stupid mistakes. We get hurt."

She let out a small surprised laugh. "It's funny—I haven't talked like this with someone in forever. And today, I actually drew some pictures—that's a freaking miracle because I've been stuck in some kind of artist limbo. I know I'm not making any sense, and I'm rambling, but it's just—just there's something about you like you *get* me, and I—can't put my finger on it, but I like it." She bit her lip.

I took her hand. I didn't ask questions. She didn't need them right now. "Come on then." I tugged her through the flat.

"Where are we going?"

"You'll see."

She followed along behind me as I led her into her bedroom and stopped at the balcony door. Rain pelted down the glass door, the drops splashing on the concrete outside.

"Let's get soaked then. No rain boots, no umbrellas, just skin and rain."

"Naked?"

I grinned. I couldn't help it. She was so damn cute. I kissed her nose. "No, silly, we'll keep our clothes on this time. If I was naked with you, we'd be fucking, not doing this." I slid open the door and pulled her outside.

She followed me and stood on the balcony as the rain came down.

I got lost a little. Watching *her*. Taking in her face as she tipped it up to feel the wetness.

She glanced over at me. "You're staring."

I grinned. "Because you look like a drowned rat." Because she looked beautiful.

She laughed. "Come on, don't make me feel like the idiot out here. This was your idea. Dance with me."

"Why are you always trying to get me to dance? What if I don't have any rhythm? I am a big bloke, you know."

But she ignored me and tugged me around the balcony in some awkward square dancing moves she insisted on.

I laughed. She laughed.

I showed her how to box waltz just like my mum had shown me.

After that, she did some baton routine she'd done at prep school.

And we just got sillier and sillier, our laughter filling up the night. We did some moves from *Grease* and *Dirty Dancing*. I looked bloody ridiculous, but I didn't care.

In that moment, life—*we*—were perfect.

I'd never been like that with a girl before. Spontaneous and fun. Real.

Later, we ran inside to get dry. She grabbed a towel for herself from the bathroom and then handed me another. I stepped inside, shut the bathroom door, and dried off the best I could while I heard her tearing apart her bedroom, slamming drawers.

I came out rubbing my hair and watched her scurry around

the bedroom.

My eyes darted to her bed, my thoughts dirty. Picturing us there. Fucking. Her mattress wasn't nearly big enough for the ways I wanted to take her.

She looked jittery as she took in my still damp gym shorts, her teeth worrying her bottom lip. She was wondering the same thing I was ... *where did we go from here?*

She'd changed into a nightie with a large white unicorn head on the front.

"Nice," I said. "You've always been a unicorn girl in my head, and now this proves it."

She grinned. "Oh? How's that?"

"You know, because you're a rare sight on campus?" I grinned.

She smirked. "Thanks. Now if I could only grow a real horn, I could stab people. Like you!" She turned and grabbed a pillow off the bed and tossed it at me. I ducked just as it sailed over my head and crashed into one of her photo frames.

She giggled.

"Oh no, you didn't." I rushed her, swooped her up and twirled her around while she screamed.

"I'm going to barf on you!"

"Liar."

She giggled and I set her down on her feet where she swayed and then grabbed my arm, her eyes laughing up at me.

Something changed in the air, that tug between us sharpening.

She caressed my arm, an unsure yet needy look on her face. "Stay with me tonight."

Somehow I sensed she didn't mean sex. Not after the guy at her door.

"Like a sleepover?"

She nodded, a tentative smile on her face. "We can watch a movie if you want. I'll even let you pick."

I didn't want a movie. I wanted her under me.

I scrubbed my face, thinking this was insane and a horrible idea, but she pulled back the quilt on her bed and crawled inside, her body sliding against the sheets. She was so bloody beautiful.

I rationalized. This *was* purely platonic. No strings. Just me and a girl in the same bed. Sleeping.

But...

I was a heartbeat away from getting in too deep.

She must have sensed my reserve. "I don't want to be alone tonight, Declan. I—I need some kindness, and you seem to have it in spades. I can't put words to it, but I feel safe with you and like nothing bad will ever happen to me again. Stay?"

"My shorts are still damp."

"Then take them off," she said, patting the bed.

I grinned and took a step closer to her, my body already tightening up at the thought of lying next to her. "Fine with me, but I don't wear underwear."

"That's a problem."

"Yeah, a big one."

She blushed, her eyes drifting down to the obvious tent growing by the second in my shorts. Her gaze bounced back to my face as she cleared her throat. "Oh. I—I don't mind if you're...wet."

"Okay," I chuckled and slid in, biting back a groan as my legs brushed the soft warmth of hers.

"You feel so good," she murmured as she turned to face me and wrapped slender arms around my chest, flowing into me like honey, warm and sweet. Our legs tangled together, seeming to know the perfect position to touch each other the most, and fuck, it felt right.

She didn't mention the movie, and I didn't bring it up.

Her body was a drug, and I wanted to consume her. I wanted to press her deep into those sheets and claim her as mine.

But I didn't.

I didn't want to be just one night with Elizabeth. *I wanted more.*

I kissed her hair lightly, and somehow, I slept.

CHAPTER THIRTEEN

Elizabeth

A T SIX ON the dot my alarm clanged me awake. Monday, the first day of class.

I rolled over, expecting to see Declan's chiseled face resting against my extra pillow, but he was gone.

Relief hit. No morning chitchat or awkward kisses goodbye. Yet ...

I was disappointed too. For the first time, I *wanted* the guy to still be there. I wanted to caress my fingers across his tattooed arm and wish him good morning. Sadly, the only thing remaining of him was the scent of his spicy cologne on my pillow. I picked it up and inhaled for exactly ten seconds longer than I should have.

I wasn't creepy at all. Nope.

I showered, put on makeup, and dressed in a pair of bright red short-shorts and a vintage peasant shirt with cream embroidery, another one of Shelley's purchases for me. We'd gotten the shirt at a consignment shop downtown, and although it had been too big, she'd taken in the sleeves and bust to fit me. She had an eye for fashion, and I tended to listen to her, especially considering I'd grown up wearing hand-me-downs from wherever my mom could get them. We'd never had much, and what's funny is I hadn't even realized it until I'd gotten in at Oakmont Prep and seen how the other half lived—fancy cars, designer clothes, Louis Vuitton backpacks.

Money and power everywhere.

I'd wanted to be part of it—desperately.

I'd figured out quick that the only way to fit in was to pretend to be like them, and I had with the help of Shelley. I'd been young and impressionable and eager to make friends—who turned out to not be real friends.

Everyone but Shelley and Blake had rejected me after Colby told his lies.

After parking my car and trekking across campus, I settled in a seat in my first class, an elective English Literature class taught by Dr. Feldman, one of the toughest professors on campus.

I craned my head to scan the auditorium, searching for Colby's sandy hair. What if I ended up in a class with him? Now that I didn't have Declan to distract me, the dread piled up. *What was I going to do when I saw him on campus?*

Blake came in and took the seat next to me. We'd filled out our schedules at registration together last spring so we could get in some of the same classes.

He tapped me on the arm. "Hey, how's it going? I wish you could have gone to lunch with us yesterday."

"Sorry, it was a hectic day." Understatement.

He exhaled heavily.

"What?" I asked.

He rubbed his face briskly and then looked at me for a few ticks. He seemed to come to some kind of decision. "I—it's just—I really need to tell you something, and there never seems to be a good time."

I cleared my throat, feeling nervous. I didn't want to have

that conversation.

He checked his watch. "We still have five minutes. Let's go outside and talk. Right now. We'll get this all out on the table, and you'll know exactly what's been wrong with me lately."

"Class is about to start and Dr. Feldman is a stickler for being on time. Why don't we meet later—?"

He groaned his frustration, his mouth tightening as he glared at me.

"Don't be that way. You're acting like a baby."

He closed his eyes and then popped them open. "Fine. You want to know what's eating me? I'm in love with you, Elizabeth, and I have been since Oakmont. You know it. I know it. Hell, all of Whitman knows it. I'm sick of sitting back and watching you screw guys and never pick me. It's a new year for both of us, and I want you to think about maybe ... me and you ... together."

No. This wasn't happening. I couldn't take this. Not with the specter of Colby hanging over me. "Blake, we did this before—"

He held a hand up, interrupting me. "That was two years ago, and you gave me up for Colby."

I stared at him, remembering all the times he'd picked me up for school when I didn't have a ride, the times he'd sat in the diner where I waited tables just to keep me company.

I *did* love him in way, but it wasn't a gut-wrenching, I-might-die-if-I-don't-see-you kind of love. It was easy and soft, like a warm blanket on a winter's night in front of the fire.

Could there be more with him?

He fiddled with his notebook, his eyes jumping to my face and then glancing back down. "The thing is, we are perfect for each other, you just don't see it. I already know everything about you. Your favorite color, the kinds of books you like to read, the songs you love. I know you want to get a tattoo, but you can't afford it. Hell, I even know you snore when you sleep—"

"Blake, stop, please. I can't do this right now. We're in the middle of class."

Pressure, pressure.

"Why not? Because you're afraid I'm right? You and I were meant to be from the very beginning, and you just got side-tracked by Colby." Intensity laced his voice, making me squirm.

My rules had no room for a serious relationship—even with Blake. "Please—just let it go."

He slumped down in his seat and shook his head angrily.

Thank goodness a sleepy-eyed Dax strolled into the auditorium right then, getting my attention. He was wearing skinny jeans, high-tops, a WU shirt, and an infectious grin that looked like trouble with a capital T. He gave Blake a fist bump and plopped down in the seat on the other side of me. Completely oblivious to the tension. Aren't most guys?

He gave me a wide grin, and I had to smile back. His face brightened even more. "Hiya. I take it you've forgiven me for being sloshed on Friday night?"

I nodded. "Declan's more than made up for your shortcomings."

He grinned and shrugged, the movement reminding me of Declan. "Indeed, he's the good one."

More students piled in, including Declan, who stalked in wearing frayed jeans and a shirt that showcased his muscled chest to perfection. My eyes feasted on his forearms, tracing the lines of his skulls and roses. Last night, he'd held me tight as if he were afraid I'd slip away—yet he was the one who left without saying goodbye.

This morning I'd been partly relieved and disappointed he was gone, but that feeling had morphed into being pissed. And me being mad over him—made me madder.

I didn't want to *care* that he'd left.

That didn't stop the heat from settling in me when his gray eyes met mine.

He walked over to us, his gaze locked with mine the entire

way.

"Hey." I cleared my throat to get rid of the nervousness. "We're being geeks and sitting up front. You wanna join us?"

He flicked his eyes from Dax to Blake on either side of me, almost as if he'd ask one of them to get up, but that was completely insane.

He shrugged broad shoulders. "I'll just sit behind you guys."

It was stadium style seating, so he had to take the stairs and then turn down the row behind us. He selected the seat behind me.

And even though we weren't touching, I could feel him there, the warmth from his skin radiating across to mine.

Dax ran his eyes over the syllabus that had been left on the top of each desk. "I'm not quite sure how I ended up here. I must have had a hangover when I selected courses." He checked out the female students who were coming in. "Although I have to admit, there are some hotties in here."

"And you?" I turned around to look at Declan. "Do you like literature?"

"I'm an English major with a minor in business," Declan said.

"No way."

His lips quirked. "Yes, way. And why not?"

"I'm just surprised. I just assumed ..."

"He's a Neanderthal?" Dax said. "Most people do, but bro here is a sucker for poems and sonnets, boring tosh that makes me want to shoot myself. He's overcompensating by opening his own gym soon."

"You two are completely opposite," I mused.

Dax snorted. "So, I'm the Neanderthal?"

I laughed. "No. Okay, maybe."

A flurry of activity came from the door, and we turned to see a petite brunette in a tube top and short-shorts make a beeline for us. Lorna from the frat house. Fabulous.

She came to a halt in front of Blake, and when she took in that there wasn't an empty seat next to him, she sent me an evil look and then moved her gaze to Declan.

"Is the seat next to you free?" she asked with a pout.

My eyes narrowed.

Had Declan slept with her?

Ugh.

Why did I care?

"Yeah," Declan nodded, his eyes off me and on her.

"Awesome," she said with a bright smile and made her way over to his aisle.

"She's pretty hot, huh?" Dax whispered to me as she and Declan took up a close conversation after she got settled. "She's limber too. All the brothers at the house love it. She can do this thing where she puts her legs behind her head and—"

"Stop."

He grinned sheepishly. "I'm teasing. It's her tube tops that keeps us riveted. Blokes keep waiting for one to fall off."

I snapped my fingers. "Shucks. If only I had the guts to wear one I could be just like Limber Lorna—my dream." I batted my eyelashes.

He laughed loudly, causing Declan to send us a sharp glare. *What was his problem?*

"If you do, pick a blue one to match your eyes. They're gorgeous," Dax said.

I blushed. "That's sweet—and oddly the most sincere thing you may have ever said to me. Thank you, Dax. I think you've more than made up for almost kissing me."

"*Almost?* Trust me, love, there was some lip-on-lip action. Don't you remember?" He leaned in and gave me a quick peck on the cheek, his full lips brushing against my skin, sending little tingles over me.

A chuckle erupted from me. With no alcohol on his breath

and no crazy party going on in the background, his kiss didn't bother me at all.

"What's so funny? That was grade-A kissing right there from the Sex Lord," he said, pretending to be affronted by my laughter.

I rubbed my lips. "You gave me goosebumps, goof."

"Goosebumps today, orgasm later?"

I barked out a laugh. "Do you ever stop with the flirting?"

"I can't. It's like I'm hardwired to get as many girls as I can. It's probably a coping mechanism because my mum died when I was young." He sent me a rueful look.

He'd said it all as a joke, but underneath I sensed the truth. "Sorry. Declan mentioned some of what you went through when you came here. It must have been hard leaving everything behind for the United States."

"Yeah, people talk funny here, and you have weird names for things. For us a lift is an elevator, a chip is a French fry, a biscuit is a cookie, a shag is a fuck, and don't even get me started on football." He waggled his eyebrows.

Declan cleared his throat, and I tossed a glance back to see him glaring at both of us. His hands sat on top of his desk, one clutching his pen tightly.

I arched a brow at him. Don't even go there with me, buddy. You have no right to be jealous. *You left me this morning*, I wanted to yell out.

Blake leaned over until our shoulders touched. He'd been quiet since the twins sat down. "Want to grab lunch later?"

I thought about it. With Colby walking around, I didn't want to be alone. "You mind if we ask these guys to come too?" I nodded toward the twins. "And maybe Shelley?" I wasn't ready for the *talk* he'd mentioned, and I needed a buffer between us.

"Something wrong with just me?"

"No, of course not. I just want to branch out and get to know more people."

Like a normal college girl.

Dr. Feldman came into the auditorium, saving me from Blake's reply. She was a tall, sparse lady with long brown hair she kept in a thick braid down her back, and her face was like stone, making you wonder if she ever smiled.

Wire-framed spectacles sat on the end of her nose as she swept beady eyes across the auditorium. "I trust you've all read the reading list I provided when you registered?"

Silence.

"I see. Another stellar class." Disdain dripped from her words. She shuffled some papers. "Well, for the first few weeks, we're going to be studying Jane Austen's *Pride and Prejudice*. I do expect classroom participation, so be aware that when I call on you you're required to stand and present your discussion."

Dax's hand shot up, and she waved at him to stand.

He did. "Do you grade on our discussion?"

She arched a derisive eyebrow. "Of course."

He shot her a cocky grin. "Brilliant, because I'm a great talker." He plopped back down.

"Any more questions before I call roll?" she asked, looking around the room.

No one moved.

"Fine." She ran her finger down what I assumed was the class roster and chuckled. "Is there seriously an Elizabeth Bennett in this class?"

I raised my hand tentatively. "That would be me."

"Please stand when you speak, Miss Bennett, so the entire class can see and hear you." She raked her eyes over me as I stood. "I confess, I'm extremely curious … did your parents name you after the book?"

I straightened my shoulders. "My parents never married, so Bennett's my mother's name. Elizabeth is just a name my mother picked. I doubt my parents had ever heard of Jane Austen." I shrugged. "I didn't discover *Pride and Prejudice* until high school."

She tapped her pencil against her leg. "Are you looking for your Mr. Darcy here at Whitman, Miss Bennett?"

My face flushed and I blinked. "I—I'm not looking for love, Dr. Feldman, just an education."

"Hmm, I see. But as humans aren't we naturally inclined to seek out love? Elizabeth found her soulmate. Don't you want to find yours?"

"No."

She gave me a surprised look. "Ah, I see. That might be a discussion for another day then. You may sit."

I sat down, relieved.

"Bugger, you could have warned me how scary she is," Dax leaned over and whispered.

I shrugged. "Wait until she asks hard questions. I heard at least half of all her students drop after the first day."

Feldman's voice interrupted us. "Mr. Declan Blay, please stand if you are present today."

Rustling motions came from behind me as Declan stood. "Present." His husky, clipped voice sent shivers over me.

She nodded, her eyes gliding over the muscles in his arms then coming back to rest on his face. "Mr. Blay, I trust you've read the required first ten chapters of *Pride and Prejudice* before today's class?"

"Not precisely."

She bristled. "I don't tolerate students who don't follow directions or complete homework assignments."

Declan cocked his head. "No, let me explain—"

She cut him off. "Please sit down so I can call on someone who's read the material."

"I'll take my chances if you don't mind, Dr. Feldman." He crossed his arms and sent her an expectant look.

She waved her hand. "Fine. Tell us about our heroine. What do you think of our Elizabeth Bennett?"

He rubbed the slight shadow on his face. "She's witty and spirited and the one least expected to marry a rich man, although she does by the end of the book." His gray eyes lazily brushed over me. "She's also a beautiful girl who likes the rain."

My heart thundered. God, it sounded like he was talking about me.

"Would you say she's the perfect woman, Mr. Blay?"

He blinked. "I don't believe in the perfect woman, just the right woman. Elizabeth knows she isn't perfect, but neither is Darcy. They're both flawed people who are at times too proud to admit their own true feelings—hence the title."

I admit it. His understanding of the theme of the book made me hot. Right then and there, I wanted to toss him down on the floor, crawl on top of him, and ride him like the Jane Austen reader I was.

"What are Elizabeth's flaws, then?" Dr. Feldman asked him.

"She's defensive—because of her family—and it affects her relationship with Darcy. She assumes he's a rich arsehole when he's actually in love with *her*."

"You seem to have a grasp on the entire novel, yet you didn't read the assignment." Her high heels clacked over to the front row so she could peer more closely at him. "Explain your-self."

"I've read it several times, Dr. Feldman, just not recently, and I was in the process of explaining when you interrupted me." He paused. "*Pride and Prejudice* is one of my favorite books. My mum read it to me when I was a kid. She was a huge romantic … and perhaps I am as well."

Girls swooned. Literally. I could hear them, melting in their seats as his softly rounded vowels washed over them.

I wasn't too far behind them. Heck, I'd already pictured us lying in a pile of old books, stark naked and smoking a satisfying cigarette after boinking each other's brains out.

Lorna clapped daintily, her eyes enraptured by Declan's question-answering skills. I rolled my eyes.

"So *awesome*," she whispered to him. "I'll have to read it for sure now."

Feldman studied him, and I thought I detected a little bit of swoon in her expression too. "I look forward to calling on you again. Please be seated."

After class finished, I turned to a glum Blake, whose hair was standing up everywhere from raking his hands through it. "Shit, this class is killer. There's no way I can do it."

"You're dropping my dream class?" I patted his hair down, some of the earlier weirdness fading.

He sighed and stood. "Yep. I'm heading over to the registrar's to take care of it. See you at lunch?" He fidgeted, waiting for me to reply.

"Sure." I couldn't say no.

We made plans to meet later, and he headed down the stairs and out the door.

I gathered my notebook and pens with a grin. Even though Feldman was tough as nails, I was excited about digging into this class.

Plus Declan was here. *But he's trouble, remember?* a voice in my head reminded me.

"You're a weird chick. You act like this class was fun," Dax said as he watched me gather my things.

"True," I said.

He laughed, and with Declan and Lorna trailing behind us, we headed for the exit.

We all came to a rather odd standstill outside the auditorium. No one seemed to know what to say next except for Lorna, who apparently knew both brothers well and kept the conversation going.

She looped her arm with Declan's. "You wanna go back to your place and study later?"

She may have liked Blake at one point, but I got the distinct impression she'd switched over to Declan.

"*Study* is apparently code for *let's have sex*," I whispered to Dax, who smirked.

"You look awesome today, by the way," Lorna said, continuing her flattery of Declan as she reached up to brush imaginary lint off his shirt.

Ugh. Enough.

I didn't want to watch this, and I came to a rapid decision.

I turned to Dax. "I'm going to grab some lunch at the Student Center at noon with Blake. You want to come?"

His eyes lit up. "Sure." He looked over his shoulder. "Hey, you guys want to join us on our date?"

"Date?" Declan came to attention, and his eyes bounced from me to Dax.

He nodded. "It appears Miss Bennett has forgiven me for trying to kiss her and has invited me to lunch. Want to join us or do you have *awesome* plans with Lorna?"

Declan cracked his neck and stared at us both, his gaze intense as if measuring the situation. "That's okay. Maybe next time," he said curtly and stalked off with Lorna half running beside him like a little puppy.

Pfft.

Dax watched her ass swing from side to side. "Guess he had plans."

"Uh-huh."

He snorted. "You have to admit. She's bloody *awesome*."

He looped an arm around me and walked me to my next class.

CHAPTER FOURTEEN

ON FRIDAY NIGHT, I fought a uni boy from Duke called Snake. Matches with Duke boys were packed events since we both had local fans. When I'd come in the warehouse, I'd also noticed a few more suits in the crowd this time, and I figured they were scouting me out for the Yeti fight in a few weeks.

I took a punch to the gut from him and gasped. People leaned back to get away from me as I stumbled around the warehouse. Some girl yelled in my face for me to get my act together.

I shook it off and rolled my neck.

Time to end this fight and start thinking about the next one.

I rushed at him, my palm strike clipping his shoulder, not the chest like I'd aimed for, yet the hit had enough force that he fell to the ground. He jumped up and barreled back at me, his legs maneuvering a jumping reverse roundhouse kick that I recognized as a Shotokan technique.

Bam! It was a hell of a move that got me right in the side. I staggered back.

He grinned as he bounced away from me. "Third degree

black belt, asshole."

"I'm better, *arsehole*."

Sure, he'd landed a few good hits—the blood that had spurted out of my nose a few punches ago could attest to that. But I had motivation and drive to win, my dream of the gym keeping me swinging.

I wiped sweat out of my eyes and squared off again. His body was lean and tall with fast reflexes, a testament to his fighting name, and I eyed him carefully, looking for chinks in his armor.

Earlier, he'd arrived in a Mercedes and had stepped out with a smirk on his face as he'd taken in the surrounding seedy area. A pretty girl had been on each arm as he'd stalked around the street like he owned the place. Cocky bastard.

I darted in and hit him with a strike to the upper thighs. He grunted and snapped back with a quick two-handed jab. I blocked them with my forearms and retreated, but he followed, still on the offensive, his elbow snapping up to catch my clavicle. I grunted and retaliated with a sideways hammer-fist strike to his gut.

Whoosh. He bent over gasping.

He got his breath and came at me again, but I blocked him. He'd grown sluggish, telegraphing his moves big time. He needed more training, and I watched the frustration grow on his face as I played with him, moving in for a quick jab and then bouncing back out of the way.

He punched at me and I ducked. He swung again, his breath winded.

That's right, pretty boy, wear yourself out.

I bounced around him and smirked.

"Kick his Dirty English ass, Snake!" one of his friends called out. "I got big money riding on this!"

"Go back to Duke, you utter twats," Dax yelled back at them, not to be outdone. Dax's frat brothers agreed.

I kicked Snake in the other leg and sent him reeling. He fell against one of the steel columns that supported the warehouse.

His eyes blinked. Once, twice.

Shit.

"You ready to call this?" I panted.

He grunted, his face set in a grimace as he staggered around me.

"We can end this right now."

"Fuck you," he said, slinging sweat-soaked hair out of his face.

"Your funeral," I said and raised my fists up.

But Snake was distracted by something in the crowd. I followed his eyes across the warehouse to see him watching one of the girls he'd arrived with. She'd apparently slipped over to a new guy, and they'd moved to an area against a back wall to kiss. Tongue action ensued. Hands rushed and roamed under shirts and down pants. They'd be shagging soon.

I looked back at my opponent, watching his face redden.

The bloody wanker was distracted by a girl who obviously didn't give a shit about him.

I grunted. *Another reason I needed to avoid Elizabeth*, I reminded myself.

"Focus. Let's do this," I snapped at Snake with a slap on the upper arm, and he turned back to face me, eyes wild.

My words spurred him into action.

He came at me again, both hands up and ready. With moves faster than I'd anticipated, he landed a strike to my spleen. I stumbled away from him to get my breath back. *Fuck.* No more trash-talking.

"Snake! Snake! Snake!" his friends chanted.

"Dir-ty Eng-lish! Dir-ty Eng-lish!" my side of the room called.

He inhaled a deep breath and flew at me, but I read his move and turned my body sideways and kicked out in a thrusting, snapping motion, the outside of my right foot aiming for his chest. He went down like a slow-moving boulder, arms splayed out and legs spread as he hit the ground.

He'd never had a chance with the girl distracting him, although I would have defeated him either way. She just made it quicker.

He moaned, and I knew he wasn't getting up anytime soon. I walked over to him. Checked his eyes, his breathing.

"You done?" I asked.

Glazed eyes looked up at me. "Yeah."

I waved for Nick to come and call it. A slick guy who wore a three-piece suit each time I saw him, he'd been setting up street fights in North Carolina for the past two years.

I looked back at Snake. "Keep a watch on your head, and if you have any headaches, see a doctor." It went unsaid that he'd have to lie about how he was injured. "And a word of advice, leave the girl at home next time."

He groaned and turned away as one of his mates came over and helped him to his feet. They stumbled away from me and out the metal doors.

Trouble. That's what girls were, right?

No way in hell would I ever let a girl distract me.

I took the cash Nick and Max counted out. This was all that mattered.

CHAPTER FIFTEEN

Elizabeth

B Y THE END of the first week of school I was back in the routine of going to class, working at the bookstore, and studying like crazy. I was off to a good start except I couldn't stop thinking about Colby being at Whitman. I looked for him everywhere now. In the grocery. In the parking lot. Outside my door?

And then there was Karl and my mom. I'd tried to call and text her several times, but she was ignoring me, and I got it. She was angry because I'd gotten upset with her and Karl at the diner. She wanted to use my story to get rich, and no way was I down with that.

By Sunday night, chocolate ice cream and relaxing were the only two things on my mind when I got home from work.

And …

I readily admitted to myself I was jonesing for some English accents, so I kicked my shoes to the floor and snuggled into Granny's couch for season two of *Downton Abbey*.

After eating a giant bowl of Ben & Jerry's and indulging in two hours of television, I stepped out my balcony door and stood there taking in the soft rain that had begun to fall. I was getting wet, but I didn't care.

Dressed in nothing but gym shorts, Declan stepped out onto his balcony. It seemed neither of us minded the weather. Like me, was he thinking of the last time it rained?

He flexed his hands, loosening the tape around them, his eyes out in the distance as if his thoughts were far away. He hadn't noticed me, and I eased further back into the shadows, letting my gaze roam over his bare chest, hard biceps, and trim waist.

Why did one guy have to look so damn good?

Did he ever wear a shirt?

I sucked in a sharp breath as I noticed the bruises on his body, one on his shoulder, another on his ribs.

"I know you're there," he said.

Dammit, there was no escaping him.

He bent over against the railing, the muscles in his back rippling, eyes still on the horizon.

And I said nothing, anger pricking at me and I didn't even know why.

But I did ... we'd spent the night together—albeit platonically—and he'd had a week to knock on my door, and he *hadn't*. He'd sat behind me in class all week but had mostly ignored me, sending eye-daggers my way when I joked around with Dax.

I didn't understand him.

And yet I did.

Both of us were afraid of getting too close.

He sighed and ran a hand through his wet hair. "I don't blame you for being quiet. I guess you're a wise girl to keep your distance." He grunted. "Which is ironic because you're the dangerous one, Elizabeth."

Me? He was the one with the potential to break me into a million pieces.

He turned to face me, his eyes zeroing in on mine, and I realized I'd walked to the edge of my balcony to be closer to him. He took in my damp nightshirt and bare feet.

My nipples pressed against the material as if they too wanted to be near him.

"Dangerous? Please. You're the one sporting new bruises," I said.

He shot me a grin. "I like it when you get feisty."

"I know." My words were quiet, remembering the night in his apartment.

His gaze brushed over my breasts like a physical touch, desire plainly written on his face.

I swallowed, feeling the invisible wires that pulled me toward him. I threw caution to the wind.

"We slept together without having sex. Do you do that often?"

His eyes smoldered like molten steel. "Never."

God, I wanted him. Desperately.

I clenched my fists. "Goodnight, Declan."

"Goodnight, Elizabeth."

"THE RESULTS ARE in, and I'm pleased to announce the prom king and queen are Colby Scott and Elizabeth Bennett," Mr. Brown, Oakmont's headmaster, announced from the gymnasium stage.

Elation washed over me in waves.

At first I couldn't believe we'd won, but when Colby took my hand to tug me toward the stage, reality set in. *This was it.*

Everything I'd ever wanted was right in front of me.

"Come on. They're waiting to crown us, babe." Colby's white teeth flashed.

I let him guide me toward the stage, my pink dress sparkling under the mirrored lights as we made our way across the basketball court, passed balloon sculptures and a backdrop featuring a cityscape of Paris. We glided up the steps and toward the center of the stage. Hands from the audience reached out to congratulate us.

Something was off …

A crawling sensation scratched at my brain, pricking at me.

I yanked my hand out of his, but he snatched it back and jerked me flush against his gray suit. "Too late, Elizabeth. This is what you wanted. Don't deny it." He kissed me roughly, his hands splayed out across my breasts.

I fumbled and pushed.

Slow motion. I couldn't move.

Wait. Had I taken something? Was I drunk? What was wrong with me?

A spotlight hit us. I saw Blake and Shelley. I saw my mother and Karl and Senator Scott, their lips curled in disgust.

Then we were in the hotel.

I was on the bed with him between my legs. Jamming into me.

No, no, no …

The terror wouldn't end.

I fought.

Stop, stop, stop.

"Elizabeth, wake up!" Firm hands shook my shoulders.

No!

I came awake screaming.

I scrambled up to the headboard. My eyes bounced around the room.

My bed. My dresser. My apartment. *Declan.* Thank God.

I sucked in a shuddering breath. My hands wiped my eyes, feeling wetness.

"What happened?" I croaked as I scrubbed my face, trying

to clear it.

He sat on the edge of my bed, and even in the dim light I could see his normally tanned face was white. "I heard you screaming from my room and came in through the balcony after I couldn't tear down your front door. Thank God your balcony door was open. You were all twisted up in the sheets ..." He stopped talking, a muscle working in his jaw.

I moved closer to his warmth and leaned my head against his shoulder. Inhaled. "You must think I'm a lunatic."

He lifted a hand to cup my head. "Do you want to talk about it?"

I bit my lip at his kindness and snuggled into his arms more fully. "No. It—it's nothing you want to know about. I just need some water."

"Okay, I'll get you some." He left and went into the kitchen, where I heard him milling around and opening cabinets until he found a glass and filled it. He came back into the bedroom and handed it to me.

Feeling nervous and just plain old shy, I scrambled to find conversation. "Did you—uh—actually jump to my balcony from yours? Wasn't that kind of dangerous?"

"Yes," he said softly. "But your front door was locked. Maybe you should give me a key."

Key? I laughed to hide my surprise. "You're just a regular Superman, aren't you?"

He shrugged, his expression giving me nothing.

I nodded.

Okay. Things were strained between us.

Obviously he was ready to go. I mean, I'd woken him up and he had classes tomorrow.

Silence ticked between us.

I kept it simple. "Thank you for coming over."

He rubbed his jaw. "If you're good then I should probably go—I guess?"

"I guess."

Neither of us moved. "You don't need anything else?" he asked.

I needed *him*. My body craved him. I was sick of seeing him for brief moments each day. I wanted more.

"No."

"Mind if I use the front door?"

I smiled. "Sure." We walked to the front door together, and he surprised me by reaching out and grabbing my hand on the way. His warm fingers stroked the tangled scars on my wrists.

He studied them. Looked back at me. "What happened?"

I swallowed. "I fell in love with the wrong guy."

I waited for him to question me or get angry at my stupidity, but I shouldn't have been surprised when he didn't. This was Declan, and he wasn't like anyone I'd ever met.

"I noticed them the night I showed you how to punch, but I didn't say anything. I'm sorry for your pain," he said, gazing down at the pink skin. "Your scars are beautiful. It means you survived. It means you're here with me." He kissed my wrist, light as a feather—and changed everything about us. "It's my favorite part of you," he said.

Big moments happen with the smallest of actions, and sometimes it's not until later we connect the dots, but in that instant, I knew that somehow, someway Declan was going to own my heart. It terrified me and excited me all at the same time.

He brushed a finger down my cheek. "Elizabeth? Do you really want me to go? Because—because I don't want to. It's been a shit week and I've barely talked to you and—"

"I want you to stay," I said softly.

Still holding hands, we went back to my darkened bedroom.

We got into bed together. Being careful of his bruises, I snuggled into his chest letting the warmth from his body seep into mine, banishing my nightmare. Wrapped up in a gorgeous body and tattoos, he was a heady sleeping aid. I wanted to yank my gown over my head, climb on top of him, and take him inside me. I wanted to ride him until all the bad memories were gone—but I didn't. I settled for keeping my clothes on and pressing myself against his hot skin, pleasure flooding me at the way his hands roamed my back, brushing against the bottom of my shirt, his fingers massaging me.

His touch was sexual.

Yet it wasn't. It was simply *more*, and I was terrified to put a name to it.

So I didn't think about it at all.

I just went with it.

CHAPTER SIXTEEN

Declan

THE NEXT MORNING I woke up around five thirty, left Elizabeth in bed, and headed to the gym before class. I'd been going early so I could catch the contractors who were working on the updates.

After the gym, I left for class and met Dax at our usual spot outside the humanities building. We hadn't seen each other much in the past few days, mostly because I was caught up in the gym and my classes while he was partying at the frat house. At least we had one class together, although it was hard to watch him sit next to Elizabeth each day and flirt with her.

"What do you think of Elizabeth?" he asked as we walked up the stairs to the third floor and came out onto the hallway.

He'd brought her up when I'd been thinking about her? "My Elizabeth?"

He paused mid-stride and flicked his eyes at me. "Yours? You shagged her?"

"No."

"I'm sensing a *but* here."

"Don't be a knobhead." I resisted the urge to shove him up

against the wall.

Jealous of my own brother. Sad.

He stiffened. "What's your deal? I'm just making conversation about a girl in class." His eyes searched mine. "And let's just say for argument's sake that I wanted to shag her—would you be okay with it?"

I shrugged. "You're your own person. Do whatever the bloody hell you want."

He rubbed his jaw, studying me with narrowed eyes. "You seem a bit off. You okay?"

Just then Nadia and Donatello came down the hall toward us, effectively ending our convo. I didn't miss that Nadia's eyes lingered on me, a pleading look in them. I ignored her for the most part, but judging from her tight face and Donatello's sullen expression, there was trouble in paradise.

They stopped in front of us, mostly because the line of bodies moving had come to a standstill. It was unavoidable we'd bump into each other. This was a small uni. I hadn't talked to her since the frat party, and although she hadn't been on my mind, her family had.

"How's your mum?" I asked, as Ninja Turtle wandered off to talk to some of the tennis lads who were standing near a classroom door.

She got misty-eyed. "She started chemo, and it goes for twelve weeks. I—I'm headed home this weekend to see her."

I nodded. "I'm sorry. Mum never took chemo. There wasn't time or any reason to."

She cleared her throat and changed gears. "On the other hand, my sorority is having our annual back to school mixer next week. You're invited."

"We're over, Nadia. I won't be coming."

Dax raised his eyebrows and bounced his eyes between us, and then over to Donatello.

"I know." Her hand caressed my arm and then dropped.

"But I still care about you, Declan. Just think about it."

She waved bye and wandered back to her boyfriend.

Dax snorted. "You're way too easy on her. Everyone here is wondering why you haven't kicked Donatello's arse, too."

I shrugged. "Some things are worth it and some aren't."

We walked into the auditorium for Lit class. Wearing a skimpy top and a miniskirt, Lorna waved at me, pointing at the same seat where I'd been sitting next to her since class started a week ago.

Dax chuckled. "Looks like someone wants to be the next girl Dirty English chooses."

But my eyes went to Elizabeth. She sat in front of Lorna, her head bent low as she flipped through the pages of her textbook. She hadn't even noticed I was here.

Dax left me to sit next to Elizabeth. He plopped down next to her, and they immediately began talking. Of course, Dax did most of the talking while she listened.

Envy ate at me. I wanted to be in his seat.

Dr. Feldman took to the podium, and I tried to focus on the lesson.

Usually, I was riveted, but today I barely listened.

My eyes were never off Dax and Elizabeth.

CHAPTER SEVENTEEN

Elizabeth

"I WISH YOU were rich like me. It's not fair you have to work all the time. And if you're not working, you're studying. It's a shame you're missing out on the true college experience," Shelley complained as I unpacked new textbooks that had come in for the bookstore. She smiled. "But don't you love me for coming to keep you company?"

I rolled my eyes at her. "Whitman isn't cheap, and we can't all have daddies that pay our Amex card every month."

She made a moue with her lips. "We could probably figure out a way for him to pay your bills too. He'd never know probably."

I shook my head. "I pay my own way. Always have. I'm here for a top notch education ..."

"So you never have to depend on a loser like your poor mom does ... I know, I know. You say it all the dang time. Trust me, you are never going to end up with some car salesman from Petal who wears Hawaiian shirts. But if you want to meet a nice, *rich* guy, then you need to get out more."

"Working makes me feel good about myself. You should try

it."

She sent me a disbelieving glare. "I just buy shoes to feel good—or jewelry. Speaking of, have you seen the new line of James Avery necklaces? God, totally gorgeous with these little silver charms everywhere. And you could totally do it, Elizabeth. Your drawings are much better than half the stuff I see."

"I—I did draw something recently. A dragonfly."

Her eyes flared. "Holy hell, that's huge. Why didn't you tell me? What are you going to do with it? Put it on a bracelet? Necklace? Make me one ... please?"

She didn't understand why I'd stopped making jewelry, not really, but her encouragement meant something to me. No one else had ever pushed me but Granny, and she was gone. "Thank you for saying that."

She grinned, refocusing. "So, let's talk about your sexy new neighbor. You had a nightmare and the English dreamboat came over and saved you from the bogeyman?"

I groaned. I never should have told her. "You can drop the baby-girl voice."

"But it's so fun. I can't believe you didn't do the deed with him. Don't you want to see if he's like Hugh Grant in *Notting Hill*? Oh, or Jude Law? Wait, how about Charlie Hunnam? Oh yeah, I'd have his babies. Well, all their babies." She waggled her eyebrows.

"My life is not a movie, Shelley."

She munched on a bag of chips she'd snagged from the café. "I beg to differ. You have to admit your life is fairly dramatic. Heck, you could probably sell the rights to it and make millions. *Chi-ching!*"

Her words sobered me, reminding me of my mom and Karl and their scheme. I pushed the worry away.

"Does everything he says sound hot? Like if he called you a bitch, you'd be like *oh, baby, say it again*?"

I cracked a grin. "Maybe."

"Oh my God, what if the twins are related to the Queen?" She pointed a finger at me, her face animated. "You could be English royalty. Heck, your name is already Elizabeth—wasn't she a queen or something? Think about it ... you in a Lady Di–type wedding dress. You already love all that Shakespeare stuff, and this would just be the icing on the cake." She started quoting famous Shakespearean lines but ended up mixing them together, tossing *Romeo and Juliet* in with *Macbeth*.

A bit later, after she'd finished, I took a deep breath. "Listen, I don't want you to freak out, but you may see Colby on campus this semester. Apparently, he's a student here now."

She dropped her bag of chips, eyes big as saucers. "What the hell? Are you okay? How do you know? Why are you not freaking out? Why—"

"I'm fine." I totally wasn't.

"He—he came to see me, but he left when Declan ran him off. So, if I act odd or whatever, it's because I'm paranoid I'm going to see him or he's going to tell people about what happened." My voice trembled.

She exhaled loudly but her voice came out hushed. "You have nothing to be ashamed of, Elizabeth, absolutely nothing. But you need to call the cops if he shows up again. Please say you will."

I nodded. But would I?

"Since your parents know his family, will you ask them if they'd heard anything about why he's transferred here? See if you can figure out what's going on with him."

She nodded, a look of worry on her face.

I pushed out a grin. "Come on, don't get glum on me. Make me laugh."

"You doing okay unpacking those boxes?" a male voice called from around the corner. Rick ambled into view. Tall with sandy blond hair and a skinny build, he'd recently graduated from Whitman and was the store manager here while he worked on his graduate degree.

He stood next to me and pilfered through some of the titles in the box. "Some of these boxes are heavy and need to go up-stairs to the non-fiction section. Let me know if you need some help getting them up the stairs." He smiled and adjusted his glasses.

I smiled back. "Okay."

We had an elevator, but I didn't say anything. He always of-fered to help me, and I thought it sweet.

I could feel Shelley's eyes on us, watching. Plotting.

"She needs help a lot, *Rick*. She needs a big old—oh, never mind." She grinned maniacally.

I shot her a look. This was not what I meant by *make me laugh.*

Her eyes said what she'd said to me many times, *That is some good man-meat right there. What are you waiting on, chi-ca? Scaredy-cat. Here, pussyyyyyyy.*

I huffed just as the café door opened and Blake walked through to the bookstore.

"What's going on?" he asked us.

"Nothing," snorted Shelley. "This bookstore needs to magi-cally turn into a night club or a frat house."

"Geez, no one's keeping you here with me," I replied. "I'm not bored at all. I'm working to pay *my* bills."

She shrugged and sipped on her soda. "This year is just so blasé so far."

"Don't you have homework?" How did the girl not get kicked out of school?

"All done." She tapped her head. "I might look like a dumb co-ed, but this brain is smarter than you think."

"Let's all do something," Blake said. "Movie maybe? I hear the new Marvel movie is showing at the Malco." He sent me a sheepish grin. "I know Elizabeth loves Thor, right?"

"Wow, Elizabeth? Is that so?" Shelley asked in a snarky

voice.

I shrugged. "Sure, what's not to like? There are big muscles and blond hair and tattoos and a hammer ..."

"Yeah, she likes big hammers," Shelley deadpanned.

"That's enough," I said.

"I was kidding." She sent me a sly look.

Blake and Rick chuckled, and even though I was the butt of the joke, it made me glad to see Blake smile. I didn't want things to be weird between us. I'd been processing his declaration of love, but I still didn't know what I wanted to do about it.

The chime on the overhead door went off as Dax and Declan both walked in the café entrance.

Shelley came to attention. "The British are coming, the British are coming."

"Stop it," I hissed.

Blake's face had grown still at our conversation, his body tense. "I don't know what all the girls see in those two—"

"—who are hotter than my hair straightener," Shelley finished.

A girl in the café waylaid Dax, but Declan strode our way wearing low-slung jeans, a Whitman shirt, and a pair of leather flip-flops.

I sighed, taking in the dark hair that curled around his ears and nape, the glossy sheen catching the lights. His steely-gray eyes seemed to zero in right on me from clear across the store, and I felt myself prepping my body for the current that would inevitably shoot through me.

He came closer and it seemed as if every eye in the place followed him.

Why couldn't I just write him off like I had all the others?

"Yep, hotter than a Times Square Rolex," I murmured to myself.

He came to a stop in front of the counter. "Hey. You good today?"

I squirmed at the attention. He meant the nightmare. It had been several days since our sleepover and he'd been checking in with me each morning in Lit class, keeping it casual but always asking if I was okay.

"Yeah. And you?"

He nodded.

Dax came crashing into us, the girl he'd been talking to tagging along behind him. "What's going on? Anybody want to come to the house and hang out?" He came over and tossed an arm around me. "Hey, love, when do you get off work?"

Blake answered. "We're going to the movies later. Sorry."

I didn't recall agreeing to a movie. Seems my friends had decided what my plans were for the evening when really I needed to get home and study.

"Sounds kinda boring, but I'm in," Dax said with a clap of his hands. He left me to toss an arm around the random girl. "You too?"

She blushed.

"Actually, Elizabeth and I already have plans tonight. I was just coming by to confirm," Declan inserted smoothly.

All eyes turned to me and then bounced back to Declan.

"Plans?" Shelley squeaked. "You didn't tell *moi*?"

"But, the movie ..." Blake's voice trailed off.

Dax's eyes widened. "Oh, I didn't see that coming."

Rick moved to the cash register to check someone out but not before looking at me with questioning eyebrows.

Seemed like everyone had a damn opinion on the matter.

"You still coming?" Declan said, a slight edge to his voice as he turned to look at me.

A hush had settled over the group.

I set down the book I'd been holding. Swallowed.

Was this a real date-date? One without sex at the end or one with sex at the end? God, I didn't know because I hadn't had a real date since Colby.

Or had he figured out I didn't want to go anywhere at all and was just trying to rescue me from my well-meaning friends? "Yes, of course," I said. "Where are we going?"

He grinned, a soft boyishness settling on his face. "It's a surprise."

Shelley giggled, abruptly clamming up when I glared at her.

Blake snapped up and took off for the café. *Dammit.* I watched him go with a heavy sigh and then turned back to Declan.

"I don't get off for another hour."

He looked at the books scattered around me. "I can help you. What needs to be done?"

"Oh, thank you, but only employees can shelve. Rick's rule. I appreciate it though. Are you sure you don't mind waiting?"

"Good things are worth waiting on."

I smiled. Breathless.

He sent me a grin. "Nice shirt, by the way." He raked his eyes over me, lingering on the T-shirt he'd given me a few nights ago. Made of thin white cotton, it featured the Front Street Gym logo, which was a black circle with two fists meeting and the gym name written around the circle. On the back of the shirt in Old English font was written *Property of Dirty English.* I'd been surprised as hell when he'd knocked on my door and handed it to me, saying he'd designed it and wanted my opinion before ordering in bulk for his gym's grand opening. It fit tight across my chest. He lifted his eyes up to mine.

"Thanks. Some cocky guy gave it to me."

He lifted an eyebrow. "He must be a nice bloke to give you a free T-shirt."

"Very. Although I think he gave me a size too small. On purpose."

His eyes landed on my breasts and he smiled before focusing back on my face. "Perhaps he never thought you'd wear it in public. Is he handsome?"

"He thinks so." My face felt like it might split in half I was grinning so big. What was it about him that had me feeling so giddy?

Shelley linked an arm through Dax's. "Well, I still want you to come along with us to the movies."

He waggled his eyebrows. "Indeed. You're far too hot to say no to. Tell me, do you dig threesomes?"

She giggled and tapped his arm. "Behave."

They got out their phones to finalize movie times, and I started in with the duties I did at the end of my shift. Half an hour later, I'd gotten the new books shelved and had broken down boxes and carried them to the back storage room. I piled them up in a corner next to the trash and then went to the broom closet. I opened it and pulled out the wide, heavy-duty dust mop.

When I turned around Blake was standing there.

"Oh! You scared me!" I laughed, clutching my chest. "What are you doing back here?" I looked past his shoulder. I didn't think Rick would mind that he was in a restricted area, but you could never tell.

He scrubbed a hand through his auburn hair roughly, making the ends stand up. "I can't believe you have a date with him after what I told you."

"Blake—"

"Since when does he get to march in here and act like he owns you?" He paced around, his movements swift and sharp, as if he were holding in banked anger.

I stiffened. "*You're* the one acting possessive. He's a good guy. In fact, you outright lied about him at the party. Care to explain that?"

His eyes widened. "I was desperate. I don't want you with him, okay? It's just—I told you how I feel, and you haven't said a word about it. You just keep going about your day, not wanting to accept that our relationship is changing. I can't just be your friend anymore and see you screw around with other guys."

I shook my head. "You're my friend. I need you." I only had two in the whole world.

He exhaled. "Just give *us* a chance. We'll take it slow, I promise. No crazy stuff." His hand reached out to touch my cheek, soft and easy as if I were a skittish animal he wanted to tame. "I won't ever pressure you or push you to do anything you don't want to do, I promise."

And the thing was, there was a tiny bit of something in my heart for him. A spark of whatever we'd had in prep school still lingering. But being with Blake meant commitment.

I—I just couldn't do it.

"Everything okay back here?" Rick's voice cut through the tension. "You need some help, Elizabeth?"

I cleared my throat and stepped back around Blake. "No, it's good. Coming out to mop soon."

Blake reached out to clasp my hand. "Wait, Elizabeth. I'm not the only one with feelings here. Talk to me."

I sighed, changing gears. Anything to get away from this topic. "Look, I have a lot on my mind right now. There's something I haven't told you. Colby—he came to see me the night before the semester started. He—he's enrolled here now. I haven't seen him since, but I'm going to. I just know it. He's not going away." I heard the fear in my voice and cringed.

He gathered me in his arms. "Fuck. I'm so sorry. What can I do to help?"

I leaned my head on his shoulder. "There's nothing to be done. It's something I'm going to have to deal with, and I really need you here beside me. I can't do it without you."

He let out a long breath and kissed my forehead. "Whatever you need, I'm here."

CHAPTER EIGHTEEN

Elizabeth

L ATER WE LEFT the bookstore and headed out to the parking lot, where Declan took the top and sides off his Jeep. We'd decided to leave my car there and have him bring me back later from wherever we were going.

I got in on the passenger side and buckled up. "Want to tell me what that was all about in there? We never made plans."

He smirked. "What? You've wanted me to ask you out since the moment you saw me at the frat house."

"You mean when you wouldn't even dance with me?" I snapped.

He tossed his head back and laughed. "You're a little spitfire. And I did dance with you on your balcony, remember?"

Fine.

He put on his Ray-Bans and grinned. "Don't like surprises, I take it?"

"No. Just tell me," I groaned.

He nodded. "Okay. We're headed to an intervention."

That didn't sound fun at all. "For what?"

His gray eyes caressed my face when we stopped at a light.

"I promise, you'll like it."

Oh shit. Lightning strikes went straight to my core.

We hit the open road and the wind made my hair crazy. It was exhilarating, but I yelled as I tried to wrestle my hair and hold it back. I needed a ponytail holder.

He reached over and opened the glove box and pointed at a pile of hair bands.

It scared me that he read my mind, but I shot him a sour look as I selected a black one. "Nadia's?"

He shrugged in that effortless way of his I'd come to recognize. Noncommittal. Mysterious as hell.

I glared at him.

But my anger only made him grin. "Jealous?" he asked.

"Yes," came out before I could stop it.

He shot me a surprised look and then turned quickly back to the road, but he kept sending me little glances as he drove, his eyes roaming my face.

"You're beautiful," he said softly. Simple words. Heavy weight. "There's no reason for you to be jealous of her. You're everything she isn't, and I like it. A lot."

When I watch romantic movies or read a book, there comes a point in the story where the two love interests are perfectly synced. He looks at her and his eyes soften. She looks at him and realizes he's the best thing since sliced bread. Kinda like when Elizabeth looks past Darcy's awful marriage proposal and sees the real man underneath the rich veneer. Or when Romeo first sees Juliet at the party and knows life will never be the same.

It happened for me just as the wind caught his dark hair and ruffled it, and in that tiny millisecond, the carefree way he smiled, the way he held the steering wheel with strong hands, the way he sent me a little searching glance as if gauging my reaction—it was enough to make me second guess everything.

But then I told myself to get my head back on straight.

He was a fighter for goodness' sake.

He was wrong for me.

Anyone was, really.

Because my heart was locked up tight, the key buried deep in my soul. And no one, not even Declan Blay, could pick that lock.

CHAPTER NINETEEN

WE BARRELED DOWN the highway and she gave me the oddest look when I told her she was beautiful.

"What?" I asked.

She shook her head as if to clear it. "You know this isn't a *date*-date, right?"

I shrugged. "I just got out of a shitty relationship myself."

"I don't mean friends with benefits either," she said.

"Did I ask you for sex, Elizabeth? Have I made a move on you?" My voice had tightened.

A soft "No" reached my ears.

"Right. I have plenty of girls willing to shag me. I don't need to go begging."

She licked pink lips, and I found my eyes lingering there, imagining my cock sliding in …

"Will you stop staring at me and watch where you're driving?" she said sharply.

I couldn't stop the grin on my face. She made me happy, and I didn't even know why. Maybe it was the way she'd looked when I'd walked up to her at the bookstore—blushing like a schoolgirl, yet with a wicked gleam in her eyes that went straight to my dick. Maybe it was the way she filled out that T-shirt.

But, maybe it was more. Deeper. I sensed a kindred spirit in her, a loner who ached to find someone to love for real. Like me.

Just one glance from her and I wanted to kiss her and make her mine. People laugh when you talk about one look at someone and you're in love, and I'm not saying that's what this was, but damn, something weird was at work here and it had me scratching my head. Was it because she was so wrong for me that I wanted her even more? Yeah. Fuck. Elizabeth Bennett had her pretty little claws in me, and God help me, I wanted her to dig them in deeper.

I pulled the Jeep into the carpark of the Front Street Gym, although she wouldn't know that since the signage hadn't been hung yet. The work crew had left for the day, so it was quiet as I hopped out and looped around to help her climb down.

She stepped down on the pavement and looked around, wary eyes taking in the two story building. "What's this place?"

I grinned. "It's my new gym."

"How can you afford all this?"

I shrugged. "I used the inheritance from my mum to buy the place, and my fighting money helps with the remodeling."

Her eyes widened. "Oh."

"Did you think I fought for fun?"

She licked her lips. "I—I don't like fighting."

I sighed. Whatever.

We stepped inside the dark foyer, the smell of sweat and rubber mats piercing my senses like a balm of cool wind on a hot day. We were both quiet as I flicked on the lights and watched her take in the wide space, imagining how she'd see it through her eyes. It was old and musty and most of the workout equipment hadn't been updated, but the boxing rings were new.

She stared at the posters in the hallway. I pointed at one of Max with his gloves in the air as the ref put on his championship belt during a mixed martial arts championship. "That's Max. He's my personal trainer, and he'll be one of my trainers here when I open this place in a few months. We've been friends for a while."

Her eyes searched mine. "You really love this place."

"Yeah. If it wasn't for this gym—for training—I'd be, I don't know, crazy? Pissed off all the time, for sure. It gives me focus."

She chewed on her lip, unease on her face.

I ignored it. "Ready for your surprise?"

She sent me a nervous look. "Yeah."

"Come on, then. Let me show you something." I took her hand and led her over to one of the red sparring mats. "I can't help but notice how wary you are with certain people, and I think you might be more confident if you really knew how to defend yourself. You need to know more than just how to make a fist. You need to know how to use it."

She looked down at the thick mat. "We're going to wrestle?"

I grinned at that image. "We're going to do Krav Maga. Ever heard of it?"

She shook her head.

"Translated it means *contact combat*, and I've been teaching it at various gyms in the area for a couple of years. Basically it's a form of self-defense developed by the Israeli military, fast, aggressive, and very effective with just a few moves."

"Does this mean you'll be touching me?"

I blinked. "Yeah. A lot."

She debated for a few seconds, a small smile curving her mouth. Full and plump, those lips on mine had been my fantasy way too many nights. "Okay, but only if you let me take you down a few times. Like flip you over my shoulder, toss you to the ground kind of take down. Maybe sit on you."

I exhaled, picturing that little scenario, and I couldn't stop the little grin on my face. "You can sit on me whenever you want."

She smirked. "Funny, Englishman. You better be nice if you don't want me to hurt you."

I laughed. This was the girl I wanted to see. Sure of herself. Sassy. Not the scared girl at the frat party.

She walked around on the mat and hopped a little on her heels. "Okay. This is going to be fun. What's first?"

"I need you to take your clothes off."

CHAPTER TWENTY

Elizabeth

OF COURSE HE was teasing me.

He chuckled. "You can close your mouth. I meant that you don't want to ruin—or rip—your jeans." He pointed to the back of the gym where the lockers and restrooms were. "Come on. I've got some extra pants for you to change into."

Ten minutes later I came out of the ladies locker room bare-footed in a pair of extra-small white karate pants.

I walked back to the mat and did a little pirouette, liking the way it made his eyes gleam with laughter.

He waited for me dressed in the same pants. His feet were bare and spread apart in a cocky stance, and even though I'd never been one of those people who got a thrill from odd body parts, his feet were sexy.

But it was his naked chest that made my heart do a loop-de-loop. My tongue wanted to lick it, but I settled for deep breathing. I recalled how wonderful it had felt to press myself against his skin the nights we'd slept together. But that was then and this was now, and it seemed as if we were slowly progressing toward more.

Keep your tongue in your mouth, Elizabeth, I told myself.

To distract myself, my eyes traced the dragonfly tattoo on his neck, my fingers itching to draw it. The tattoo seemed so incongruous with the tough guy he was, yet it fit him. He had a softness to him, and I think I'd sensed it from the first moment we'd met.

"Come here," he said. Silkily.

I went without hesitation. "What?" I asked.

He reached out and gathered the bottom material of my shirt and tied it in a knot that rested on my tummy. Tingles went over me at the brush of his fingers against my skin. "Now, you're ready."

"Thank you," I murmured, looking down at the peek of my tummy that showed through. I suddenly felt alive. Wired.

He nodded as he bent down to readjust the sparring mat, and I saw the scars on his back again.

"What happened to your back?"

He stood back up and faced me, his face like stone.

I saw the distance growing in him, as if he didn't want to talk about it.

"If—if you ever wanted to tell me about it, I'd listen …" My voice petered out.

"I don't."

Sadness filled me. There was so much more to him than just being the hot guy with the sexy accent. "I won't judge you, Declan. I have my own scars."

He exhaled, studying me. "I got into a scuffle with my father and went through a plate glass window when I was fourteen. My back took the worst of it."

"That sounds awful."

"I spent that whole summer sleeping on my stomach, waiting for the stitches to heal." He looked at my wrist. "What happened?"

Images of the hotel zipped through my head, and I opened

my mouth to tell him, I mean really tell him what had happened to me, but I didn't. Old habits die hard.

I looked away. Swallowed. "I can count the number of people on one hand who know why I slit my wrists. I—I'm not ready to tell you."

"Blake knows?"

I heard the jealousy in his voice.

"Yes."

He tightened his lips. "Right then. Let's get to work."

I nodded, relieved he was letting it go.

"When we get down to direct man-on-man sparring, I'll ask you to wear protective gear and wrap your hands, but for today, we're just going to talk about stance and some basic moves to get you comfortable. Okay?"

I nodded, and that seemed to be all he needed to go into full-on teaching mode. He had a beautiful voice for it, clear and low, yet commanding. I could see the appeal in taking a class from him. I bet the women hung on his every word.

"You don't want to give your opponent any leeway. Be cognizant of your environment and if you can get help. If you can't, then be prepared to put up a hell of a fight. Most importantly, be aggressive and do whatever it takes to defend yourself. Punches, kicks, elbow strikes, knees, and even biting and scratching. Just don't freeze up like you did the night Colby showed up."

I smirked. "Sounds like a cat fight I saw once on the quad freshman year."

He smiled as he adjusted my shoulders and stance. "This kind of fighting is much more premeditated. Just keep your strong leg in front of you. Put your hands up in front of your face just below eye level. Your hips, eyes, and lead shoulder should always face your opponent."

I followed his instruction, my heart thundering at our closeness.

He had me shifting my weight around on my legs to get comfortable.

Back and forth. Again. And then again.

He demonstrated an uppercut elbow punch for me, positioning his body next to mine as he rotated his hips and shuffled forward at an imaginary attacker. He moved like lightning strikes in the sky. Fast. Brilliant. Too hot to hold. I repeated his kicks and punches again and again until I began to feel a tight burning in my thighs and arms and buttocks.

"You'll need to exercise to get stronger muscles," he told me later as I failed miserably at a good front kick. "The thing to remember about a kick is you go for his twigs and berries. If you can't, aim for a knee or his neck or nose. Just get the kick in and get out."

I grunted and wiped sweat from my face.

"Tired?" He paused in demonstrating the kick once again.

I shook my head. Liar, liar. But watching him move his powerful body around was invigorating.

Who needed Gatorade when I had a hot dude showing me his moves?

A few minutes later, we faced off on the mat. "Come at me with some heat. See if you can sneak in my circle and land a tap on my arm."

"What about the protective gear?"

He waved me off as he positioned himself in a defensive stance. "We're fine for today. You won't get in."

Won't get in?

I puffed up my chest and shuffled toward him like he'd shown me, hands up and ready to strike. I bounced around back and forth, angling for a spot on his body.

"Come on, Elizabeth. You're taking too long."

I moved around him, looking for a way inside, but each time I rotated around him, he'd pivot his body toward mine.

"Move slower," I snapped.

"It doesn't have to be perfect, Unicorn Girl. Just get a tap in."

"Don't call me that."

I shifted and he followed.

"I can't!" I yelled at him. "You're too big and fast."

He sighed and rolled his neck. "Pretend we're at some party and we just met and I'm going to throw you down and take whatever I want ..."

I don't even remember lunging for him. I don't remember telling my fist to slam his face, but it did. His head jerked back, mostly to avoid my punch, but some of it still connected.

I gasped. "Declan! Why didn't you defend yourself?"

He blinked a few times. "Damn. I didn't say break my nose; I said *tap*."

I fluttered around him, feeling terrible. My hands cupped his face, our chests touching. "God, I'm so sorry. Are you okay?" I ran my fingers across his jawline, fingering the stubble there. "Want me to get some ice? Maybe a bottle of water? Do you need to sit down? God, I'm talking too much, aren't I?"

He wore a bemused expression. "I'm fine. You caught me by surprise is all."

"I could have hurt you," I wailed. "And then I'd feel horrible. You've been nothing but good and wonderful and sweet to me and I ..." I sputtered out of words, scared at what was on the tip of my tongue. God. *What was wrong with me?*

"Maybe I do need water." His voice was weird, his eyes as well, the gray taking up most of his irises.

"Declan, your eyes are dilated. Are you sure you're okay? Do you have a concussion?"

He groaned and shut his eyes.

"Declan?"

He stepped back. "It's not the hit, Elizabeth. It's *you*."

I hissed, something in my heart shifting as he opened his eyes and stared at me. With longing. With heat.

I imagined fireworks went off somewhere in the distance.

Change happens to all of us. Sometimes you want a new haircut, sometimes you want to try blue cheese instead of ranch, and sometimes you just want to ignore your head and go with what you desire the most. Mostly it's a gradual process, but not with Declan. I wanted sex on a mat in an un-air-conditioned gym with a hot as hell British guy pounding into me, no matter the consequences. Fuck my silly sex rules. I wanted him.

He studied me. "If you knew what I was thinking, you'd run like hell."

"Are you thinking about tossing me on the mat for real?"

He lowered his chin, his eyes at half-mast. "Yes."

I felt drunk at his words. Dizzy with need.

I shivered at the heat that raced up my spine as he stood there looking at me with those molten eyes.

Wanting me.

God, I was sick of being a walking, talking dead person when it came to real emotional need. I just wanted him, hard and fast.

"Kiss me, Declan. *Please.*"

"I've been waiting forever for you to say my name like that," he said in a low voice and tugged me against him. His hand swept over my face, pushing back the hair that had fallen forward.

I clutched him, my hand snaking around the taut muscles of his neck, my nose inhaling the scent of male and sweat. His lips took mine hard, and I moaned at the slide of his lips against mine, at the way he dominated me. His arms held me prisoner in a jail I wanted, my hands clawing at his shoulders, pulling him closer. More. *Yes.* He tasted like the most delicious dessert, rich and decadent.

"Yes," I murmured and rubbed my hands over his back greedily, searching out the hard muscles and indentations, wanting to map his skin in my brain and sear it to memory.

He held my arms up and tugged my shirt off, tossing it aside without even looking to see where it went.

I didn't care either.

Hurry, hurry, take me, I said in my brain, but he went excruciatingly slow, his hands cupping my breasts through the nude bra I wore. He palmed them with one hand while the other slipped to my back and unsnapped it.

It fell unnoticed to the floor.

He massaged me, his eyes meeting mine as he bent to take a nipple between his lips, his teeth teasing and then sucking it into his mouth. Pleasure raced over me as he tugged and twisted.

I tossed my head back and gasped, my hands tangling in his hair, clutching him tighter. I was going to combust before we'd even gotten to the good stuff.

His touch was rougher than what I was used to. More masterful. Confident. Sexy.

"This is so good," I whispered.

"It only gets better," he murmured and captured my peaks again, his tongue and teeth lashing at my now tender skin.

His hands were everywhere, as if he couldn't get enough, and I loved the greedy way he touched me. He knew every nerve ending that would send me over the edge, and I strained closer, wanting more of him, my hands now gripping his broad shoulders just to keep standing.

Sensing my collapse, he eased me down to the mat and then stood over me, his eyes burning.

"We shouldn't do this," he said, chest heaving. "We're completely wrong for each other, and I'm not even sure you like me most days."

"I agree. But don't let that stop you."

He huffed out a laugh and tore out of his pants and tight athletic boxers, his cock bouncing out and straining for me. I sucked in a shuddering breath. Thick and hard, it was the biggest one I'd ever laid eyes on. My lower regions twitched.

He grinned. "You're looking at my manhood like it's a stick of dynamite about to explode."

"Is it?"

His eyes laser-locked with mine. "Indeed."

He knelt down, and a painful dawning hit his face. "I don't have a condom. This was the last thing I expected would happen." He cursed and rubbed his face briskly. "Fuck. I'm sorry."

Disappointment seared me, my body crying out for him.

He brushed a strand of hair out of my eyes. "I'm clean, though. I've never had sex without one. Not once."

I'd never let a guy near me that didn't have a condom, but I came to a rapid decision. "I'm on the pill. If you say you're safe, I believe you, Declan."

He kissed me hard and swift. "Thank you for trusting me."

I stared into his eyes. It wasn't so much trust as need riding me. "I will cut your cock off if you give me a venereal disease. Got it?"

He chuckled. "I'll let you, love. Just the thought of your hands on me makes me happy."

He slid down to lie next to me, the press of his body like nirvana. Strong arms wrapped around my shoulders as he gathered me close, and I moaned. Finally.

His hands roamed lower, his fingertips sliding my underwear and pants down my legs. His eyes followed their path. "Your legs are so damn long. I keep thinking about them wrapped around my hips ..." He groaned, his mouth dipping down to kiss my tummy, my hips, the bend in my knees.

I groaned and spread my legs as his fingers burrowed in and slid into my center, dipping in and out. He spread the wetness around, pressing and teasing and strumming me with his touch.

I writhed and arched closer while he bit his lower lip, watching me twist to get him closer. Deeper.

There. Yes.

I moaned.

He worked me hard, yet gently, ghosting over the bundle of nerves in my G spot, thrumming them like a guitar string.

More. I wanted him everywhere.

He read my mind and maneuvered between my legs, placing them on his shoulders and then taking my center in his mouth. Hot fire flashed over every inch of me, and I gasped out as he delved deep into my recesses, his fingers playing at the heart of me. He parted my labia, his tongue searching for tender skin. His mouth worked me, rubbing and plucking with his lips.

Intense need built. I gasped out his name.

He looked up at me, eyes heavy with lust. "You like?"

I nodded. No one had ever done this to me. I'd never trusted them to.

"Don't stop," I murmured.

He didn't deny me, plunging two fingers inside me, his tongue pulsing over my skin. His mouth took my clit captive, nursing it with soft strokes.

I screamed his name and snapped into a million pieces, the fragments scattering and falling all around me like stars from heaven. I gripped the edge of the mat and rode it out, my inner muscles clamping down and contracting under his mouth.

My body sagged onto the mat.

I cupped his face when he looked at me, a grin of satisfaction tipping up his lips. "I've been dying to do that since our first kiss in my apartment. You taste better than I ever imagined." And then he kissed me hard, letting me taste myself.

I clung to his shoulders and gazed up at him. "I don't know what to say except thank you for that."

His hands caressed my face. Sweet. "I want you like I've never wanted another girl," he whispered.

Oh. My heart thundered in happiness. *Was he for real?*

We kissed again as he eased between my legs, his hands brushing my thighs, little electric pulses shooting over me.

I let him on top of me, even though my rules clearly said he shouldn't.

He held the base of his erection with one hand and worked into my sheath inch by inch. "You're tight, Elizabeth," he groaned. "So good, love."

I moaned at how he felt, every nerve in my channel clinging to him. He held me for a few moments without moving, letting the fullness resonate and sink in, then he thrust in further, pushing down his cock, making even more room.

I parted my legs more, every inch of me wanting to take all of him until finally he seated himself all the way in. I cried out at the heat from his size and how it burned in a good way.

His head dropped to mine and he kissed me deeply just as he stared to move steadily, his cock pumping slow and then faster, slow and then faster, his pace controlled. He was a man who knew how to work a woman, who'd done this more times than I wanted to think about it. He shifted and reached underneath me to raise me up, giving him a more direct angle into my center.

Sweat dripped from both of us as he pressed hot kisses down my chest and captured a nipple, nipping at my skin as he throbbed inside me. He owned me, his hands clutching my hipbone to push in faster.

He went harder, his eyes wilder, his hands going everywhere, thrumming and circling my clit, demanding I come. He grunted in a primitive way, and I raised up on my elbows, wanting more friction, more of him and his coaxing fingers. I rotated my hips against his skin as we slapped together, up and down, slow and fast. His thrusts were sharp and sure, the pleasure mounting higher and higher.

Sharp sensation gathered at the base of my spine, and I tossed my head back and pushed against him, swiveling my hips with his, making him hiss and his eyes glitter.

I was close, so close.

He smacked against me, knifing inside me, his body a blur, a muscled, well-oiled machine that could go on and on. "Come again, Elizabeth."

I shivered at the authority in his voice. "Yes," I gasped.

He panted. "Good. I'll follow."

He pushed my legs down into my chest until I was imprisoned and went at me with a new vengeance. He hammered into me without mercy, all gentleness gone. One of his hands spread me apart, his fingers stroking my lips and clit, delving into softness.

"So gorgeous." His voice was hoarse. "You're mine, love. And I'm going to make you come hard."

With a snarl he pressed my knees down tighter.

This. I'd never had this feeling. I wanted to soar. I wanted to scream at the top of my lungs. I wanted him to fuck me and never stop.

More, more, give me, give me. I didn't care that he had me pinned down on the mat. I didn't care that he was taking me hard. I wanted sex like this with him. He was in control, and I reveled from underneath him, begging him for more, urging him to send me over the edge. "More."

He barked out a laugh and pounded me, his arms squeezing my thighs together and getting a new angle.

I went to the moon as I lost my mind, my muscles clenching against him, grasping at him, milking him.

He went with me with a loud roar, his neck muscles in stark relief as the pleasure knifed through him, his cock tightening and expanding as he held on to my hips, thrusting hard. Heat flooded my core as he came inside me.

Our pants filled the air as he released my legs, but still he moved inside me, his eyes heavy. "I can keep going. Can you?"

I sucked in a shaky breath. Laughed.

"You laughing at me, Unicorn?"

I cupped his face, entangling my hands in his hair. "Never. That—that was the best sex I've ever had."

He smiled. "I'm not surprised. I aim to please."

I laughed at his cockiness, but I knew he was teasing.

He'd done way more than just please. A giant stick of dynamite has just gone off inside me.

CHAPTER TWENTY-ONE

Declan

S HE WAS SO damn beautiful underneath me with that soft look in her eyes. From the moment we'd met, she'd had a vulnerable coolness about her, a quality that told me in no uncertain terms she'd been hurt. So seeing her now, all relaxed with a happy glow on her face, made me feel bulletproof.

I collapsed next to her on the mat and gathered her in my arms. She was warm, her skin damp from our lovemaking. I gazed down at her, my hand stroking her gently after the roughness, brushing against her tummy. I cupped her full breasts and lightly kissed each rosy, still erect nipple. I made my way up her body until I kissed her on the nose, my thoughts still dirty, my cock throbbing to dive back inside her and make her come again.

She hit all my senses when it came to the way she looked, the blond hair that was most decidedly natural, the curve of her face, the dramatic sweep of her eyebrows that lent her an exotic look—all of her was perfect.

Sex was the language she and I had got exactly right from the very beginning, the level of heat I felt for her more intense than anything else I'd ever felt.

It had just taken us a while to nail it home. Literally.

I grinned. "I wasn't kidding. I can go again if you're up for it."

She snorted, blue eyes dancing. "Please. No. You're insane right now."

"Insanely hot."

She grinned at me and then looked down at her legs. "I'm still quivering."

I was too, but I kept quiet. She did that to me when no girl ever had.

She played with my arms, tracing designs over my tattoos. "Besides, this is the part where you're supposed to whisper sweet nothings in my ear about how beautiful I am. Cuddling and hand-holding, all that jazz."

I cleared my throat. "My dearest Elizabeth, your eyes are the most beautiful blue I've ever seen, like the color of the Blue Man Group. Let me count the ways I love them. I love them more than fish and chips. I love them more than Dr. Feldman's class. I could …"

She slapped me playfully on the arm. "Okay, that's enough with the cheesy poetry."

I kept my face blank. "Too bad you'll never know now how much better it could have got."

She paused, stopping her laughter with her hands. "Wait. You are teasing me, aren't you? 'Cause that was crap."

I shrugged my shoulders.

"Ugh, I hate it when you do that noncommittal shrug. I can't figure you out."

I grinned. "Good."

I rolled her onto her back and kissed her again, this time more insistent, my hands cupping her face. She craned upward, wanting more, her hands sliding and rubbing my lower back, her nails digging into my arse.

I flipped us over and rolled her on top of me.

"What are you doing?" she breathed down at me.

"This." I spread her apart and seated her on my now fully erect cock.

She tossed her head back and moaned as I held on to her hips and shoved up, twisting around in her pussy.

"Ride me," I said.

She rode me like a horse, bouncing and gyrating. Her tits bounced with each thrust, their nipples straining toward me. I couldn't let them go unattended. I squeezed them together and divided my time between them both, my tongue tasting her sweat, my nose inhaling her skin.

I plowed into her sweetness, letting her take control, her body jerking up and down. We worked each other, my cock sliding nearly all the way out and then back in. She panted, her long hair sticking to her face as she ground herself against me.

She cried out when I started pumping harder, getting deeper, wanting every single inch to be encased by her. Everything faded away, and all my eyes could see were her.

Her, her.

It was intense and crazy and wild and soul-wrenchingly good.

I wanted to go slower this time. I did. I wanted to savor the sweetness of us. But I couldn't. My need was too sharp, too fucking primitive.

She seemed to sense the same urgency, as if this moment might be our last.

"Lean over me," I told her after a while. "Let me do the work."

She moved over me, and I took over, my cock jerking in and out of her, needing to be the one she wanted, the *only one* she ever wanted.

We moved together like we'd made love a million times. I captured her breasts and sucked hard, my free hand finding her tender nub and coaxing it. Stroking her to the rhythm of my cock.

She screamed my name and came, her muscles clenching around me.

She collapsed on top of me, but I wasn't done, pounding into her, skin on skin, chest to chest.

It was electric and hot as hell.

I threw my head back against the mat and yelled as I came, my hands holding her tight.

So tight.

Never let her fucking go.

CHAPTER TWENTY-TWO

Elizabeth

THE NEXT DAY was Saturday, and my cell phone rang at exactly eight o'clock in the morning.

Who on earth would call this early?

"Hello?" I managed as I sat up in bed. Last night had been wild, and my body was still reverberating with little aftershocks.

"Miss Bennett?" a crisp female tone said.

I cleared my throat. "Yes?"

"This is Sylvia Myers with Myers' Jewelry Store." She paused as if waiting for me to reply, as if she were returning *my* call.

"Hi?"

Myers' was one of the premier jewelry stores in the Raleigh-Durham area. I'd been in there a few times to window shop and get ideas, but their prices were way out of my league.

"I'm calling you about the images you emailed our office? We'd like for you to come in and meet with us next week to discuss perhaps purchasing some of your designs."

Images? I hadn't sent anyone pics.

I sat up straighter in bed, brain racing. "I see. Which ones were you interested in, Ms. Myers?"

A shuffling sound of papers came through the phone. "Your personal assistant, Shelley, sent over several drawings, but the ones that caught my eye were the silver pieces, the butterfly ring in particular and the scroll bracelet. We have a shop in Asheville where your artisan type of jewelry would sell quite nicely. Would Wednesday at nine be okay to meet?"

Shelley!

Just when I thought she was full of crap and as empty-headed as a balloon, she'd gone and done something so incredibly ... sweet.

But why would they want my designs?

Because they're beautiful, a small part of my heart whispered. *At one time, you believed in yourself. Do it again!*

I scrambled around for a pen and a notebook I kept on the nightstand. "I have classes all morning, and I'm not done until one and then I have to work ... but I can probably get off. Would three o'clock be okay?"

God, what was I doing? I hadn't designed anything new in years. All I had was the old stuff. And how the hell had Shelley even gotten ahold of my old designs?

"I didn't realize you were a college student, Miss Bennett. I assumed you were a professional designer with experience. Your logo on your email says you own a company called Darcy Designs."

Darcy? Nice name. Props to Shelley for remembering *Pride and Prejudice*.

"Yes, that's right."

"How old are you? You sound rather young on the phone and honestly we're looking for dependable artisans at the moment, not young college students." I heard her tapping something, and I imagined her sitting behind a big desk in an office, regretting calling me.

I sighed. "I am a full-time college student."

"I see." But I could still hear the uncertainty in her voice. She seemed to come to some kind of decision and cleared her throat. "Okay. I'll see you Wednesday afternoon at three at our main jewelry store in Raleigh." She rattled off the address. "Good day, Miss Bennett." She hung up.

I sprang out of bed like a scalded cat.

I'd gotten an interview for my designs. Holy cow. Exhilaration filled me along with a good dose of fear. I could do this, right? I had to try. Because existing like I had been wasn't working.

And then thoughts of Colby seeped into my brain. I hadn't seen or heard from him in two weeks, but somehow I knew he was out there. Lurking. Waiting for me.

I shuddered and pushed those morbid scenarios away and raced out to my balcony. I wanted to see Declan. When we'd gotten home from the gym last night I'd given him an awkward kiss goodnight at my door then I'd come in to crash. But, he hadn't been far from my mind all night.

I leaned over the railing. "Wake up, you sleepy-headed Englishman, I have big news!" I called over to him. "Huge!"

I counted ten seconds and he suddenly appeared, his hair standing straight up and eyes blinking in the morning sun.

I nearly clapped, but stopped just in time.

"What's going on?" He scrubbed the dark shadows on his chiseled jawline, looking like a million bucks. No man had the right to look that good this early.

And, of course, he slept in the nude. Gloriously. Fantastically.

"Declan! You're flashing the whole complex." I tore my eyes off his perfect body.

"I thought something was wrong with you," he half shouted as he went back inside his bedroom and then came back out wearing a pair of tight black boxers. "This do, madam?"

I ran my eyes over the snug lines. Not by a long shot. I

could see exactly how monstrously large he was. And hard.

His eyes went to half-mast. "You're looking a little too hard, Elizabeth. Focus on my face, not my body."

He sent me a searching look, and I figured it was last night hanging between us.

I just didn't know how to handle all this *feeling*.

I waved him off. "Forget your cock. I got a meeting on Wednesday with a jewelry company about a design opportunity. This could be the beginning of something I never thought could come true." It still might not.

A wide grin split his face. "Hang on, I'm coming over."

"What? No, you don't have to do that. I just—I don't know—wanted to tell someone."

"And you told me first?"

I nodded.

"Stand back," he said, and before I'd barely gotten out of the way, he'd jumped from the top railing of his balcony to mine. He landed right in front of me, his bare chest within inches of mine, and before I could even think about how nervous he made me, he swung me up in his arms and spun me around. I squealed, the sensation of being back in his arms heady.

He dropped me unceremoniously on one of the chairs I'd put out there.

"I say this calls for a celebration," he said, plopping down next to me in another chair. "Let's go out for breakfast. My treat."

An unfamiliar lightness came over me. Things were changing fast, but I didn't dwell on it. "Okay."

He nodded. "Where do you want to go?"

"I don't care." And Lord help me, I didn't care where I was with him.

Just this one day, I promised myself.

He leaned over and before I could pull back, he'd kissed me on the cheek. "Done. Get dressed and I'll knock on your door in thirty minutes."

While I watched with bated breath, he jumped back over to his own balcony and went inside his bedroom.

CHAPTER TWENTY-THREE

Declan

CAME BACK inside from the balcony with a grin on my face as I scrambled around to get ready to take Elizabeth to breakfast. After a quick shower, I shoved on jeans, a Front Street Gym shirt, and flip-flops. Done. I couldn't fucking wait to be near her again.

Last night had been incredible, but it wasn't just about the sex. It was *her*.

The way she'd danced in the rain; the excitement in her eyes when she'd talked about her jewelry interview; the way she struggled through her fears. I wanted all of her.

Was it stupid that I wanted to tell her everything about me?

How much I'd loved my mum and missed her?

How I wanted to finish my gym and work on a UFC title?

How I imagined taking her in every position imaginable?

Yeah. Best to wait on that.

I knocked on her door five minutes later, and we walked to Minnie's across the street from our complex. Our hands brushed against each other as we crossed the street, and my cock tightened. Just the simplest touch and I was ready to take her back to my place and show her exactly how I felt.

Minnie's was a popular uni hangout and was busy, but we found a booth in the back.

We ordered and got our food and dove in, the camaraderie between us not surprising me at all. I'd sensed from the beginning that we were more alike than she realized.

We were deep in a discussion about a trip I wanted to take to London next year when all hell broke loose.

As in, my ex showed up.

Nadia walked up to our table with Ninja Turtle following dutifully behind her, shooting me cautious looks over her shoulder. I cracked my neck and rolled my shoulders. Nadia's gaze went from me to her and back to me, lingering longer than necessary.

My lips compressed. Could I *not* get away from her? "What do you want?"

Elizabeth looked up from tucking in a good-sized chew of French toast, saw them, and coughed, then grabbed her glass of water to wash it down.

"Who's pissy today?" Nadia huffed in a delicate way that didn't detract from her pretty face. "Lose a fight last night?"

Elizabeth stiffened and bounced her eyes from Nadia to Donatello and then back to me. I set down my fork. *Dammit.*

"Good morning," Elizabeth said, obviously trying to cover up the dead air as her eyes encompassed them both. "You guys coming or going for breakfast?"

Please say going.

Nadia kept her gaze on me. "Going. But if you want some company, we'd be glad to stay?" She didn't wait for my response but flicked a strand of hair over her shoulder and glanced back at her boyfriend. "Isn't that right, Donatello?" She laughed but it sounded off. Not her usual sparkly self. My eyes went from her to the Brazilian, noticing his tense shoulders and tight jaw.

Was she nagging him the way she'd done me?

I grunted. Hard to believe with the pedigree he obviously had, but some girls are hardwired to never be happy, and Nadia was one of them.

He mumbled something about tennis practice, but Nadia had already slid in next to Elizabeth on the booth, leaving him no option but to sit next to me.

There we sat in a weird, four-person tableau.

I ran my eyes over Nadia, my heart and head both affirming that I wasn't in love with her anymore. I doubted I ever had been.

For the next five minutes we made small talk about the weather, classes, and what we were doing the following weekend. Nadia's voice was slightly shrill at times as she threw question after question at us. Digging. She wanted to know if I was shagging Elizabeth. I was ready to snap, especially when the waitress came by and set down coffees for both of them.

Nadia speared Elizabeth with her gaze. "Hey, don't you date Blake?"

Elizabeth shook her head. "We're just friends."

"But you do spend a lot of time with him, right?" she asked pointedly. "I see you with him everywhere on campus. It's not surprising people assume you're dating." She traced her finger on the table. "Does *he* know you're not dating?"

"Enough with the questions," I snapped, yet, at the same time, I waited for her response. Blake was something we hadn't really touched on, but I knew she had strong feelings for him as a friend. I hated the motherfucker. Okay, maybe that was a tad extreme, but if he wanted Elizabeth as his, he was going to have to go through me to get her.

Shit. I scrubbed my jaw. I sounded like a Neanderthal—or a possessive boyfriend.

Elizabeth straightened her shoulders and cleared her throat. "The truth is, I made a pact freshman year to never date while at Whitman."

"So … there's no one you're seeing right now?" I asked, trying to keep my voice even.

She licked her lips, eyes darting away from me. "No. I—I don't do serious. That's how college should be, right?"

Everything in the restaurant zoomed out and anger sliced through me at Elizabeth's glib attitude. I clenched my fists under the table and tried to catch her gaze, but she was poking at the food on her plate.

Did our night mean nothing to her?

Didn't I have the answer right in front of me?

Fuck!

I exhaled and grabbed my coffee before I said something I'd regret in front of Nadia, who'd eat that up.

Nadia smiled broadly, looking smug, her eyes going back and forth between us, picking up on the obvious cues. "How fascinating and very modern of you." She touched Elizabeth's hands to get her attention. "And in case you didn't know already—*I mean, who doesn't?*—Declan and I dated for over six months, and even though we didn't end up together," she paused on a nervous laugh, "I can attest that being friends was the best thing."

Elizabeth nodded. "Of course."

"In fact, Declan's the only person who understands how my mom having cancer is ripping me up inside. Isn't that right, Declan?" Nadia insisted.

I shrugged as Ninja Turtle stiffened.

Nadia focused back on Elizabeth. "So where are you from, Elizabeth? I'm dying to know more about you."

Elizabeth muttered something under her breath.

"I didn't catch that," Nadia said.

"I said Petal, North Carolina."

She nodded, a superior look on her face. "I'm from Raleigh. My parents own the Ridgley Hotel chain. I guess we're kind of Whitman royalty around here. But Petal, North Carolina … hmm

… small town, I'm guessing, but now that I think of it, it does ring a bell. How far is it from here?"

"Give the girl a rest. You're getting on everyone's nerves," Donatello snapped as he pulled out his phone and began to check it.

Elizabeth exhaled. "No, it's fine. Petal is a small town a few hours east of here, close to the coast."

Nadia snapped her fingers. "Colby Scott! He's from Petal! He's Senator Scott's son, and we used to play together when we were kids and our parents hung out at the Raleigh Country Club. You know him? He's going here now."

My entire body went on alert. *Colby Scott?* What the hell? The guy who'd been at her door that night? After the incident, I'd run his name past the campus police and even the Raleigh Police Department, but his record had been clean. I'd tried to dig around for his address, but so far I'd gotten nothing.

Had she outright lied about knowing him?

"I know him." Elizabeth's face had turned ashen.

Nadia clapped. "Small world. Whatever happened to him? Is he as handsome as he was when he was ten?" She giggled. "I need to call him up, remind him he promised to marry me when we were kids."

Elizabeth didn't answer but looked down, her curtain of blond hair hiding her face.

"You okay?" I asked softly.

She lifted blue eyes to mine briefly before she dropped them again, but not before my heart stuttered at the pain I saw etched in her gaze.

"Did you go to high school with this Colby guy?" I insisted. "Is he the one who came to your flat?"

"Yes." Her voice was whispery.

The tension ramped up.

I found myself leaning over the table to study her closer.

I looked at the bangles on her wrists. At the scars underneath. "Is he the one who did that?"

Nadia cocked her head, sniffing a secret. "One what? Did I miss something?"

Elizabeth seemed to gather herself, her hands fluttering around her face as she pushed hair back. She squirmed in her seat, fiddling with her purse and then drinking a sip of water. "I—I used to date Colby. It was a long time ago, and I'm sure he's forgotten about me now." Her throat worked, the only telltale sign she was lying through her teeth.

I sank back in my seat, rage and anger building. *Colby Scott.* I repeated it in my head. My breathing kicked up and it was all I could do to sit in that booth and pretend like I wasn't about to lose my shit.

Nadia seemed oblivious to everything, probably too caught up in her own issues. She looked at me "I've tried to call you a few times—left some voicemails and texted."

"I've been busy." I took a sip of coffee, trying to compose myself so Nadia wouldn't see how torqued up I was.

"With Elizabeth?" she asked with a wry smile at both of us.

"With *everything*, Nadia." I sent her a hard look.

What the hell was wrong with her?

But I didn't care. All I wanted was to get Elizabeth out of here and figure out what was going on.

Ninja Turtle stood up from the booth. "I'm going to the car, Nadia. I have to make some calls. Make this quick. I won't wait all day."

He stalked off and out the doors of the diner.

I focused on Nadia. Exhaled. "Look. It's obvious things are rocky with you and Nin—your boyfriend, but you shouldn't involve me. You're only making things worse by continuing to chase me. Especially when I am here with someone." I kept my gaze off Elizabeth, but I knew she was watching us intently.

Her face fell, tears blooming. "God, I made such a mistake, Declan, a *stupid* mistake. I was trashed and angry with you when

I slept with him. I didn't know what I was doing. I—I thought you'd forgive me. Just—I still love you."

Her face twisted with tears and she nibbled at her lips, and my eyes went straight there. It was a reflex, and it didn't mean jack, but there it was and I knew the moment she saw it because she got a knowing gleam in her eye.

"You might try to deny it, but you still care about me." She leaned over. "Let's talk. I can come to your place or you can come to mine? Please, Declan."

Elizabeth suddenly commented, "Uh, Donatello just pulled out of the parking lot." We all turned to watch as his red Porsche spun out in the gravel and pulled onto the street.

Nadia wailed. "And now I'm stuck in this godforsaken diner. And I can't walk in these heels. This is just perfect," she said bitterly.

I tossed my head back and groaned at the cocked-up situation.

Elizabeth let out her own sigh of exasperation and shooed Nadia up until she could scoot out from the booth. She faced us both. "Well, I don't blame Donatello," she said. "You guys obviously have a lot of history to talk about anyway, and if I'm here—"

"That would be great," Nadia murmured, wiping her eyes and sending Elizabeth a grateful look. "Thank you for being so nice when I obviously crashed your breakfast."

Elizabeth's lips tightened. "I'm not nice. You're simply extremely annoying. You're like a cat in heat when it comes to Declan and frankly, I'm sick of it."

Nadia gasped.

I grabbed Elizabeth's hand. "No. Stay. Just ... wait a fucking minute. We haven't had a chance to talk about us—about last night."

Things were happening too fast. She'd just told me in so many words that I meant nothing to her as well as the name of the guy who'd hurt her.

I needed time.

She shook her head. "No, really, I have a million things to do today, and I can't handle any more stupidity."

"Elizabeth, wait a fucking minute—"

She held a hand up, her cool mask already in place, reminding me of the girl who'd walked in the frat party. "Save it. I've heard enough, seen enough. Enjoy your talk."

CHAPTER
TWENTY-FOUR

Elizabeth

NGER BURNED WHEN I left Minnie's. I was pissed at
Nadia for chasing after Declan right in front of me, but I
was also ticked at him because I'd seen a look he'd given
her and part of me felt like he still had feelings for her.

I stomped across the street and back to my apartment, and if
I had a theme song for the breakfast fiasco, it was a toss-up be-
tween "Love Bites" by Def Leppard or "Done" by The Band
Perry. Both about love and letting that shit go.

Love … I'd bled for it. I'd tasted the destruction of losing
your heart, and no matter how beautiful Declan was inside and
out, I couldn't endure heartbreak again.

I went up the breezeway and saw my mom standing at my
door. Her shoulders were slumped as she banged on my door.

I inhaled sharply, remembering our last meeting at the diner. Worry gnawed at me once again about Karl and his crazy
plan to blackmail the Senator. He was bad news for her, just like
all the rest.

"Hey, I'm here," I called out. I infused my voice with enthusiasm, but I didn't know how much more I could take when it

came to her. But she was all I had left now that Granny was gone, and it's hard to let go of family no matter how shitty they treat you. Sure, I had a few cousins out there, but they were in Petal and the majority of them didn't associate with my mom. She'd always been bad news, borrowing money that she never intended to pay back and generally being undependable.

She met me on the staircase, and I smelled the stench of stale cigarettes on her wrinkled clothes.

"Thank God you're here," she exclaimed. I didn't miss the busted lip she'd tried to cover up with her pink lipstick. Her eyes darted down to the parking lot and back to me.

"What's up?"

"Let's get inside and I'll tell you everything. I need some coffee." Her voice was sharp as razors.

We got inside and I made us coffee. She stirred in cream and sugar as she sat at my small table and watched me. "You got any food here?"

"Sure." I got up and made her a quick breakfast of scrambled eggs and toast. It wasn't much, but it was all I had in the pantry at the moment.

"Are you going to tell me why you're here?" I asked as we sat together a bit later.

"Can't a girl come see her daughter?"

"You never have."

She frowned, chewing her food. "I don't have anywhere else to go."

"Karl hit you," I stated.

She touched her lip gingerly. "It wasn't his fault. I smarted off to him, and usually he's sorry after a fight and buys me flowers or takes me on a trip, but this time ..." she rubbed her arms "... he's fit to be tied."

"We can call the police. At least get a restraining order against him."

She paled. "No! I—I still love him, Elizabeth, and we'll

probably get back together once all this Senator Scott stuff flies over."

My mouth dried in fear. "What? Don't tell me you're still on that, Mom?"

She cleared her throat, eyeing me nervously. "Karl ... he really wants to bring Colby to justice—"

"No, he wants money from the Senator. There's a difference," I bit out, getting angry now. "Why did you even tell him? You—you're supposed to be my mother, and you know how I feel about what happened. I don't want anyone to ever know."

She picked at her chipped fingernail polish. "People in Petal know."

"Yeah, and they think I'm a slut." I slammed down my coffee cup.

She winced. "Look, it's a lot of money. I'm tired of struggling and never having anything. Plus, I think the Senator needs to know about his son."

"Why do you even care? You didn't when it happened." The words were out before I could pull them back.

"Don't ever say that, Elizabeth," she said sharply. "You were such a good kid, and I knew I didn't have to be on top of you all the time. It's not my fault it happened on a weekend I was gone. And then you changed, keeping to yourself, never calling anyone, never going out, acting like you hated me ..." Her hands fluttered around. "I—I know I'm not the PTA mom or the one who spent money on you—because I didn't have any— but I did the best I could." She pulled out her Marlboro's and lit one.

I took a deep breath, steeling myself. "What happened with Karl and the Senator?"

She sucked her cig. "Karl called his office for several days until he finally got through to his personal assistant, but she wouldn't allow Karl to speak directly to him. He put a bug in her ear that it was about his son. That did the trick. He called us back the next day and Karl said his spiel. He asked for fifty thousand or we'd sell your story to the press."

God, their stupidity made me sick. Nausea rolled. I jerked up and got a glass of water.

She sucked on the cigarette, the butt burning a bright red. "The next day, the IRS showed up at Karl's car lot and closed it down, claiming he owed back taxes—which might be true, I don't know—but he had to close his shop and he can't open it until the IRS finishes their investigation, which might take months. They confiscated all his files and froze his money. He's convinced the Senator sent them. His whole life has been that car lot and if he doesn't have that, then, well, he's broke."

She continued. "Karl called a reporter with the *Raleigh Herald* and said he had a story about Senator Scott's son and a girl he raped. They agreed to see him and pay him for the story, but once he got there, they had a team of lawyers waiting with all these papers and wouldn't listen to a thing Karl said because they needed a firsthand account of the attack—and a police re-port."

I sat back down. "They're a reputable newspaper. They can't print hearsay."

She nodded. "That's why Karl's angry and upset. Well, that and the car lot—obviously."

"So he hit *you*?"

"It'd all be fine if you'd just tell your whole story how you let that boy rape you."

"I didn't let him," my voice cracked.

She barely noticed. "I want Karl back," she said glumly.

I stood up, my chair scrapping across the tile. "God, for once in your life, do the right thing and forget him," I snapped. "Stop ruining my life to get what you want!"

Her lips tightened. "I don't want a lecture from you right now." She sighed, looking exhausted. "Now, if you have a place for me to sleep, that would be great. That is unless you don't want me here and I'll just leave ..."

I stopped and stared at her. Part of me wanted her to leave, but I just couldn't kick her out. She *was* my mother.

"There's an extra bedroom across the hall from mine. It's not much, just a twin bed."

She nodded and headed down the hall, but then turned around. "I'm sorry to bring all this to you, baby, but—just keep an open mind about Karl."

"Just get some sleep, Mom. We'll talk later."

But we didn't talk later.

A few hours later I went out to the grocery to stock up on things she'd like, mostly chips and pizza and soda and cigarettes, and by the time I'd returned it was dark. I walked into an empty apartment where she'd left me a hastily scribbled note on the kitchen table.

Karl picked me up. He found a newspaper in New York to take the story. I'm sorry.

Love, Candi

I sank down on a chair in the kitchen, groceries forgotten as fear crept into my heart. I battled with tears of frustration, my hands clenched around the note. No matter how hard I tried to push the shadow of that awful night away, it continued to haunt me.

CHAPTER TWENTY-FIVE

Elizabeth

SUNDAY WENT BY, and I kept waiting for Declan to confront me about our convo at Minnie's, but he didn't. I'd knocked on his door a few times, but he was never there. I pictured him in some seedy boxing ring getting pounded into a pulp. Then my imagination would switch to him kissing Nadia. God.

Was he angry with me for the way I'd left things between us? No doubt.

But why hadn't he knocked on my door? I didn't know.

I'd replayed our night at the gym over and over in my head. My body longed for more of him, and it frustrated me. There were absolutely no repeats in my sex life.

On Monday, I got to class late, but thankfully Dax had saved me a seat and Feldman was also late.

I took it and opened my books, fighting the major disappointment that Declan wasn't in his usual seat.

I looked at Dax "Where's your brother?"

He shrugged.

"It's not like him to skip class. He isn't injured, is he? From a fight? How can you let him continue doing that?" I closed my eyes briefly. "Why does he do it?"

Dax's lips tightened, and it was the first time I'd seen him with a truly unhappy expression on his face. "For money so he can open his gym. It's his piece of home that he doesn't have here in the states." He looked down and then back at me. "I know everyone thinks I'm a joke, but I—I get him. His dream is to be his own man and break away from us—from me. I wish he'd just take my half of the money, but he won't. In case you haven't noticed, Declan's stubborn."

"Yeah."

"Miss Bennett, care to tell us what you're discussing in the middle of my class?"

Shit. Caught. I shook my head. "No, sorry, Dr. Feldman."

She tapped a pencil against her desk. "Then perhaps you'd like to answer some questions?"

Not today. Please. My mind was everywhere but on this class.

Dax's long frame stood and half the auditorium sighed. "I was the one talking the most, Dr. Feldman. I'd be delighted to answer your questions," he said in his clipped accent that I could tell he laid on extra thick.

After class, he met me outside the humanities building. I had a math class next, but decided to skip it to find out more about Declan. We found a bench in the quad near a fountain that was popular and took a seat. We chatted about what he was doing in his classes and how he struggled to keep his head above water, and I could tell that even though he wasn't an A student, he did try. I didn't want to pressure him to talk about Declan even though I was dying to know more.

"You're a good listener," he said after a while, giving me a gentle poke in the ribs.

"You're easy to listen to."

"Not to mention how hot I am."

I rolled my eyes. "You're full of crap."

He tossed an arm around me. "You better believe it, love."

I toyed with my backpack. "So about Declan ..."

He sighed and took my phone and typed in some digits, giving me a self-satisfied smirk.

"What are you doing?"

"Texting Declan and telling him to meet us for lunch."

"Lunch? What if I already had plans? And use your own phone." I tried to jerk it back, but he held on to it.

"But he might come if you ask. Dude doesn't even budge for me." He handed my phone back. "Here, I'm done. He now thinks you want to see him at the student center in half an hour. He also thinks you want to shag him in the science lab later."

My mouth parted. "Seriously?"

He laughed just as my phone pinged and I saw it was from Declan.

"What does it say? Is he excited?" he said in a girly voice, leaning over my shoulder to read my phone, his dark hair tickling my arm. Of course, Dax had lied about the shagging text, so I didn't smack him.

"He said 'Okay.' That's vague," I muttered.

"Hmm." He sat back and scratched at his unshaven jaw as if what he had to say he'd thought about carefully.

"What's up?"

He sent me an unsure look. "It's just, Declan really likes you, but Nadia yanked him around pretty good, and I just don't want you to do that to him."

"How do you *know* he likes me?"

He sent me an exasperated look. "He gave you a cute nickname for starters. And he watches you like a hawk in class. He's rather jelly, my bro, but when he loves, he loves hard."

"What do you mean?"

He sighed. "He puts his all into whatever he does. Fighting. His gym. Me. When we first moved here and were the new kids at our private school, we were both scrawny, and of course, we talked funny. He lashed out at the wankers who teased me and ended up with the rep as the guy with a chip on his shoulder, which wasn't true. But word got around and pretty soon rednecks were showing up and trying to push him around. Mostly he tried to stay out of trouble, but senior year while he was on a date, he got jumped by four guys behind the bleachers at a football game. He'd filled out by then, and it took three to hold him down while one pounded him with brass knuckles. When he came to, he was lying on the ground and they were all laughing and tossing back their beer. He got up and beat the bloody hell out of them, even chased one down the highway. Then the cops showed up. It was a hell of a night. Father was not pleased."

"Was he hurt?"

"Spent the night in the hospital, but the other guys were worse."

He grunted. "He's always been the better guy than me. Smarter, quicker, kinder. He even pays his own uni fees. When I grow up, I want to be just like him."

I smiled. Declan was all those things and more. Sexy, sweet, hung.

He shot me a cocky grin. "You got a crush on him."

"I do not."

"You do."

"Do not."

"You so bloody do. Now shut the fuck-all up about it."

"*I do not.*" I stood up and stamped my foot on the sidewalk.

"Then let me come over to your place tonight. I'll show you my sexy underwear—Union Jack flag and all."

My mouth flapped open. "No. That's just weird. You're like … a brother."

"Okay, gross, but you aren't seeing anyone else, so why does it matter? I'll be one of your famous one-night stands, no problem."

I closed my eyes. "Dammit, does everyone know about that?"

"It's a small university, but your friend Shelley also likes to talk when she drinks." He grinned. "She's been popping in at the frat house a lot lately. She and Blake are thick as thieves."

Ah. Interesting.

He continued. "You have feelings for Declan. I know it because your eyes get all mushy when he walks in a room."

"You're an expert on me?"

A self-satisfied grin curved his lips. "I'm a psych major, remember? And not nearly as stupid as you may think."

"You're a lunatic major more like it."

He leveled me with a serious stare. "I wish I was more like you. You don't care what other people think and you've made your own way at Whitman—which sounds a lot like Declan—but you're also completely gorgeous and unaware of it. Hell, I could have fallen for you in a heartbeat if you'd given me any indication we had a chance." He smiled at my widened eyes. "You met me first, but I was drunk and Declan wasn't. Not that that mattered. Once you took one look at him, you'd chosen him already. Fate. Karma." He smirked. "Yeah, I believe in all that silly stuff. Anyway, I'm not here to hit on you—too late for that—but I am telling you not to crush his heart. He's had enough of that already."

This was family. Love. Emotion swelled and impulsively, I hugged him tight.

I pulled back to stare up at him. "Is he back with Nadia?"

"No, but I heard Donatello broke up with her, so she's free." He took my hand. "Come on, let's go see him."

On the way over, Shelley and Blake texted us and wanted to meet for lunch too—even after I told Blake that Declan was coming—so we arranged to meet outside the student center and walk in together.

All I could think about was seeing Declan again.

My eyes searched the milling crowd until I found him standing next to a big column outside the entrance to the stone building. His dark brown hair was disheveled as if he'd raked his hands through it. As I watched, he took his bottom lip between his teeth and pulled as he read *Pride and Prejudice*.

He checked every box I had.

"He's a dream," Shelley purred next to me.

"He's okay," was my reply.

"Girl, you crazier than my mama when she's got her menses and runs out of coffee."

She grinned and gave me a hug. She'd been over to the apartment for the past two nights to keep me company. Between Declan and the whole Mom and Karl mess, I'd needed a friend. I'd also cooked dinner for her both nights in appreciation of her getting me the jewelry interview.

I pulled her aside. "Heard anything about Colby?"

She nodded, a worried expression on her face. "Officially, the word is he left NYU because he wanted to be closer to home." She rolled her eyes. "As if anyone would miss Petal."

I nodded.

She held a finger up. "The gossip is he got caught sniffing coke at a party the cops busted. He got off, thanks to dear old dad, but he also got kicked out of school—and went to some fancy rehab. Looks like our perfect poster boy isn't so clean anymore."

She sent me a hard look. "And if he comes to your house again, you have to call the police. You can't take any chances, especially if he's doing drugs. Think about it, Elizabeth. He was always on the edge in high school, and I guarantee you, Colby on drugs is crazy as shit. As soon as you see him, you run straight to Declan's or you dial 911. Okay?"

I nodded. "Okay."

Declan looked up at that moment, his gray eyes zeroing in on mine, and I lifted a hand in a wave. I shoved thoughts of Colby away.

He tucked his book in his backpack and headed our way.

"Just watching him walk is like art moving." Shelley sighed.

He stopped in front of our crew, gave Dax a fist bump and nodded at the rest of us. We all headed inside Zoe's, a pizza place.

Declan slowed his steps until he was walking next to me. "Hey, you. Been wanting to talk to you."

"Hey." I set my pace with his. "You didn't come to class today."

He sighed and tucked his hands in his pockets. "Yeah. I had an appointment at a bank. We had some flooring issues come up at the gym, and I went in to see if I could adjust my loan." He rubbed his jaw.

My lips parted. He needed more money? "I wish I could help you."

He shrugged. "I've got a plan. Always. But enough of that." He sent me a serious look, his eyes roaming over my face as if he were devouring it. "I'm sorry about Nadia showing up at the diner ... and then we didn't really get to finish talking about everything."

"About having sex and how great it was?" I inhaled.

He raised an eyebrow. "Yeah. Wanna meet tonight?"

"I get off work at seven."

"Hey guys!" Nadia waved, a bright smile on her face as she said excuse me's and cut in front of several students so she could be directly behind us. "Are you having lunch too?"

What the hell. She was like a tick you couldn't get off a dog.

And this whole showing up everywhere we were? Not cool.

She smiled. "So happy I saw you! I wanted to tell you good luck on your jewelry interview."

I blinked. How fake could she be? I'd just told her how annoying she was the last time I saw her.

She bobbed her blond hair. "Oh, don't look so surprised. Declan told me all about it. Do you make rings? I'd love to see them sometime." She flashed her right hand where a huge diamond rested. "Daddy gave me this one on my eighteenth birthday, but I'd love something more quaint."

I looked at Declan. "You tell everything you know?" I left *asshole* off.

He frowned. "We were talking at the diner—after you so abruptly left—and I happened to mention why we were at Minnie's to begin with—"

"Oh no. Did I say something wrong?" Nadia said, biting her lip and batting her lashes. "Please don't misunderstand. It's just Declan and I have a deep friendship. We *will* talk even if we don't date anymore. I hope that doesn't bother you. Oh, but you guys aren't dating anyway, right?"

Oh, she didn't fool me.

Just the thought of her with Declan made me want to pull every hair on her head out. In clumps. Hell, it made me want to pull every hair on *his* head out.

Maybe some chest hairs too.

But I reminded myself that Nadia was a pro at manipulating people, and I refused to be toyed with so easily. Two years ago, I'd let myself break in half when girls had trash-talked and run me into the ground, but that wasn't ever going to happen again.

Bitchy girls with a hard-on for Declan would *not* determine my happiness or lack thereof.

Declan took my hand and laced his fingers through mine. His thumb caressed my palm. Did he know I was jonesing to smack her? "You ready to eat, love?" he asked softly.

I speared a last look at Nadia's face, her eyes locked on our intertwined hands.

The cave woman in me wanted to jump on her and have a tussle right here in the cafeteria. But I was better than that.

I nodded at Declan. "I'm starving."

"Oh, and by the way, Elizabeth and I *are* dating, Nadia," Declan said. "Now if you'll excuse us, we're going to eat lunch."

What? I felt my eyes widen, but I played it cool.

What on earth was he up to? Was he just trying to get rid of her?

She blinked rapidly, her mouth opening and closing, and then she turned and flounced off.

As soon as she was out of earshot, he turned to me. "You know me telling her about your jewelry was completely innocent, right? She twisted that to make it more than it was." He studied my face. "I don't want Nadia. I think you know exactly what I want."

Okay.

I didn't bring up his comment about us dating as we went through the line, got our pizzas, and found the large table where our friends were already seated.

Because you like the idea.

"Sit here," Declan said to me, pointing to a seat next to him as he sat down when Blake motioned for me to sit next to him.

I sent Blake an apologetic smile as I sat down next to Declan.

Just then a text came in on my phone, and I pulled it out of my backpack.

I read the text and the air got sucked out of me.

So you're blackmailing my father now? Not smart, Elizabeth. Call me ASAP. See you real soon, babe ...

Emphatic. Sure of himself. Colby Scott.

I wanted to hurl the phone across the room but settled for gripping the edge of the table.

I jerked up from my seat and grabbed my backpack.

"Where're you going?" Dax and Declan both asked at the same time, the similar timbres of their voices striking.

"Home."

"But, you still have classes," Shelley said with a quizzical look. "You've never missed a class in your life, even when you had the flu ... Crap, you look like death warmed over." She scowled. "Was that your mom on the phone?"

Deny, deny, deny.

I clutched my phone to my chest. "Just not feeling well. Later guys."

Blake stood up. "Wait, I'll walk you to the parking lot."

"No, I will." Declan stood.

Everyone looked at each other, uneasy glances going between Blake and Declan.

"I don't need a babysitter." I pivoted on my heels and had just cleared the door that lead to the outdoor quad when I felt Declan behind me. He pulled me to a stop and I whipped around.

His eyes searched mine. "Why are you so upset? One minute you were glad to see me, and the next you can't get away fast enough. What's going on with you? Was it Nadia?"

I shook my head.

He narrowed his eyes at me. "Has Colby been to see you?"

"No. I—I just need to get home. I don't feel well." I twirled around, but his voice stopped me.

"You're running, Elizabeth, but it won't do you any good. You can't fight what we have."

His words went straight to my gut, and I turned back to face him.

His eyes bored into mine. "Can't you see what's happening between us? We keep pushing each other away because we're scared. But that night at the gym—it wasn't just sex for me, Elizabeth. I want you *for real*, all the good and bad parts together."

I shook my head. "I don't know what you mean."

A muscle ticked in his jaw. "Stop denying *us*."

Us? The colony of butterflies in my tummy went crazy.

He continued. "You have wounds. Deep ones. I see that.

You're living in the past with no hope for the future, but you *do* have hope. I saw it when you talked about your jewelry. I saw it when I made love to you. Just—open your heart. Let me in." His words were insistent, his eyes soft. Earnest. I sucked in a sharp breath.

God, he was beautiful.

So was Colby.

Didn't he see that I couldn't change for him? Did he really think I would hand him the razors to cut out my heart piece by piece? It wasn't just a paper thing you could tape back together.

"My heart is not easily mended," I whispered. "And you—you have the potential to rip it apart permanently, so much more than Colby ever did."

He exhaled. "I will never hurt you."

"Colby said that too," I said bitterly.

"Listen to me, Elizabeth," he clasped my hand, his gray eyes peering down at me intently. "I've known since the frat party that we have a connection. There's a magnet in my chest that's drawn to yours. Maybe it was lust at first sight. Maybe it was the vulnerable way you looked at me, but mostly, it—it was the dragonfly. This feeling … it's crazy and I can't define it, but I think—I think I'm falling for you."

Love?

Love cuts out your heart piece by piece, feeding it to the boy you love.

But this is Declan. He's different, a small voice whispered.

But …

"What do you want from me?" My voice was torn, my emotions all over the place.

He cupped my cheek, his thumb caressing the curve of my face. "The truth. How do *you* feel? Do you hate me? Do you want me to kiss you?" His full lips tilted up in a sweet smile, like he already knew the answer. I guess he did.

He leaned his head down and pressed his warm mouth

against mine. The pressure was gentle and sweet at first, but like everything between us, it got hot fast. His hand snaked into my hair and cupped my head as our tongues tangled, massaging, our passion rising with each dark stroke. God, yes. I wanted this. Him. Forever.

But all I could think about was Colby. I eased back from him and rested my forehead against his chest.

Afraid to look at him. Afraid to face the truth of what I had to do.

He tilted my chin up, his eyes heavy with desire. "Don't pull away, Elizabeth. Not from me."

But I did.

I exhaled heavily, all the while trying to mentally distance myself from his heady maleness that made me want to crawl into him and never leave.

"Come with me and we'll get out of here," he said quietly. "Just—don't tell me what I think I see on your face."

I closed my eyes. No, this had to stop. If he wanted the truth, I'd give it to him.

"Wait," I said, taking another step back. "You haven't heard everything. Colby—he chased me relentlessly, and I just couldn't wrap my head around why a guy like him wanted me. I didn't have rich parents or the right clothes or even a car. I wasn't popular, although that changed once he made it known he wanted me. Suddenly I was part of the in-crowd. Girls wanted to be my bestie. Guys talked to me. Looking back, I see now I was merely a trophy to him, the girl he couldn't have. The virgin." I bit my lip hard.

Declan's face tightened.

My gut churned with memories, but I couldn't stop. I had to get it all out this one last time. "He—he bought me flowers, texted me fifty times a day, and I was too naïve to see what was right in front of my face. He was a player who'd left a trail of broken hearts—but he told me I was *different* and that he'd change for me." I sucked in a deep breath, forcing the words out. "Prom night he provided the alcohol and drugs. Things got hazy. One moment I was dancing and the next I was in a hotel room with my dress ripped apart. It wasn't what I wanted," my voice cracked, and I yanked it back under control. "That night, darkness slithered its way into my heart, and I vowed to never fall in love again. Two days later, my mom still wasn't home from Vegas, and I—I slit my wrists to end the blackness inside me. I—I never want love to push me to the brink of ending myself again."

Declan had taken to pacing during my story, but now he came to a standstill and looked at me, his fists clenched at his side. "I'll kill the bastard."

My voice quivered. "He's untouchable—even for you."

"Did you report him?"

"And ruin my life? Put myself through a pointless court battle and public censure? I'm a nobody!"

"Never say that." The tightness around his mouth softened as his eyes searched mine. I pulled back from him even more, my eyes everywhere except on his face.

He saw too much.

He gathered my stiff body in his arms and held me.

But I couldn't relax. I wanted to hide away forever. I wanted to disappear.

"I got you, Elizabeth. Let me take care of you. Let me be the one you run to. We can figure it all out together."

My breath hitched. I debated on telling him more about Colby, about the text and the threat behind it, but I couldn't involve him. I couldn't lead him on. Because in the end, I could never love again.

"Elizabeth?"

I gazed up at him. "Declan …" My voice trailed off, unable to form the words that teetered on my lips.

"What's wrong?" he asked, eyes clinging to mine, hope on his face.

"I—I can't." My voice sounded strangled.

"Tell me why."

Emotions warred in me, part of me wanting to sink into his arms and throw caution to the wind, but the other side ...

"Why won't you let me in?" he insisted.

"*You know why*," I said, closing my eyes briefly and pulling back.

"Say it. Get some guts and just fucking say it. You *know* how you feel about me." His hands clutched my arms.

"Because I—"

"Yes?"

.I shook my head and swallowed down the words in my heart and went with the ones in my head. "I—I can't be with you. You're all wrong for me. You're a fighter and you're beautiful and you'll break my heart. You're just another one-night stand, okay? That's it. Nothing more. Just—just leave me alone. *We're done*." I jerked away from him, chest heaving.

Immediately, I wanted to yank the words back, but the rules girl in my head told me to run and end this misery.

So I did.

"Wait," he barked out, but I moved furiously through the quad, dodging students as I bolted for the parking lot.

CHAPTER TWENTY-SIX

AN AVALANCHE OF emotions slammed into me as I watched her weave through the quad. Running from us. She'd rejected me, just as if she'd reached in my chest and squeezed the fuck out of my heart.

So much for putting it out there on the table and taking a chance.

She was falling in love with me too, but the kicker was she didn't want to.

I knew it. She knew it.

I watched her until she got to the street, her lonely figure hunched over as she checked the crosswalk and then crossed hurriedly, headed for the carpark. She moved like the devil was behind her, and dammit, I didn't want to be the person who put that freaked-out look on her face.

I'd just wanted to see where we could go from here.

I wanted her in my bed at night and every morning.

I wanted her in my skin.

I wanted her in my soul.

And I wanted in *hers*.

Yet …

She was afraid because of Colby Scott. *Fucking rapist.* My anger skyrocketed, my blood racing through my veins when I thought about him.

I was going to kill him. Slowly and with my bare hands.

Fuck. I rubbed my hair, my hands tugging on the ends. But it wasn't just Colby keeping us apart, was it? There was the fighting, and no way in hell was I giving up my dream. I lived and breathed by my fists. My gym meant everything to me, and maybe I'd even shoot for a UFC stint when I got settled.

With a heaviness in my chest, I stalked back toward the cafeteria and people shuffled to go around me on the sidewalk. Considering the mix of what I was feeling, there was no telling what was on my face.

Dax had come outside and walked toward me. He pulled up next to me, a wary look on his face. "Where'd she go? Did you cock it up?"

I exhaled, trying to let go of the lingering frustration. "She went home, and no, I didn't *cock it up* for your information. I told her I wanted more, and she told me to stay away. Oh, she also said I was nothing but a fuck to her. Nice little conversation."

He opened his mouth, but I held my hand up. "Not now. I don't want any bloody questions. She told me how she felt, and I am officially finished."

His mouth tightened. "I just want to help. I like her and I think she's good for you."

"Yeah? She doesn't want *me*, brother."

But she's afraid, a voice reminded me. So? I had my bloody pride too.

He let out a sigh. "It's just—there's something about the two of you…the way you look at her…bollocks, I don't know. You should go after her. Don't give up so soon."

Leftover anger flared again. "Great. Romance advice from

the guy who's never had a serious relationship. Thanks but no thanks."

"Don't be an arse."

"Don't be a nosy parker," I snapped. "You don't know what the bloody hell you're on about."

"You're my twin. I can read you like a book. You're half-way in love with her already."

I barked out a laugh. "Maybe if you did read a real book, you'd pass your classes."

"Knobhead. You don't know when to shut your gob do you?"

"Back to the name calling? Very mature," I said with gritted teeth. "You best take a step back, brother, and think about what you're doing."

We faced off with each other, our eyes glaring as the moments ticked by.

Suddenly he relaxed his stance, his shoulders dipping as he took a step back and surveyed me critically. He waved his hands at me. *"This.* This is how I know you're in trouble when it comes to Elizabeth. Your fists are clenched, you've got this crazy look in your eye, and your hair looks like squirrels are living in it you're pulling on it so much. You're in deep shit, and you don't know how to handle it."

I rubbed my temple, my anger cooling rapidly. I shouldn't be angry at him. This wasn't about Dax. This was about her.

His eyes went to something behind me. "Bollocks. Here comes more trouble."

I turned to see Nadia approaching at a fast pace, her hips swinging as she crossed the quad and came to a halt in front of us. Her voice was slightly breathless. "Hey, I saw Elizabeth running away from you from inside the cafeteria. Is everything okay?"

"Stalker," Dax muttered.

Her green eyes hardened as she swiveled toward him.

They'd never really got along; mostly because she'd been jealous of the closeness he and I shared.

I gave her my noncommittal shrug and made to walk off from both of them when she grabbed my hand. "Wait. I—I need to tell you something about Elizabeth. Remember us talking about our mutual friend Colby? I talked to him yesterday, and he told me the truth. She's got an absolutely terrible reputation in Petal—"

I jerked back from her as if she scalded me. "Shut up, Nadia, you don't know jack," I snarled. "Don't ever say his name again. He's a—" I caught myself when her eyes flared wide. I couldn't betray Elizabeth.

"He's a what?"

"Nothing. Just stay away from him—and me."

She gasped but quickly recovered. "Why? You can't just say that and not follow up." She hitched her bag up on her shoulder. "Is he not who I think he is?"

Dax smirked and raked his eyes over her. "Is anyone? Sometimes you have a girlfriend who says she loves you but then she screws a Ninja Turtle."

She reddened, her eyes glaring. "Stay out of this, Dax. I'm talking to Declan. Not you."

He nudged his head at me. "Look at him, Nadia. He isn't thinking about *you* or your shit. He was over you the day you cheated. He wants Elizabeth. Scoot on along now little slag."

Her lips tightened. "I know what that word means."

"Indeed," he smirked. "That was my intention."

She flicked a strand of hair and huffed, but he wasn't done yet, and I wondered if it was because he'd never seen me this worked up over a girl.

"By the way, I hadn't had a chance to say anything to Declan yet, but I ran into one of your sorority sisters at the Tau house last week. I flirted a bit—as I usually do—and suddenly we were involved in a deep conversation about you. She just so happened to mention that your mum is not at home these days, but is in fact currently on a two-month-long cruise around the world. Interesting. It must be hard to get chemo out on the ocean."

She paled, her eyes flaring wide. "Wha—What? Who told you that? She—she's home."

He smiled. "Then why are you stuttering? The thing is, I'm guessing you made that story up so Declan would talk to you again so you could manipulate him into feeling sorry for you and eventually taking you back. It needs to stop, Nadia."

Several seconds went by until finally her shoulders dipped in defeat. Tears spilled down her cheeks. She turned to me, a pleading look on her face, and I read the truth there. I expected her lies to bother me more than they did, but the truth was I hadn't loved her enough, and the only feeling left was pity.

All my emotions were too wrapped up with Elizabeth. She was all I could think about.

I exhaled heavily and walked away.

I didn't have shit to say to either one of them.

I just wanted to be alone.

And later? I wanted to fight.

CHAPTER
TWENTY-SEVEN

Elizabeth

HATED THE color pink, any shade of it.

The soft pink like you'd see on a baby blanket, the hot-pink shade of lipstick that Mama sometimes wore, and even shades of maroon pricked at me. For two years now, the mere idea of wearing that color made my stomach churn. My prom dress had been a glittery, delicious pink, the shade of strawberry ice cream, with sparkles.

But as Shelley and I walked down Freemont Street on our way back from my meeting with Sylvia Myers for my jewelry interview, I came to a complete halt in front of a consignment shop window. I'd been in the store before to hunt through their old books or to look for good quality used clothing. The artist in me loved the unique and eye-catching window displays the owner put together.

Today, the display blew my mind. Everything was pink.

Shelley stopped next to me, her fashion designer eyes raking over the ensemble inside. "You like the dress? Kinda dated for you, don't you think?"

"It's beautiful," I said, my eyes running over the window.

At the ceiling were pink papier-mâché clouds with a crystal chandelier hanging in the middle. Below that was the only mannequin, a tall blond wearing an empire-waist dress with heavy lace dripping from the sleeves and the tea-length hem. It was romantic and *pink*, and nothing I would ever wear—yet something about it called to me.

Next to the mannequin rested a pink and white distressed desk with an old typewriter and a collection of books on top of it, their spines facing outward, giving me a clear view of the titles. *Pride and Prejudice* was right on top. Darcy came to mind ... then Declan.

I sighed, my eyes taking in the dress, part hippie chick, part vintage—*and probably out of your budget*, I reminded myself.

"It looks like someone vomited up cotton candy everywhere," she said. "Besides, I thought you boycotted pink?"

True. "I wonder how much it is?"

"This place is reasonable. Plus you've got some money now." She grinned widely and leaned in to give me another excited squeeze. She'd been bouncing along beside me since we'd left the interview, and her enthusiasm was contagious. I smiled back. I had to admit, I was giddy myself considering Sylvia had just offered me a thousand dollars for three of my jewelry drawings which she'd then hand over to her artisans in Ashville to recreate.

Letting go of those designs had felt like a small step on my way to finding the artist inside me again, as if I'd climbed a hill and reached the top. It wasn't quite the mountain, but I knew if I kept putting one step in front of the other, eventually I'd get to the summit.

And then I thought of Declan. Again. What if he was everything I'd been unconsciously searching for these past two years? What if he was *the one* I was meant to love—right in my hands—and I was letting him slip away? Emotion swelled in my chest. Telling him to leave me alone had been one of the hardest things I'd ever done, and I hadn't been able to sleep or think about anything but him for the past two days. His face. His eyes. His cocky grin. *God, his kindness.*

Before I knew it, we'd stepped inside the shop and were met by a sales lady.

"Can I help you, dears?" the older lady asked.

"I'd like to look at the dress in the window," I said.

She showed us how to get up to the display through some rickety steps to the left of the window. "Go on up there and have a look, everyone does. It's a small space, but you can move around. Just be careful."

We nodded and went that way.

"Best we can estimate, the dress was manufactured here in the US. It's a hundred percent silk with a lace overlay," she called out from behind us as we stepped into the brightness of the window.

We checked the price tag. One fifty. Pricey.

I fingered the soft lace at the sleeve.

Why did I even want it? Where would I wear it?

"Try it on," Shelley said in a hushed voice, which was odd, yet it was as if we both sensed the precipice I was standing on.

Without thinking too hard, I found myself whisked into the dressing room by the saleslady while Shelley followed to help me into the dress.

The material slid over my neck and arms, and when I turned to look in the mirror, the girl I saw there wasn't the same one from Monday, the one who'd told the most beautiful guy he was only a one-night stand. *This* girl—she was almost radiant. Happy.

"What do you think?" I asked, and I heard the uncertainty in my voice.

Shelley's face lit up in a big grin. "You're gorgeous in it, of course, but you'd need to give it to me so I can do my thing. Maybe chop off the length—but keep the lace—and bring in the waist so it isn't as loose." She sighed heavily.

"What?"

"Pink always was your color …" I figured she was remembering the day we went shopping for our prom dresses and no matter what store I went in, I always gravitated toward the pink ones.

"Buy it, Elizabeth. And then fucking wear it—heck, even if it's just to class. Prove to yourself that Colby doesn't matter anymore, that he may have taken something precious from you, but he didn't ruin you forever." A mist covered her eyes.

I put my hand on her shoulder. "Oh, Shelley. I adore you. Thank you for being my friend through all of this."

She shook her head and wiped at her eyes, a rueful grin on her face. "God, I'm so stupid. Sorry. It's just—seeing you walk into that interview today with your head held high and now you're trying on *this* dress? I feel like I've been waiting forever to see this moment."

Emotion welled, and I hugged her hard.

I realized it was time to stop being a coward.

KNOWING AND DOING are not the same thing. I spent lonely nights in my bed, wishing I'd have a nightmare so Declan would come wake me up. Hold me. I was pathetic, and if I was a drinking girl, I would have used alcohol to make it better.

Declan was doing exactly what I'd asked him to do: leaving me alone.

The night after I'd bought the dress, I invited Blake over, mostly because I was jittery about Colby. We went out to the balcony to sit for a while, and Declan had been out on his, his elbows propped up on the railing, his bare chest glistening in the moonlight. I'd said hi. He'd nodded his response and stalked back inside. Later, after Blake had left, I'd heard a girl's voice coming from his side of the wall, and when I'd gone out to take the trash to the dumpster, I saw Lorna from Lit class leaving his place. She'd flounced past me on the stairs with a knowing smirk on her lipstick-smeared face. Sharp pain knifed into me at the thought of him kissing her the way he'd kissed me.

Had he already moved on to the next girl? Was that how little I meant to him?

You did this, I reminded myself.

By Friday, I walked into Lit class determined to confront him and make him talk to me. He was already sitting next to Lorna, both their heads bent in a low conversation. *Today*, I told myself, *talk to him. Tell him how you feel.* And, God, I wanted to tell him—but my insecurities and fear needed him to show me he still wanted me first.

Dax sat next to me and poked me on the arm. "Hiya, girl. You okay? You look odd—well, you're always odd—but you look stranger than usual today."

I took a deep breath. "It's just I hate seeing Declan with her," I whispered as I nudged my head to the couple behind me.

He flicked his eyes to the couple and then back to me. "Yeah? If it bothers you, then do something about it. It has to be you now." His eyes studied mine. "You feel me?"

I nodded and then Dr. Feldman came in the auditorium. I pushed Declan out of my mind and focused on Darcy instead. At least a fictional character couldn't hurt me.

CHAPTER TWENTY-EIGHT

Elizabeth

ON SATURDAY MORNING, I tried to psych myself up to approach Declan, but he wasn't home. I knew because I constantly watched for his Jeep in the parking lot. By lunchtime I was restless, so I drove by his gym. His car was there, but then I couldn't bring myself to stop and go in.

While I was driving home, an idea struck.

With determined steps, I went into the extra bedroom. I unpacked my jewelry tools from their boxes and spread them out on the desk, running my fingers across the cold sheet metal.

A shift occurred inside me, small yet significant, something that had been building for the past few weeks. I let go of the constant control I kept over myself, and suddenly my fingers itched. To create.

I looked deep inside myself and asked tough questions.

Where was my power?

Where was my belief in myself?

It was here all along, a small voice said.

Using 18-gauge sheet metal, I measured one of the bigger ring sizes on the metal that I thought would fit him. Without thinking too much about the significance of it, I etched one of the dragonfly designs I'd drawn earlier to what would be the inside of his ring. After that, I used my saw to cut out the band, filed it, and then used my butane torch to make the metal more pliable. I pickled the piece with vinegar and hot water, getting rid of some of the oxidation on the surface. Next, I used my pliers to shape it into a circle and then soldered it with my torch to connect the edges. After pickling it again and filing and sanding down the seam, I slipped it on a metal rod and began the hammering process, the tinkling sound echoing through my apartment. The last step was to toss the ring in my jewelry tumbler and let it roll around, getting polished. I took it out and set the ring down on my nightstand to dry.

I stared at it with deep satisfaction. He'd have a small piece of me even if he didn't want my heart anymore.

My phone pinged, reminding me that I had dinner plans with Blake and Shelley. Shelley had said a band was playing, so I spent extra time getting ready, putting on my newly altered pink dress and a pair of silver strappy heels. It was a bit overboard for the restaurant, but I didn't care.

That dress was my armor, proof I was changing a little bit every day.

At the last minute, I ran back to the bedroom and straight to the jewelry box, I found a chain, slipped Declan's ring on it, and clasped it around my neck.

Perhaps I would never give it to him, but I wanted it against my skin.

When I walked out, I saw his Jeep in the lot. Before I could second-guess myself, I knocked on his door. Emotion was clawing at my chest, and I was teetering on the edge of—*what?*

What was I going to say?

Was I going to beg him to give me another chance?

Maybe.

But he never answered.

"WHOA, LOVE," SAID a male voice. "You better slow down there or you'll fall." Strong, tattooed arms reached out to steady my momentum as I stumbled walking inside Cadillac's.

I'd know that husky voice anywhere.

Declan.

I shouldn't have been surprised to see him here. It was Saturday night, and if there weren't any frat parties, this was the place to be. He wore jeans and a nicer shirt than usual, and I found myself remembering how he'd looked in his gi pants with his chest bared and scars showing.

Heat curled in my core. This was the first time he'd touched me since the day on the quad.

He raked his eyes over me in a leisurely fashion, a slow perusal that started at my heels and worked its way up to my dress. "You look nice," he murmured.

I nodded. "What are you doing here?" I asked, looking at his face, devouring his chiseled jaw and full lips. I squirmed, remembering that mouth on my body.

I peeked over his shoulder into the dining establishment. *Was he alone?*

Ah. Dax and several of the fraternity little sisters sat at a large round table toward the back, near where the band was setting up. Lorna was there, of course.

I let out a long breath.

"I'm here with friends. What about you? You with Blake?" His voice had snarled that last bit, and I stiffened. Blake had actually cooled it with the pressure and I wasn't sure why, but part of me wondered if he was afraid of Declan.

"You're not saying anything." He leaned on the wall to get out of a patron's way, putting us closer together. His finger reached out and traced a line across my cheek. "I know this look. You're worried." He paused, his brow wrinkling. "Colby?"

And I heard it then, the slight slur in his voice, the smell of alcohol on his breath.

My heart stuttered. I reared back. "You've been drinking?"

"I'm twenty-one. Would you like one?" He held up a bottle of dark beer, and I felt stupid I hadn't even noticed. I'd been too busy taking in the rest of him.

"I don't like it," I snapped.

"Good thing I'm not with you then." He tipped it up to take a sip.

We stared at each other as the seconds ticked by, that familiar zing between us tugging at my heart. I closed my eyes so I wouldn't want him so much. Even knowing he'd been drinking—*I didn't care!*

"I came to your apartment tonight, but you weren't home. There was something I wanted to give you."

He cocked an eyebrow. "You ready for round two already? I didn't think you did that, you being strictly a one-time shagging kind of girl."

My chest rose. "Don't be a jerk. Don't you think I'm hurting? I'm going crazy thinking about you—"

Blake and Shelley stepped inside the door, laughing as they came over to us. Blake gave me a gentle hug and sent Declan a glare.

Declan sent me a conflicted look as if he had more to say, but then he straightened up from the wall, his muscles rippling and flexing. "Good to see you. I need to get back to my friends."

Such cool politeness.

And then he stalked away to join the boisterous group at the back. As I watched, Lorna immediately got on one side of him and another girl on the other, both of them vying for his attention.

See, people are never who you really think they are. He's

just like all the rest, the rules girl said in my head.

"You okay?" Shelley asked, her voice tentative.

I shook my head. My chest felt like it was caving in. We weren't even friends anymore. "I can't stay here and watch him."

Blake nodded. "I agree. Let's go back to your apartment and order in pizza. My treat."

I nodded and glanced down at my pink dress. I wanted to get it off as soon as possible. "Just get me out of here."

CHAPTER TWENTY-NINE

Declan

I WASN'T A *pussy. If she didn't want me, I'd just forget about her,* I told myself as I sat back down and took one of the tequila shots sitting on the table.

Dax sent me a wary look. "You've had enough."

"It's enough when she's out of my head." I nudged my head at Elizabeth, who stood at the door, a wounded expression on her face.

As a rule, drinking was something I rarely indulged in, but over the past few days, I'd worked on pushing Elizabeth out of my head. Or I'd tried to. Drinking dulled the pain briefly, but it was never enough.

I let her go the only way a guy knows how. I focused on girls who wanted me.

There's no point in chasing a dream if it doesn't want you back.

And I couldn't stop the thought that maybe she *was* really in love with Blake but was denying it to herself. Maybe I was completely wrong about her feelings for me.

Since she'd told me to stay away, I'd seen them together

everywhere. In the student center. On the quad. At her place.

I hated him for no reason other than he had her attention and I didn't.

I lifted my beer and took a drink.

One particularly bad day after realizing Blake was in her apartment, I'd called Lorna to come over to my flat. My head had been all twisty, and I hadn't cared who I was with, my body jonesing for a release to make me forget about Elizabeth.

I'd kissed Lorna and eventually we'd ended up on my bed, but my heart hadn't been into it, and before long I stopped us.

Being with Lorna had been wrong. And I don't even know why.

I didn't owe Elizabeth anything.

But …

The clarity hit me. I wasn't *just* falling in love with Elizabeth; I'd gone completely over the edge as if someone had shoved me off a skyscraper and I was freefalling toward the concrete.

She was my queen and I wanted to be her king. I wanted to sit at the throne of her body and love her forever, but it wasn't just about sex, although that had been over the fucking moon. No, with us it was about two broken people who looked deep into the eyes of the other person and just—meshed. Call it fate or destiny or just plain old karma, but whatever it was, the moment I watched her dance in the rain, my heart had known, only it had taken my head a while to catch up.

"She's leaving," Dax leaned over and told me.

"I don't care. Fuck her."

"Yeah, right." He considered me, his gray eyes worried. "You need to get your head straight before the fight with Yeti."

I turned my head to see her walk away and, *fuck*, part of me wanted to run after her.

And tell her what?

Was I ready to put myself out there again for someone with

commitment issues?

Lorna's heavily made-up eyes slid over me suggestively. "You want to get out of here, babe?"

I tipped up my beer and took a good long swig. "What've you got in mind?"

She licked red lips, her eyes gleaming with seduction as she pushed her tits in my face. I stared down at the creamy globes. I could have those in my hand tonight. "Whatever it takes to make you happy, Declan."

Make me happy?

Nothing.

You are not to think about Elizabeth again, I told myself.

I scooted in closer to her, the scent of her perfume clogging up my nose. I toyed with a strand of her hair and gave her a broad smile. She leaned into the crook of my arms and kissed my neck, her mouth hot as she nipped down the column of my throat.

She slid her hands between my thighs and pushed down on my cock through my jeans. It didn't even twitch.

Dax slapped his hand on my shoulder. "Let's go, bro."

I blinked up at him, and the room spun. I waited for the pleasant buzz of beer to kick in, but all I got was an empty feeling in my gut.

He sighed. "Come on, let's get you out of here before you do something you'll regret."

Lorna pouted. "But the night's just getting started—"

I stood up with Dax's help.

"Sorry, love. It's not in the cards tonight," he told her.

He leaned me against him and we made our way out the door of the bar. We stumbled toward his beamer, one big dude holding up another one.

"I love you, you know that, right?" I murmured.

He huffed, tugging me along. "Yeah, man. Me too. Now get in the bloody car."

"Wait." My eyes searched the carpark, hoping she was still there. "She's gone," I said.

He sighed and opened the door for me. "You got it bad, bro. I'm sorry it's not working out."

"Yeah." The first woman I'd ever loved, and she didn't want me.

I slid into the passenger side, exhaled heavily, and then promptly threw up in his car.

A FEW HOURS later, I felt sober. Mostly. Maybe the puking had helped.

I tried to go to bed, but I couldn't sleep, so I got up and took a hot shower. Water dripped down as I palmed my cock, thinking about Elizabeth under me, her soft skin against mine.

I got out and dressed in a pair of silver gym shorts and padded out to the balcony.

My eyes went to her darkened flat. Of course, she was asleep. Right? It was three in the morning.

I didn't care.

I took a running leap and jumped the distance, sticking the landing with a soft thud. Her glass door was unlocked—I had to get on her about that. But for now, I slid it open quietly and eased inside, peering around until my eyes got used to the darkness.

I came to a halt as the glare of headlights from the carpark hit me in the face.

What the hell was I doing?

I'd just waltzed in uninvited. She'd be angry if she woke up and saw me here. Right?

What if someone was with her?

Fuck! Fury rushed at me and I scrubbed my hair, my eyes devouring her form underneath the covers. Just one single form.

She rolled over, a soft sigh escaping as she settled back into her pillows.

Things—life—had been tough for me since Mum had passed, but I'd done the best job I could, trying to be the person she'd have wanted me to be. Living with my dad had shaped me into the guy I was now. Tough. Hard. But underneath, I've longed for the deep love between two people that Mum had always told me was out there.

I paced around her room.

But Elizabeth didn't want those things, so why was I sneaking into her bedroom like some lad with a woody?

Say goodbye?

Maybe.

I sighed.

I had to if I wanted to keep my sanity. I had a fight to think about and she was a big distraction.

But …

Could I let her go forever?

Could I pass her in class and smile when I saw her with Blake?

Could I watch *them* fall in love someday?

Could I run into her years later at a park and see her playing with a toddler that wasn't mine?

I was too proud to beg and too angry to think straight. Hell, maybe I was still sloshed.

God, I needed to breathe.

I exhaled.

I had to tell her goodbye.

Yeah. After all, what other choice did I have?

CHAPTER THIRTY

Elizabeth

SUNDAY I WOKE up depressed about seeing Declan out drinking.

Was he just like all the rest?

I cranked up Pink on my phone, plugged it into the speakers, and spent the rest of my day tinkering around with my sheet metal.

Later that evening, I tried calling my mom again. I'd been trying to reach her since she'd left here last Saturday. Today she actually picked up, and after a brief conversation, she admitted they hadn't sold the story and were on their way back to Petal.

Thank God.

I let out a huge sigh of relief. At least there was that working in my favor.

Dax called and asked to meet me to take a peek at my Lit notes for an upcoming test, so I headed to the student center.

I arrived and found him sitting in the back at a booth, looking as sexy as ever in a black band shirt featuring the Beastie Boys. I plopped down across from him and handed over my notebook. Seeing him reminded me so much of Declan that my heart ached. "You could have asked to see Declan's notes, so why don't you tell me exactly why you called me."

He cleared his throat and settled in over the table with his hands folded, a serious expression on his face. He let out a deep breath. "I don't know what kind of jacked-up thing you and my brother are doing to each other, but he's bloody well gutted ... *and* he has a huge fight on Halloween with some albino freak. Not good. If you still want him—and I know you do—then you better get it sorted and let him know. If you cock this up and ruin his fight, it's all on you, love."

"Tell me how you really feel," I murmured.

He smirked. "That's the fuck-all truth of the matter."

I sat back in the booth, worry and fear settling in my gut. Halloween was two days away. I licked my lips. "You really think he might have trouble with this one? Because of me?"

Dax sent me a hard look. "I don't know. I'm sick of both of you. Maybe if you'd two figure your shit out, he'd be fine."

"Don't manipulate me, Dax. We have issues to work through. Plus, I don't like violence, and I can't condone it," I snapped. But even as the words came out of me, part of me yearned to see Declan use his body again. My mind flashed back to the night he'd hit Colby. While I'd been terrified at first, afterwards, I'd been in awe of his power and agility. And his alpha instincts made me hot as hell. I sighed.

Dax shrugged.

Fine. I changed gears. "What about Lorna? He was with her last night, and he didn't seem to be pining for me when she was hanging all over him."

"He isn't with her, but he's a fool 'cause I'd be shagging that in a heartbeat. I wouldn't wait for you, but he is."

My face must have telegraphed my feelings on that because he held his hands up. "Don't get angry. One day he *is* going to pick someone else. He is my brother after all." He exhaled. "So get over your past and get over the fighting and go after your goddamn man."

I toyed with the scars on my wrists, avoiding his eyes. The standoff between Declan and me wasn't really because of his fighting. Maybe it had been part of the reason at first, but mostly it was still *me* being afraid to take that final step and admit my feelings.

To open up myself up to potential heartache.

But didn't you promise yourself you'd be brave? a small voice reminded me.

Yes, and I had in small steps, slowing climbing that mountain.

But isn't it time to take a leap?

I stood to leave. I eased my necklace off, the one with Declan's ring, and handed it over to him. "Will you give this to him? It's the first piece I've created in two years, and it—it has a dragonfly engraved on the inside. He told me the significance, and I haven't been able to think of anything but him, so I made it." My voice trembled.

He studied it, then looked at me. He nodded, a solemn expression on his face. "I will."

He stood up as well and wrapped me in a hug. "Two days," he whispered in my ear. "Don't forget."

CHAPTER THIRTY-ONE

Elizabeth

MONDAY MORNING I went to Lit class but neither Declan nor Dax were there. I assumed Declan was getting in last-minute training or rest. After working at the bookstore, I came home and cleaned out the fridge and then wiped down the baseboards while the television showed episodes of *Downton Abbey*. It kept me busy and my mind off of things I didn't want to think about.

That evening, a knock came at my door.

I opened it and Declan stood there, leaning against the doorjamb, his stance tense, as if he were holding himself in check.

"Hey," I said. "How are you?" I could barely breathe for taking him in, my eyes soaking in the broad shoulders and muscled biceps.

He nodded, rather formally. "Good. I don't mean to bother you—"

"You aren't. I'm just here … alone. Catching up on *Downton Abbey*. And cleaning. I need to do the kitchen and bathroom next, maybe my closets." I stopped. "I'm sorry, I'm babbling." I forced a laugh.

His face never changed.

"Do you want to come in?" My voice shook, and I coughed to make it stop.

He cleared his throat. "No, I was just popping by to tell you I asked a cop friend to investigate Colby. He said he's living in some apartments on the south side of Whitman." He sighed. "I've been checking out the carpark and your place from my balcony every night, and if I'm not here, I call the campus police and they've done some drive-bys. I know things have changed between us, but I'm here if you need me."

Oh.

"Thank you. That means a lot." *Please come inside.* I fidgeted with the door handle.

His phone buzzed, and he pulled it from his pocket and checked what I assumed was a text message.

"Someone important?" I asked. I tried to keep the resentment out of my voice. I really did. I had *no* reason to be jealous. I'd had my chance.

He flicked his eyes at me. "My date."

My heart dipped. "Is she pretty?"

He shrugged.

Pain ricocheted through me. Stop, just fucking stop it already.

I picked my broken heart up, dusted it off, and shoved it back in my chest.

I caught a flash of silver on his hand and froze. My breath snagged in my throat. "You're wearing the ring I made you?"

He grew still, his thumb flicking at the sterling silver band on the ring finger of his right hand.

"It looks great," I murmured. "I—I had to guess at the measurements, but it seems like I got it right." I held myself together. Not letting him see how emotional it made me to know he was wearing it. Did he love it as much as I did? Did he think about me at all?

"Thank you for the gift." He fidgeted. "I think about y—my mum when I wear it."

"I—I didn't expect you to wear it on a date."

"Jealous?"

I stiffened. "No."

"Liar." He shrugged, a sad smile on his face. "Whatever. I don't really have a date, not unless you count the gym. She can be a bitch sometimes."

Yes.

"Declan, I—I want you to come in. Please. I need to tell you …" I stopped, afraid to finish the sentence. I swallowed.

He rubbed his cheek, the dark shadow there a testament to his virility, his maleness. His eyes were a stormy gray as he gazed at me, as if a thousand turbulent emotions churned inside him. "It's late, Elizabeth. I need to prepare for tomorrow, and I didn't come here to argue with you. Just to tell you about Colby."

But I didn't want to argue.

He took a step back from my door and sent me one final look, his gaze distant as it raked over me.

He was done with me. I'd waited too damn long.

I sensed it deep in my soul, that fragile connection between us being pulled taut until it was ready to snap. I wanted to bend over and cry.

And then he was gone.

HALLOWEEN ARRIVED.

I went to class in a daze and by three I was at the bookstore to work my shift. Rick had said we could wear costumes to work, so Shelley and I had done a quick power shopping trip to pick me up something at the mall. I'd ended up choosing a lime green Tinkerbelle costume with a shimmery tank and tutu and pointy ballet flats with a fluffy ball on the toe. Itchy and uncomfortable, I went with it. I didn't care.

Weighing heavily on my mind was the fight, but the deal was no one knew exactly where and when it was unless they were part of some inner circle. Shelley and Blake weren't, so we waited to hear through the grapevine.

Shelley and Blake had stopped by the store on their way out to a costume party at one of the frat houses. She'd chosen a zombie cheerleader costume and Blake was a zombie football player. They left to hit the parties, and I stayed behind to finish my shift.

Three hours after they left, my phone pinged.

Shelley.

CALL ME ASAP, her text read.

"Excuse me, I have to get this," I told Rick and went to the back storeroom.

I texted her, **What's wrong? Still at work. Can't call. Text me.**

Declan is fighting in an hour!! was her response.

I called her quickly, my voice hushed. Rick had a strict no cell-phones-at-work policy. "What's going on?"

"He's fighting at a warehouse on Water Street, the one next to the old cotton gin." She rattled off an address. Her voice lowered. "This place is going to be insane with music and drinking and all kinds of shit. I don't know if you can handle it."

My chest rose as I inhaled. I'd already forgotten the address. "Text me the address, and I'll meet you there."

CHAPTER THIRTY-TWO

I ROLLED MY shoulders and paced around the small area behind a screen that Nick, the fight organizer, had set up earlier
in the warehouse, trying to block out the blaring music and
flashing lights behind me. Max had counted over five hundred
heads at the door earlier—the biggest turnout ever. I checked my
wrapped fists and my cup. All was good. I let out a pent-up
breath and air-boxed to keep the adrenaline pumping. I was
ready to knock this out.

Dax popped around the screen. "This place is a bloody freak
show. Students are here in costumes from the frat parties. Suits
are everywhere. Fuck, it's crowded." He grimaced, his face torn
as if something was bugging him.

I paused my boxing. "What's going on?"

He fidgeted and scratched his head. "I didn't want to tell
you, but I figure it's better coming from me than suddenly seeing
her in the crowd—Elizabeth's here."

I stepped back from the screen, my eyes skating through the
crowd. "Where?"

He shook his head. "I saw her when she came in, but then

we got separated. This place is a madhouse."

I exhaled. Dammit. Now I had her to worry about. "Make sure she gets out of here, okay?"

He nodded and looked over at Yeti. "He's fucking huge, man. He looks like an albino rat on steroids ... that's very hungry."

I slapped him on the back. "Relax, his reach sucks."

He nodded, his face still unsure, but he gave me a fist bump. "Kick his arse, brother. I got money on you."

"Done."

He stalked off but stopped a few feet outside the makeshift ring—chalk lines on the ground—jostling around with some of the more hardcore students for a good view. He was never too far from me at a fight. Max came over and took up position in my corner.

Nick blew a bullhorn, signaling the start of the match, and the music grew louder as I stepped into the twelve by twelve ring. Fucking joke. This fight had no rules and no one ever stayed inside the lines.

Yeti came in like the monster he was, his beefy body circling mine as we sized each other up.

We started out slow, each of us testing, until about sixty seconds in when he launched himself at me. Crisp fists landed on my gut, and a powerful one hit my shoulder as I pivoted away.

I inhaled at the pain, sucked it up.

Now it was on.

I clenched my fists and ran for him and got in four hits to the chest, sidestepping back when he retaliated by striking heavy with his right, aiming for my throat and chin.

He missed.

I attacked again, my palm strikes ripping into his shoulders and gut, slicing up to get to his lungs to knock the breath out of him. Punch. Punch. Punch.

He grunted. Blood flew through the air. The crowd

screamed.

Yeah. Go down, fucker.

He tore away from me and paced, his face red as he shook it off, but then he grinned, teeth showing. Apparently, Yeti didn't wear a mouth guard.

A flash of blond hair in the crowd grabbed my attention, and his palm strike connected squarely with my ear twice, *bam, bam,* then he flipped around and elbowed me in the gut, his other fist connecting with my temple when I bent over.

Dots flashed in front of my eyes.

The room faded.

Wake the fuck up.

My chest heaved as I sucked in air and stumbled away from him.

He tossed back his head and let out a roar. The crowd egged him on, clapping and calling his name.

I shook the hits off, rose up, and went at him again, this time using an elbow strike combination with leg kicks. He took both hits to the chest and went down to his knees. Success. I pounced and we wrestled to the floor, the hard concrete grinding in my shoulder as we grappled for control. I used a forearm submission move.

I pushed him down and got in one … two … three quick punches.

Dir-ty Eng-lish! Dir-ty Eng-lish! the crowd chanted.

He goosed up with a head-butt as I pounded him; I swerved.

He bucked up again, this time stronger. My purchase slipped. *Dammit.*

Not yet.

He grunted and blood spurted from his face as I hit his nose with my palm.

I lowered him closer to the ground until his nose kissed concrete.

"Fight's over, Yeti," I muttered, and in the millisecond it

took me to breath those words, he contorted, loosened the hold and jabbed with his knee, connecting with part of my upper throat.

I gagged and fell back.

Girls screamed. Guys yelled. Max yelled from the sidelines. No clue what he said.

Bugger!

I lost steam. Fast. I couldn't fucking breathe.

He grinned maniacally and came at me, jabbing at my face. He got my right eye. I kept moving. Avoiding. Dodging. Trying to breathe.

Using all the strength I had, I rolled my hips and retaliated with a jab-cross. The left hook went straight for the liver and the right aimed for the area under his heart. I yelled as it ripped out of me.

He stumbled backward into the crowd, who shoved him back in.

I growled and tore into him, swapping messy blows and kicks, neither of us willing to give in. I scanned the crowd as I paced, looking for blond hair.

I found Elizabeth. *And Blake was with her?*

Slam! His knee did a punching stab and hit my liver. I crumpled as pain ricocheted through my lower body. Gasping for air, I arched back just as he missed nailing me with a high left leg kick. I swayed around the ring.

Shit-motherfucking-hell.

"Fight's over, English," he taunted as he landed another jab to my gut.

Again.

Again.

Air whooshed out and the room spun. My bare feet fumbled around the ring and I tripped and fell to my knees.

Air. Needed fucking air.

Sirens reached my ears first. Then the screams of the spectators as they ran for the exit doors.

"Cops are coming," a mummy screamed as he ran past and then climbed out one of the windows that lined the south side of the warehouse.

Now it was a madhouse.

Yeti did a crude gesture with his dick and then pointed his finger at me. "This isn't over. You got lucky this time, English. Next time, I'll kill you *then* I'll fuck you." He rocked his hips and laughed. As I watched him, he jogged over to his manager and then darted out a door that led to a myriad of offices in the back. I had no clue if there was an exit back there.

"Let's get the hell out of here," Max yelled as he grabbed my arm and tugged me toward the main doors of the warehouse.

"Wait," I wheezed out and pulled loose from him. "Where's Dax?" I scanned the room, looking for his build. "And Elizabeth? She's here somewhere."

"Don't be an idiot. You're the one they'll arrest," he yelled at me.

The sirens blared loud now, the flashing blue lights ricocheting into the cracked windows.

I turned to him. "Go on. I'm coming right behind you."

He groaned and gave up on me and ran for the door.

I stood in the middle of the chaos. Most of the place had emptied except for the people who'd been on the top level and were trying to maneuver the rickety stairwells.

No blond hair. No Dax as far as I could tell.

"This way!" a voice called from across the warehouse, nearly thirty feet away.

Dax stood at a broken window, poised to crawl through. Elizabeth stood next to him, her eyes like saucers. She motioned with wild hands for me to come on.

The squeal of tires came to a stop outside the warehouse. Car doors opened. Voices yelled.

I sprinted toward them. Dammit, I was too far away.

"Push her out first," I yelled. "Cops are right behind me."

He got what I meant and hoisted her up, careful to avoid the jagged shards of glass. Her legs disappeared over the edge.

"Go, Dax!"

He shook his head, a pleading look on his face as he watched me run through a group of girls who'd had too much to drink and were trying to get out.

He sent me one final look and jumped through the window. Through the panes of the glass, I saw his shadow grab Elizabeth's and run for a neighboring building's ally.

I ran hard toward the window and dove headfirst through it. Hitting the ground, I rolled back to my feet and kept moving.

Shouts came through the window from the interior of the warehouse.

Shit. The cops had come inside.

Go, go, go, I told myself.

I turned the corner of the building and darted down the dark alley where I was hoping Dax had gone. They weren't there, so I kept running between buildings and calling their names. My fear was the cops would spread out, but with five hundred people going in every direction, I hoped they had their hands full.

Where were they?

I turned down a small side street nearly a block over when I saw them waving at me as they waited next to a dumpster in an alley.

I jogged over to them.

Dax sent me a wild look. "Cops? What the hell? That's never happened—and my car is parked over there," he wailed as he bent over to catch his breath. "Fun times, bro."

I moved my attention to Elizabeth, who stood frozen as she watched me, her chest rising rapidly.

Her eyes suddenly widened. "Your hands are bleeding."

I looked down, realizing I must have cut them when I'd hit the ground running.

She picked them up to inspect them and dabbed at them with the end of her tank. "This is crazy. We need to get you to the ER."

My first instinct was to pull away from her touch, especially since my hands were swollen from fighting, but I didn't move, the heat of her body intoxicating. She smelled like lemons or something fruity and I wanted to pull her to me and inhale deeply. "I'm fine," I said gruffly.

"You're not fine!" she snarled. Angry.

God, I loved that fire in her eyes.

"Why do you care so much anyway?"

She puffed up even more, blue eyes flashing as she dropped my hand and took a step back. I took in the soft curves of her breasts as she crossed her arms, the way her throat moved when she swallowed. My body tightened, my cock hardening. I told myself it was the usual leftover adrenaline, where I felt like I could fuck forever, but it was all her.

I wanted her, my pride be damned. All the turmoil from the past few days disappeared, and she was all that mattered.

I turned to Dax. "Go get my car. It's three blocks east of here in an open lot on Chester Street. Key's on the top of the driver's side tire." I paused. "And give us a few minutes before you come back."

He rose up, his eyes jumping between me and Elizabeth. "Okay," he said uncertainly. "You guys good here in the alley? Elizabeth?"

I cocked an eye at her, letting her see the heat in my gaze. *You are mine*, it said. "You okay alone with me?" I asked, a twist to my lips, daring her to say no.

She nodded and Dax ran off into the darkness, but neither one of us watched him leave, both of us wrapped up in each other. She was still angry, and I was just horny.

"Declan—" she started.

"Come here."

She licked her lips. "Why?"

"I've been fighting, my blood is practically boiling, and I need you ... *now.*"

Her nose flared and the pulse in her neck kicked up. I wasn't alone in this, and I was done rolling over and giving up on her.

If she wouldn't come to me, then I'd go to her.

I wiped the blood from my hands on my shorts until most of it was gone, seeing that my cuts weren't as bad as I'd thought. My bruises would probably be worse. I glanced up to see her watching me. I moved closer to her until I had her backed her up against the metal building behind her, but I kept a few inches between us as I propped both arms up on either side of her head.

"Now ask me to kiss you," I said, staring down at her.

She panted, her eyes filling up with darkness, her pupils telling me the truth. Her top teeth bit into her plump lower lip, and my eyes went straight there. I was going to suck that mouth hard tonight, and she'd beg for more.

"Are you hot for me, Elizabeth? Did watching me fight get you excited?"

She closed her eyes and shuddered as if just the sound of my voice got her off.

"Are you?" I asked again. "Because I want you so bad I can't even think straight. I see you walk across campus or on your balcony and I want to run to you. I see you in class and, shit, I want to scoop you up and kiss you until you can't breathe. I think about you in your bed at night all alone and I want to slip inside, crawl in your sheets, and hold you. Fuck you."

I ran my fingertips across her lips. She moaned, her tongue dipping out to taste my skin. "Would you like that?"

She nodded, her eyes still closed, her neck arching up to mine. "Kiss me, please, Declan."

"No. You kiss me. I need to know you want this too."

She made a whimpering sound in her throat and moved her

mouth a whisper away. Blood pounded in my body as she looped her hands around my neck and arched up to press her lips against mine. She was tentative, like the first kiss she'd given me, but I wasn't having any of that. Groaning in satisfaction, I gathered her closer using my forearms, my hunger rising with each stroke of her tongue against mine. The press of her breasts against my chest made my cock pulse with need. She sighed and gave into the deepness I wanted, her tongue rubbing against mine seductively, her breasts and hips pressed against mine as I rocked against her.

"I want it all, Elizabeth."

Her hands grasped my shoulders and clung, her nails digging into my bare skin. "Me too."

We devoured each other, our lips searching cervices and hidden places. Our tongues tangled with open mouths.

Fast and hot. Hurry, hurry.

I nipped at her collarbone. "Take your shirt off. My hands are shit right now, and I'm trying to not get any blood on you."

"I don't care. Touch me." She lifted her shirt up at the hem and whipped it off, revealing a white lacy bra. My mouth went straight to her breasts, where I licked and bit her nipples through the material, the moisture soaking through, exposing her.

She twisted and writhed against the building, her hands tangling in my hair.

"You feel so good," she murmured, her hands sweeping across my chest. "Can I touch you? Are you hurting anywhere?"

"Not right now."

Her hands drifted across my chest, tracing down to my navel, the softness of her touch driving me crazy. She stopped at my waistband and I tossed my head back.

Yes, baby, yes.

"Wait," I said and reached inside to take off my cup, throwing it on the ground.

She slipped her hand in my shorts and fisted the pillar of my cock and pumped me, her fingers ghosting over the head, making me hiss.

"I love this ... the sounds you make, how you look at me like I'm the only girl in the world," she said.

"All for you." I ripped the button on her skirt with my thumbs and shoved it down, my eyes heavy as I took her in with her lacy bra and panty set.

She curled a leg around my hips to pull me back, and I went with her up against the wall again, my hips holding her hostage.

"It's damn inconvenient, but once again I don't have a condom," I said around her breasts, my mouth moving from one to the other, sucking the globes deep inside my mouth.

"You trying to get me pregnant?" She let out a breathless laugh.

I froze.

She whimpered. "I was kidding. I trust you."

I trust you ...

So many things hit me at once. Her pregnancy comment, and how the thought of putting my seed in her to make a baby didn't freak me out like I thought it would. The way her body felt against mine. How I'd been waiting for this moment forever. I rested my forehead against her face. "Look at me. I mean really look at who I am."

Her face softened. "I am."

"I'm the guy who's going to take you up against this wall. I'm going to bury my cock in you and own your body and you're going to love it. But I'm not going to hurt you. Ever."

She smiled. "I know."

I grimaced. "It's killing me that I can't put my fingers in you. Is my mouth okay?"

Her eyes glittered with heat. "Are you kidding me? *Yes.* Please use your mouth."

I fell to my knees and tossed one of her legs over my shoulder as she arched back. She was soaked, and I centered on her nub, my tongue coaxing and flirting with her core, mimicking the motions of what my cock would soon be doing inside her.

My hands itched to touch her sheath, to delve into its sweetness, but instead I cupped her breasts and squeezed. She gasped out my name and swiveled toward me. *More.*

She pulled my head back and stared down at me, a wild look in her eye. "Declan, *please.* I can't wait any longer."

I stood, my hands picking her up as her legs went around me. I knifed inside her, and my body sang in relief, the intense pleasure of sliding into her making me yell out.

"I don't want to hurt you," I whispered in her neck as I pumped gently, easing in more and more of my length.

"You won't," she whispered.

I pumped soft then hard, seating myself until I was all the way in.

Her fingers dug in my shoulders and spurred me on, her small hips jerking to get more, her body clenching and sucking me.

I roared. She was mine, and I knew I'd never want another girl for the rest of my life like this. Using my chest, I pressed her further into the wall and pounded her with an unflinching rhythm, my cock bursting already to come. She felt so damn good bareback, her hot, velvet core wet with need. I hammered in and out, thrusting with powerful strokes. She moaned when I locked my arms on either side of her, holding her tight so I could angle down to press my pelvis against her sensitive skin. I rocked against her nub, my hands cupping her arse, positioning her to take every single deliberate stroke.

She tugged at my hair and yanked my face up to hers. "Whatever you're doing, don't stop."

"Never."

I snatched her lips and kissed her roughly while she clung to my scalp, her fingers digging in. My mouth went deep over hers.

The sounds of us, her gasps, my grunts, the smacking of our

bodies ...

"You, all for you."

She screamed out her orgasm, her legs locking around my hips.

I let out a shout as I came inside her, the most intense pleasure I'd ever felt shuddering through me, a wave of heat and desire and need that culminated in one burst of sensation. My body rippled and jerked with aftershocks, and I panted over her, my chest heaving like I'd run a marathon.

CHAPTER THIRTY-THREE

Elizabeth

E HANDED OVER my skirt and shirt, a little smile on his full lips as he watched me dress. I took my time, liking his hot gaze on me as I slipped them back on, my legs and arms loose from our crazy sex.

"Orgasm aside, I'm really pissed at you right now."

He speared me with a cocked eyebrow as he adjusted his shorts. "Do I have to ask?"

"That fight," I called out, getting worked up again at his blasé attitude. "You're taking a huge risk for money, I get that, but if you get caught you can go to jail. It might be hard to run a business from a cell, Declan."

"You're gorgeous when you get your knickers in a twist, you know that?"

I crossed my arms. Why was it so hard to be mad at him? He raked his gaze over me and rubbed his jaw, that intense look on his face like he was going to devour me. Again.

He grinned. "I almost got my arse kicked, and I don't even give a damn because we're going back to my flat for the next round. I want you naked and in my bed, and I'm going to make love to you until you aren't mad at me anymore." He reached out and tentatively touched my face with his swollen hands.

Well. I couldn't say no to that.

WE DROPPED DAX off at the Tau house and then went to Declan's apartment. He immediately went to the bathroom to clean up the blood and wash out the cuts. Dax and I had tried to get him to stop by the ER, but he refused, saying he'd had worse, and in the long run, it meant less questions being asked.

Speaking of questions, even though we'd had make-up sex in the alley, I still didn't know where things stood between us.

I'd been rummaging through his fridge when I heard him shout from the bathroom. I tore open the door and found Declan pouring a bottle of antiseptic over his hands. Bruises that I hadn't seen in the alley before, ugly, purple splotches, decorated his ribs and back.

Anger filled me. Dammit, I wanted to kill the Yeti. Declan wouldn't even be paid for this fight. My hands fluttered around him. "You can't do this again. Please tell me you won't."

"We're getting in this shower together, and there will be very little talking involved."

Oh, he was frustrating. I put my hands on my hips. "No."

He didn't say anything as he packed up his gauze and put it back in the cabinet, his face a mask. With his back to me, he shoved his shorts down, his back rippling with hard muscle as he bent over to turn on the shower. Water beat down, tapping on the ceramic.

"What? You're just going to ignore me now?" I huffed, part of me lusting after his body, the other part of me wanting to smother him with my pitiful nursing abilities.

"If we're going to do this thing …" My voice trailed off when he bent over to get a towel, his forearm brushing against the skin on my shoulder. I hissed. *God, he was beautiful.*

"And I know you're trying to distract me, so just stop being all sexy and listen to me—"

He stepped in the shower and closed the glass door, effectively cutting me off.

I huffed and paced around, mulling.

Why was he so stubborn?

I came to a stop. It was no wonder we were in love with each other; we were just alike, neither one of us willing to budge.

I stopped in my tracks. My heart jackhammered. Love? Had I just thought *love*?

I realized a thousand things at once, as if they'd been there the entire time, just waiting for me to see them. Of course it was love.

Loving Declan was like the rain storms I loved to dance in. Crazy and unpredictable, sometimes turbulent, sometimes gentle. I didn't know if I was going to be struck by lightning, but one thing was for sure, I wanted him anyway. Fighting and all. Somehow we'd make it all work. If he could accept my past and love me anyway, then I sure as hell could handle whatever the future brought for us.

I'd wasted so much time with my one-night stands and rules about life. It had never been about proving to myself I could be normal and have sex and not let Colby win. For two years, I'd been punishing myself. I'd hunkered down in my grief and tried to end it all. Why had I let a mere boy destroy me?

I'd been scared for too damn long, denying myself the pleasure of falling, of that feeling you get when butterflies go crazy in your tummy. I'd been shoving them down, swallowing them whole.

Not anymore.

I jerked my shirt off and then my skirt, my hands ripping at my bra and panties. My body was already throbbing with arousal, but more than that—we needed to talk.

I yanked open the glass door. "Do not shut me out. I have something to tell you ..."

I stopped and swallowed. He was wet, his hair slicked down as water coasted lazily down his throat to his chest, past the V in his hips and right to his hard-as-steel length.

I stepped inside and shut the door. I sensed something big—other than the size of his appendage.

"Are you ready to risk your heart, Elizabeth?" he said softly, watching me.

"Wha—what?"

He sent me a heavy look, laced with heat. "Right now, in this shower, you are going to tell me exactly how you feel about me."

I shivered at the authority in his voice. "Is that an ultimatum?"

He stroked his hard length, eyes on my face. "Do you want this?"

Yes.

But first ...

"This—this is going to sound really weird, but ..." I swallowed, getting my nerve up. I mean, I thought he was in love with me, but was he? I sucked in a sharp breath and gathered my courage. Be brave. "I—I have a mountain to climb in life, and I want you next to me. I want you to walk up it with me—behind me to give me a push or next to me when I need to hold your hand. And when there's a jungle there, I want you to fight with me. We'll have machetes, and it will be tough some days when I try to figure out who I am and what I need, but with you next to me, it'll be okay. I want you to carry me when I'm tired, and I'll carry you when you're tired. I want you to rub my fingers when I've worked a hard day making pretty things, and I'll rub your muscles when they get hurt. I want to be the blanket that covers you when you are cold. Or vice versa. I want all of it—all the blood, sweat, and tears—no matter what dream you decide to follow. I'm here. Forever. I love you."

"Unicorn Girl, God, I love you too." Tears misted in his eyes and he blinked them away as I did a double take. He wasn't the kind of guy who'd *ever* cry. He gathered me in his arms and kissed me deeply, his mouth soft and tender.

After a while, we pulled back. "And I'm sorry for ignoring you for the past few days and not seeing what was right in front of my face. I—I was scared."

He kissed my nose. "I knew you loved me—or I hoped you did. You couldn't stand it when you saw me at Cadillac's with Lorna. Hell, you couldn't stand it when I deliberately flirted with her in class just to get you going. But you rejected me, and shit, it felt like you'd knifed me in the gut. I never want to have that feeling again. I never want to be without you by my side. And I hate to bring up Nadia, but you have to know that I never loved her—not really. Not like this need I have for you, to sink into you and never come up for air."

My heart filled with emotion, and I battled my own tears.

He sighed, his face softening. "The moment that dragonfly landed on you, I knew you were going to rock my world. It was my mum, telling me to *see* you."

I traced my fingers across the tattoo on his neck. This beautiful Brit was hers. "Nothing matters without you. My past, my rules. It all seems so unimportant now."

He picked me up and kissed me while I laughed against his lips. "This shower is kinda on the small side. Let's get out and get in the bed."

His slippery fingers skimmed down to cup one of my breasts, his touch circling closer and closer to my nipple. "Always in a rush," he teased, his fingers finally making contact with the nerve endings on my nipple. I hissed, the sound reflecting part torture, part pleasure.

I encircled my arms around his neck and leaned back, giving him more room to play, more skin to see. He slid his hands down to my waist and toyed with my bellybutton.

"I'll never have enough of you. I think about this constantly," he said, easing his hand down further to palm me. "When I fought, when I worked out, when I ate, when I was in class. All I wanted was you under me and whispering how much you can't live without me."

He slid a finger inside me. "This. You. Me. I want it forever."

I didn't give him a reprieve either. I knew what made him sweat, my hands coasting over his chest, flicking at his nipples with my nail, making him groan.

I moaned as his finger pushed deep into my center, sliding against the wetness. He strummed me delicately and then harder, his fingers like magic.

"Declan," I murmured, tasting how his name sounded when I knew that he loved me and I loved him.

"Elizabeth," his voice huffed out.

Passion slammed into me like a tsunami.

Tingles built in my spine, the heat building as I relaxed against the shower wall while his hands worked me. Teasing. Stroking. His touch consumed every single cell in my body, the drive to possess him and be owned by him. "I'm going to come soon," I gasped.

He moaned and twisted me around until I was facing the wall. His lips landed on my neck and he sucked hard. I called out, and he did it harder. Making me squirm with need. I gasped. "What are you doing?"

"Making you mine and letting everyone fucking know."

He moved me again, facing me toward the shower. With a gentle pressure from his hands, he bent me over. "Put your hands on the wall and hang on," he said softly.

He ran his hands down my back, and I felt him grasping

himself as he slid into my sheath, softly at first, but then wilder, going deeper, and I tightened my muscles, accepting all of him, clenching against him. His body flexed and stroked, sliding in and out like a well-oiled machine.

"You feel so good. Never want to stop this." His hands tangled in my hair and pulled.

His hand cupped one of my breasts, pulling on the nipple. I angled my hips higher to get more of him, to feel every single inch.

He pounded into me, his hand curving over my hips, the touch rough and then gentle. I got lost in the sounds of our sex. I went deep, my mind and body feeling part of his, as if we were one.

He grabbed my chin and turned my head around to stare deep in my eyes as he slammed his cock home. "We've got all night to do this."

I closed my eyes in ecstasy.

CHAPTER THIRTY-FOUR

Elizabeth

THE NEXT DAY neither of us wanted to get out of his warm bed, but by seven I was back at my place showering. Declan was skipping classes to go talk to his father. He'd been tense most of the morning and didn't want to say why, so I let it go.

After my first class I had a small break so I went to the Tau house to see Blake. It was ten by then and most of the brothers were up stirring around from whatever Halloween debauchery they'd gotten into the night before.

I asked where Blake's room was and made my way up the stairs. I knocked briefly and when no one answered, I eased into the darkened room. He'd pulled the shades down and then tugged the curtains all the way closed. I smirked. Preparing for the next day hangover?

I heard a grunt, and my eyes went straight to his bed. That was when I noticed he wasn't alone. Long, curly red hair was splayed out, half on his pillow and half still under the covers. I froze and squinted to make sure I wasn't seeing things. A girl's arm popped out from the covers and I saw a ring I'd made.

Shelley and Blake? It seemed crazy, but then I remembered

all the time they'd been spending together. Here at the house ... the parties.

Neither had seen me yet, and I couldn't stop the silly grin that spread across my face.

I eased back out of the room on tip-toes, not daring to call attention to myself or embarrass them, but I practically rubbed my hands together in glee when I thought about how I was going to surprise them both with my knowledge.

I clicked the door shut and left.

THAT AFTERNOON I finished my shift at the bookstore and headed back to the apartment. My mind and body yearned for Declan, but just as I pulled in the parking lot, he was pulling out, a passenger inside a Lexus with an older gentleman who was the spitting image of Declan and Dax. *Father?* Where were they going?

I debated on calling him and just then he sent me a text.

I love you so fucking much. I need you bad, but my father is demanding I go to dinner to talk money. I'll be home soon.

But he wasn't.

I waited for him. And waited.

At midnight, I gave up and went to bed, crawling beneath the cold sheets.

Where was he?

CHAPTER THIRTY-FIVE

Elizabeth

A METALLIC SOUND reached my ears. I looked around the dark bedroom, checking out the balcony door, but it was shut. It hadn't come from that direction, I decided, my attention instead focusing on my bedroom door that led out into the apartment.

It came again, a gentle scraping noise.

I tried to put a name to it and decided it was like the sound someone makes when they scratch metal with a sharp object.

Declan? My heart warmed, and I couldn't stop the smile that spread across my face.

The sound came again, this time sharp and clear as a bell, and a malign tingle went down my spine.

Something was wrong, very wrong.

I was fumbling around on the nightstand for my phone when the overhead light clicked on, blinding me.

I held my hands up to shield the light and blinked.

Gasped.

A hurricane ripped through my chest.

Colby.

His hands twitched, calling attention to a roll of duct tape and a small silver knife. His nose had a slight bend to it, testament to the night Declan had broken it.

He rushed me and I scrambled up to a sitting position, but my reactions were sluggish.

He lunged over me and I twisted away on my stomach, aiming for the end of the bed, but he caught my ankle and yanked me back. He flipped me over to my back and covered my mouth and most of my nose with his hand. "You were always a bit of a handful."

I struggled and his grip tightened, the pressure against my mouth hard enough against my teeth that I tasted the copper.

He laughed, a jagged, breathless sound. "And don't act so surprised to see me. After all, you sent your mom and her boyfriend to blackmail my father. Did you really think I was going to let that ride?" His nose flared, anger sparking in his gaze as he put his nose next to mine.

"You really should have called me back and talked to me. We might have been able to figure this whole thing out, but you didn't, and now I have to talk to you in person."

God help me, I couldn't breathe. Not really. Small amounts of air sucked in and then rushed out of my nostrils. Dark spots danced in front of my eyes, and I clawed at his hands, my nails digging in to get some muscle, but he laughed and elbowed me in the ribs.

Whoosh.

The room spiraled.

He was going to kill me. Here in my bed. He was going to finish what he'd started two years ago.

My lungs burned, ready to explode.

My body ached for air. God, help me. Someone, please.

I whimpered and kicked up at him, trying to find purchase on his shoulders, his legs, anywhere. That didn't work, so I tried to buck him off me, my hips still able to move.

He *tsked* and maneuvered me up on the bed and straddled my chest with his legs. "I'm going to take my hand off your mouth so you can breathe, but if you scream, I will knife you right here, do you understand?"

I nodded, fading fast, adrenaline the only thing keeping me awake.

He eased his hand back a millimeter at a time until finally I had more air.

I opened my mouth and gulped in fresh oxygen, filling my lungs.

Yes, air, air, air!

He shoved my chin up to close my mouth and slapped a piece of duct tape over my mouth as his other hand imprisoned my wrists.

I grunted, not able to move. My eyes watered. Death loomed.

Don't give up! the girl inside me yelled. *You did once. Never again.*

I flailed around, using my elbows like Declan had taught me to knock him in the nose. He screamed in pain and pounced on me harder, using his knee to pin me in place on the bed. He fished around in his pocket and pulled out a zip tie and tied my wrists together. Sweat dripped from his face into my eye, and I cringed.

I sucked air in through my nose, imagining the picture I made, my wrists bound, a piece of duct tape across my face as I lay crosswise on my bed. Memories from another bed flew at me, things I didn't want to remember.

Straightening his shoulders and rolling his neck, he paced around my room.

He wiped a shaky hand across his mouth. "I had plans, Elizabeth. Hell, I had plans for the good life and then you start calling Father and his assistant, telling them lies about us. You're a little slut and you want to backtrack and tell everyone that I raped you." He barked out a laugh. It was weird and off.

His eyes flared wide, the bloodshot veins like roadmaps. *Was he high?*

He crossed his arms. "Father called me all high and mighty and asked me all these crazy questions about you. He was already pissed at me for getting kicked out of school, you know, and his words to me were to 'take care of it.' Now, maybe that meant paying you off, but you see, I really think he meant for me to do whatever necessary to make sure your little story never reaches the papers or the police."

No! I shook my head from side to side rapidly. My eyes beseeched him. *Please. Mama and Karl had given up,* I wanted to scream at him. *It was over. Over!*

He licked his lips, hungry eyes raking over me. "You know, I remember that night at the hotel. Do you?" He ran his eyes over the scars on my wrist. "I heard about this. I really did a number on you, didn't I?" He lifted his eyes to mine. "That's some powerful shit, when you can make someone try to off themselves."

I froze.

His eyes clouded in a faraway look as if chasing a memory. "You drank that vodka like water, and when I put that Molly to your lips, you lapped it up like a baby kitten looking for a milk coma." He sat down on my bed, his fingers idly toying with Granny's quilt. "I had to have you, I guess. You'd been telling me *no* for weeks and you're the type of girl who wants too much, and I was sick of kissing your ass. I wanted you, and, in the end, I got you, didn't I?"

He was going to kill me this time. He was on something. I knew it by the way spittle came out of his mouth.

I closed my eyes, fighting to keep the hysteria at bay.

Fighting to keep my imagination from running crazy.

I whimpered, an image of Declan in my head, his broad shoulders, his warm gray eyes, his sensual mouth that I'd never taste again. I pictured the future, us having babies—twins—me working on my jewelry while he made a living at the gym, going to the UFC. Dax popping in for dinner ... laughter.

Simple and easy.

Just love. True love. Epic kind of love.

Colby speared me with his gaze, bringing me back. "Truth is, things got kinda out of control prom night. I didn't mean to hurt you—or hit you—but that's what happens in the heat of the moment. You were so helpless—I liked it. You get that?" He squeezed my cheeks together, his hands rough. His tongue snaked out of his mouth as he licked his lips. "You were good, Elizabeth. I liked hurting you."

I closed my eyes.

"Don't do that!" he barked. "I still have things to say to you."

My eyes flew open. He kneeled onto the bed, eyes protruding with anger. "I came down here to get rid of you, but first, all this talk about prom ..." He laughed bitterly. "Well, it's got me excited, babe." He jerked my hands up and pressed them against his crotch. "See? My dick is hard."

CHAPTER THIRTY-SIX

Declan

A LITTLE AFTER midnight, my dad dropped me off at my flat. We said goodbye, and maybe I sensed something new between us. Respect? I didn't know, but we had spent the last few hours at a steak place, working through the details about a huge-ass loan I was taking from him. I'd had to swallow some of my pride to ask, but in the end it was worth a future with Elizabeth. Maybe she was okay with my illegal fighting, but I didn't want to put any kind of stress on our relationship. Reality had hit me like a ton of bricks last night as I'd held her in my arms. Yeti wouldn't be my last illegal fight, and there'd never be enough money for the gym. Of course, I'd given him a choice: either he gave me a loan or I continued to fight. He'd been furious at first, especially since he hadn't known about the fighting, but in the end, he'd agreed to a loan.

I climbed the steps to the stairs and popped open my phone to search for a text from Elizabeth. She'd sent me a few, the last one around eleven.

Should I let her sleep and talk to her tomorrow?

I stopped in front of her door and knocked but didn't get an answer.

I knocked again. Her car was there.

Did she not want to talk to me?

Was she tired from last night?

I stalked back to my place and unlocked the door. Just as I was opening the door to go inside, something pricked at me. I stepped back onto the breezeway, a sense of urgency gnawing at me.

I scanned the carpark. All looked well.

But then...

My eyes went to Minnie's Diner across the street. Parked in the back was a sports car, its lines sleek and powerful even in the dark. Porsche?

What the fuck?

CHAPTER THIRTY-SEVEN

Declan

BANG!

My shoulder crashed into the door and the cheap wood cracked. I rammed my hand inside and turned the knob. I don't know why I didn't just run back into my place and cross over the balcony, but this seemed faster.

A light burned from underneath her bedroom door and I headed that way. It was locked too. *Fuck!*

I kicked in the door and slipped inside, ready to kill whoever was here.

But what I saw made me pause, every nightmare ever imagined playing out in front of me.

Colby stood behind a bound and gagged Elizabeth on her knees, a knife at her throat.

"Don't come any closer," he warned, pushing the knife in far enough that blood bloomed on her neck and dripped down.

I jerked to a halt and held my hands up. "It's cool. Just don't hurt her, and all of this will work out."

He inhaled sharply, his cold eyes leveled at me. "Oh? Like you hurt me?" He tightened his grip around her shoulders, and I watched as her eyes flared wide.

I wanted to rip his throat out with my bare hands. My chest heaved and it sounded loud in the quiet room as we faced off.

"I don't see a way out of this that works for you," I said softly, backing away from him while angling myself toward her dresser.

He grunted. "I do. You think you can touch me? Don't you know who I am?"

I nodded. Oh, I knew exactly who he was. He'd hurt my Elizabeth.

I looked at her. "It's going to be okay, love. I got this, okay. I will never let anything bad happen to you, got it?"

She nodded.

"Shut up! Stop talking!" he yelled at me, his knuckles white, still holding the knife against her throat as he pulled her up and forced her to walk to the bathroom. He shoved her inside and she fell to the floor. "Get in there until I figure out what to do with both of you." He slammed the door and paced around me, his face contorted in a snarl. He eyed me warily, taking in my body.

I made myself look small, huddling in the corner. Waiting. He was bound to make a move with the knife, and I had to be ready.

The sound of sirens pierced the silence.

Feral eyes roamed around the room as if looking for the origin of the sound and then focused on me. "You called the cops." He tightened his grip on the knife.

I shook my head. "It's a college town. Cops are out everywhere. You can still leave and nothing bad will have happened. I don't want to hurt you."

God, I wanted to kill him.

I was going to kill him.

The sirens got louder and louder, and he paused, his head cocked toward the balcony. The flash of blue lights came in through the window, and he looked back at me, his eyes bulging with rage.

I lunged for him, avoiding the hand with the knife.

We fell to the ground in a tangle of limbs and the knife skittered across the floor.

Fists flew, mostly mine, but some of his hits connected with my bruises and I flinched, ripples of pain in my body.

I tore into him with palm strikes and punches.

He might be a crazed fighter hoped up on adrenaline, but I was the goddamfucking talent.

And I was going to kill him.

My strikes zeroed in on his temple. A palm strike to the face, one to the ribs, and another to the liver.

His head dangled, wobbling like a broken doll's. His eyes shut.

He was out.

I exhaled, the sound of Elizabeth beating on the bathroom door permeating my senses.

I wiped my face, feeling the trickle of blood. I didn't want to scare her more than she already had been. I stood and looked around for something to tie up Colby with before I'd let Elizabeth out here.

A red-hot pain sliced into my leg. Colby had come to—had he ever been out?—and had grabbed the knife and plunged it into my thigh.

I roared, the rage in me skyrocketing. The room spiraled as I spun around and launched myself on top of Colby. I slammed a fist into his face. Another to his groin.

Oh yeah, I liked the sound he made when that connected.

The bathroom door collapsed and Elizabeth's body lay on top of it, her eyes frantic as she took me in. I laughed rather oddly. I guess she'd beat it down to get to me.

Her, her. That was all that mattered. Shit, I didn't want her to be scared.

Nothing would ever happen to her. I loved her. I wanted to be with her forever. I wanted to make babies with her. I wanted to wrap her up in a cocoon of love...

And just then, things got hazy. I felt weak. My blood was everywhere, pooling on her tile.

Shit. Wait. Got to save her.

Fading.

Everything went black.

CHAPTER THIRTY-EIGHT

TOUCHED HIS face. Cool. He was pale, too.

I worried my bottom lip with my teeth and pulled up the hospital sheet to tuck it around him more securely.

He'd almost died in front of me. Tears pricked at my eyelids, but I beat them back when I saw his hand twitch. Time to be strong.

His eyes fluttered.

Long black lashes—God, how had I never noticed how beautiful every single hair on him was?—lifted and he gazed up at me, at first disoriented, but then a slow dawning in his eyes.

"I'm alive?" His voice sounded like it had been dragged over gravel.

"Halleluiah! He speaks," Dax shouted out with whoop from a green recliner where he'd been sleeping for the past few hours.

A pretty nurse popped her head in and looked at Declan. Smiled. "You're awake. Great. I'll let the doctor know."

"She can check out the Sex Lord anytime," Dax snarked.

He then leaned over and inspected Declan. "You'll live, I guess. Just my luck."

"Arsehole," Declan muttered at him. "Always thinking about yourself."

I smiled. If he had died—God, I would have wanted to go with him.

He focused back on me. "What happened? I blacked out ..."

I watched his face as he pieced it all together.

I nodded gently. "You've been here for about twelve hours. The police arrived just after you went down. They arrested Colby and called an ambulance for you." I licked dry lips. "He—he nicked your femoral artery. If it hadn't been for the quick-thinking policeman who tied off your thigh, you would have bled to death." I took a deep breath. "You spent four hours in emergency surgery to repair the vessel—a kind of graft. You probably won't be able to walk without crutches for a few weeks."

"I'll live then." His eyes devoured me, raking over my face, my lips. "How are you? Did he hurt you?"

I shook my head. "Just what you saw. I told the police what happened."

"Everything?"

I took his hand and squeezed. "Yes. They've arrested him, but his dad has already made a statement on television. He said he knows Colby's innocent, so we may have a bumpy road ahead of us."

"Like hell we will." Winston Blay walked in the room, his suit wrinkled from being up all night with Dax and me. We'd spent the last few hours talking a lot, and I'd filled him in on everything about Colby and what had happened to me. He'd been surprisingly understanding, and we'd formed a bond while waiting for Declan to pull through surgery. He'd told me how he was glad Declan had come to him for money instead of continuing the illegal fights. In the end, I think all he wanted was for Declan to find some happiness. "He may be a Senator, but I'm an ambassador, and no jerk-off southern good ole boy is going to try to kill *my* son and think he's going to get away with it."

Dax did a fist pump. "That's what I'm talking about."

I leaned down to Declan. "Your dad has been on the phone all morning, lining up lawyers and talking to bigwigs. He's been good to me, too. He found my mom and Karl in Petal and they're at their local police station now, giving a statement about how they tried to blackmail the Scotts'."

That seemed to satisfy Declan. He gazed at me. "God, I was so afraid I was going to lose you forever. I—I don't think I would have survived that."

I kissed him, not caring that people were watching, but Mr. Blay and Dax discreetly left the room. I pulled back and rested my face against his shoulder. "No, I was afraid you were dead. I—I can't even think about it."

Declan patted the covers. "Get in the bed with me."

I eyed him warily. "You've got too many wires hooked up to you to get freaky."

"I don't want to shag you. I want to love you." He sat up in bed and scooted over. There was barely room for me, he was so big, but he tugged me down until I was lying across him, his hard body warm against mine. He pushed a hand through my hair to cup my head. "When I get out of this hospital bed, I am taking you away from this town and we are going to be alone, without the gym or uni or family or anything. I have some things to show you."

"Good things?" I teased.

"I want to take you to London and show you where I grew up. I want to visit my mum's grave with you and tell her how I found the perfectly broken girl to fall in love with. I want to watch you eat a proper shepherd's pie—maybe show you how to make it."

"I don't cook. All I can make is ramen noodles."

He smiled. "Then I'll eat ramen."

Poor guy.

I laughed. Giddy. "You really do love me," I teased. "I'm

yours, Declan, and I will do my best to make you happy and never live with any stupid regrets. I promise you I will always focus on the future." I pressed my lips to his lightly. "I'm not going to judge myself on the past. I don't live there anymore."

He studied me as I talked, and when I stopped, his mouth captured mine, his tongue sweeping out and plunging deep. I sank into him, immersing myself in his scent, his warmth, his bulk. He kissed me soft and sweet, then hard and dark, just like I liked it.

I came up for air. "It's you, always you, my Mr. Darcy."

"I love you too, Elizabeth Bennett."

We lay together cuddled up in a tangle of limbs as the sun peeked over the horizon. Two years ago, I'd watched another sunrise and had vowed to never love again, but this, this was different.

This was the beginning of my life.

I'd sensed it from the moment I saw him at that frat party, that movie-worthy experience we sometimes get when we sense a shift in the atmosphere as if something extraordinary is about to happen. It had. I'd found him even with my rules dragging me down. And we'd have troubles like all young people do. Love is never perfect, in fact, it's the exact opposite of perfect, but that's okay, because it gives you room to grow and explore. There'd be times when we'd bicker and argue, but we'd have great make-up sex too. And no matter what came our way, I was in this for real. If he wanted to use his fists, I'd stand in his corner and kiss him before he put his gloves on.

He'd do the same for me.

"What are you thinking?" he asked a while later as we snuggled.

I turned my head on the pillow to face him. Some of his color had come back and it made me glad. "My mind is racing, thinking about possibilities. Our future. What I can do with my jewelry. What you can do with your gym. I—I just haven't been this happy or excited about life in a long time. And you're in the hospital, which makes it even more weird." I plucked at the covers. "I feel like I've been going through these small yet monumental changes over the past few weeks, and I owe it all to you. Loving you is the best thing that's ever happened to me." I bit my lip to keep the tears at bay.

He studied me for a while, his gaze full of complete understanding. "You and me, we got this. I'm going to spend the rest of my life loving you. I'm going to give you whatever you want, Unicorn Girl. I'm going to kiss you every single night. I'm going to fuck you and then make love to you. I'm going to give you kids. A home. Happiness. All of my heart."

Joy filled my soul. "Will you read Jane Austen to me naked?"

He barked out a weak laugh. "I'll do one better. I'll make love to you and quote the whole bloody book at the same time."

"Mm, I could get used to that."

"Just making sure you get what you want, love."

We laughed and held each other close as sun rose higher in the sky.

EPILOGUE

Elizabeth

One year later

I SETTLED IN on the bench and gazed at the garden surrounding one of the water fountains in Hyde Park. I looked around for Declan, but he'd left to grab us water from one of the vendors near the entrance.

It was a chilly yet beautiful October morning and we were in London for the week to catch up with old school chums and family members of his mom's.

I sighed. It had been a wonderful year considering the hell we'd been through.

I was in my last year of school, but I'd given up my job at the bookstore to work on my jewelry. Meyers had offered me another contracting design job, and when I wasn't studying, I was working on new creations.

Blake and Shelley were together. Most of the time. They fought a lot, and I didn't know if it was going to work out, but I had my fingers crossed.

Dax was his usual self, partying at the frat house and sleeping around. I knew the real man though. Underneath that shiny veneer was a guy looking for love.

My mom had left Karl, and the last time I'd seen her, she'd already found a new guy—a drummer she'd met at a concert.

Declan's father had given him and Dax a graduation gift of several hundred thousand dollars, therefore canceling the loan. Mr. Blay swore it had always been his intention to give each of his children a college graduation present, and the boys didn't argue. Mr. Blay and Declan had formed a kind of truce, and while it wasn't a total reconciliation, it was progress. Dinners at the Blay mansion were still a bit testy and odd, but I was content. Another mountain for us to climb, and we were armed and ready.

It was the best family I'd ever had.

As far as Colby went, he was in jail awaiting trial for first-degree attempted murder for me as well as a count of second-degree attempted murder for Declan. With the duct tape and penknife, it was going to be extremely difficult to prove his innocence. Senator Scott's personal assistant had also come forward, revealing the blackmail scheme hatched by Karl and Mom, giving Colby plenty of motivation. His sentencing could be up to life in prison without parole. He and his father had done their best to get him out on bail, but because he was a flight risk, it had never come to fruition.

He'd been charged with rape as well, which has no statute of limitations in North Carolina, but the burden of truth rested with me, and my lawyers would have a difficult time proving it. There were pictures of me drunk at prom and the chaperones had tossed us out for being intoxicated. But I'd decided to tell my whole story in court, and Shelley and Blake would also testify. We didn't know if it would be enough to convict him, but I was in it for the long haul. I was worth it. Declan had told me that a long time ago outside the truck stop, and now I believed it.

Declan came back from the refreshment stand with two bottles of water, his long legs crossing the park as a group of women across the fountain ogled him with hungry eyes—but he ignored them, his gaze locked on mine.

The gym had opened officially in February, and we'd had a huge grand opening party this past May. We were living in an apartment he'd had renovated in the back, and it was small, but for now, it was just us and it was enough.

He smiled at me as he sat down next to me and took my hand to hold it. We'd been coming here each afternoon to take in the pretty flowers and people watch.

Just then, a fluttering flashed across the bench and landed next to us. A dragonfly.

I let out a small gasp and went to nudge Declan, but he'd already seen it.

"She knows I found you," he murmured and wrapped me up in a hug. We watched as the blue insect hovered around us, flitting from one side of us to the other for the longest time, until finally, she flew away …

The End

Dear Reader,

Hearing from you is very important to me. Honestly, it makes my day because I love to talk about my characters like they are real people (they are in my head!). So please drop me a line on my website or on Facebook. Book reviews are like gold to indie writers, and you have no idea how we relish each one. If you have time, I'd appreciate and love an honest, heartfelt review from you. Thank you for being part of my fictional world.

Ilsa Madden-Mills, NYT and USA Today best-selling author

MY OTHER BOOKS:

Briarcrest Academy Series
Reading Order:

Very Bad Things
Very Wicked Beginnings
Very Wicked Things
Very Twisted Things

ABOUT THE AUTHOR

NEW YORK TIMES and USA Today best selling author Ilsa Madden-Mills writes about strong heroines and sexy alpha males that sometimes you just want to slap. She's addicted to dystopian books and all things fantasy, including unicorns and sword-wielding females. Other fascinations include frothy coffee beverages, dark chocolate, Instagram, Ian Somerhalder (seriously hot), astronomy (she's a Gemini), Sephora make-up, and tattoos. She has a degree in English and a Master's in Education.

Sign up here for her newsletter to receive a
FREE Briarcrest Academy novella ($2.99 value)
plus get insider info and exclusive giveaways!

http://www.ilsamaddenmills.com/#!contact/ckws

For more information about the next book
and to order signed books, please visit my social media sites:

http://www.ilsamaddenmills.com/

Ilsa Madden-Mills Facebook
(https://www.facebook.com/authorilsamaddenmills)

Ilsa Madden-Mills Goodreads Page
(www.goodreads.com/author/show/7059622.Ilsa_Madden_Mills)

Ilsa's Instagram
(http://instagram.com/ilsamaddenmills/)

Ilsa's Twitter
(https://twitter.com/ilsamaddenmills)

ACKNOWLEDGEMENTS

THERE ARE SO many fantastic people in the indie world that made this journey possible. Please know that my gratitude in no way lessens as the list continues.

For my husband who has stood by me every step of the way. You and me, babe, against the world.

For author Lisa N. Paul—We're both hardworking writers living similar lives, only we're too far away from each other, and it drives me crazy. I don't know what I'd do without your calls each day. Thank you for all the giggles and lunch dates that we've never even had in person. Most of all thank you for being my dear friend and being there when I need advice.

For author Tia Louise, my twin brain, and author Scarlett Dawn, my cheerleader—I can't think about you guys without wanting to sing "It's Getting' Hot in Herre" and smoke cigarettes. I adore both of you tremendously, and the next time we get stuck in an elevator together, I plan on bringing more alcohol…and a bikini.

For all the girls in my author group (Fuck That Noise), the best group of writers and storytellers around. We're small but we are MIGHTY. I appreciate each and every one of you!

For Debi Barnes—you are a gem of a blogger and an even better friend. Thank you for all your help with DE.

For my graphic designer who sacrificed time to make my cover one of a kind—S.k. Hartley, you are the best!

For Rachel Skinner of Romance Refined, my awesome and sweet editor who is extremely tough on content and exactly what I need. She worked with my crazy schedule when she didn't have to, and I love her for her kindness.

For Jimmy and Jenn Beckham and Tia Louise—thank you for proofreading and helping me polish.

For Miranda Arnold of Red Cheeks Reads: my wonderful and talented PA. HOLLA! Haha! So happy we connected through our love of *Very Bad Things*. Thank you for being a go-getter for me. Race to the end, baby!

For the admin girls of Racy Readers: Erin Fisher, Tina Morgan, Elizabeth Thiele, Miranda Arnold, Stacey Nickelson, Sarah Griffin, Heather Wish, Heather Reed, Kinsey Taylor. You ladies are responsible for the great reader group we have. It's one of the best ones ever, and I thank you for your constant support, ideas, and love.

For Julie Titus of JT Formatting: the best formatter out there. I appreciate you so much! :)

For the ladies of The Rock Stars of Romance who worked tirelessly and answered all my questions and offered advice: Lisa and Milasy and Dawn…you are the best!

For my Ilsa's Racy Readers Group: you may be last on this list, but you are the BEST. You picked me up when I got knocked down and made me laugh when I needed it the most. Thank you all for every shout out and each review you posted. Thank you for sharing a part of yourself in our group.